The Nightroad

Anthology One

The Nightroad
Anthology One

By

JG Benedict

Media Hatchery
Orchard Park, NY

ISBNs
Paperback: 978-1-955180-12-2
Hardcover: 978-1-955180-14-6
eBook: 978-1-955180-13-9

Library of Congress Control Number: 2024921121

Cover artwork © 2024 Megan Benedict via Canva

Printed and bound in the United States of America
First Printing 2024

Visit JGBenedict.com

Published by Media Hatchery
P. O. Box 554
Orchard Park, NY 14127

MediaHatchery.com

This project is made possible with funds from the Statewide Community Regrant Program, a regrant program of the New York State Council on the Arts with the support of the office of the Governor and the New York State Legislature and administered by GO ART!

For Megan, Jackson, Elwood, and Mylo,
without whom, none of this would be possible.

When the forest burns along the road

Like God's eyes in my headlights

And when the dogs are looking for their bones

And it's raining icepicks on your steel shore

—Chris Cornell, *Rusty Cage*

Contents

Prologue: Rook's Story, Part 1

The headlights of the dark blue sedan flickered in the unnatural gloom. There was something about the light, or lack thereof, on The Nightroad that made Ford Greene (whom the others among Exodos Omnis called Rook, on account of him being a rookie amongst their ranks) deeply afraid. Why did it always remind him of dying? The tall, ex-basketball player shifted in his seat. A black and grey scruff was beginning to grow on his dark chin and cheeks; he lamented what his appearance must have been becoming in his newfound life, constantly on the move. He had undoubtedly been more comfortable on the arc with the game hanging in the balance than he was in this damn car that was too small for him—traveling to meet God-knows-what in this infernal darkness. He shuddered and tried not to think of how far away from free throws and sporting events his life had gone.

His condition must have been apparent, for it roused his companion from his entranced driving. "You look more spooked than usual, Rook. I'd have thought you'd be getting used to this by now." The plainness with which he spoke did little to calm Rook's nerves. At that moment, they were somewhere in between the safe, rational, real world and the dark, unknowable gulfs that surrounded it, racing through said darkness on a two-lane asphalt highway. It was a place that shouldn't physically have been possible. Yet they persisted, chasing some mysterious vehicle that had been laying waste to the surrounding landscape for the past three days. And he was expected to get used to it? "Man, how could I ever?" His answer came out in response to both his thoughts and his partner.

Gordon Knox (whom the others all called "Critter") simply scoffed. "You know, big-time athlete like you used to be, you'd think you'd be made of slightly tougher stuff. Tonight is child's play compared to what shit we usually get into. Especially with *that* baby." Critter motioned to the mechanical contraption sitting in the back seat, his handlebar mustache framing the smirk beneath his trucker hat.

The device, which looked for all intents and purposes to have come off a low-budget movie set, rattled in its seat as if in response. The collection of flimsy-looking tubes and brightly colored wires, loosely attached to what appeared to be an overturned cooking pot, was a Class-B hypersonic mine, Rook had been told. A large red button sat on its base near the center, with warnings of caution scrawled around it. The idea that this thing was highly lethal was laughable given its appearance, Rook thought. Both he and Critter wore special frequency-regulating earplugs all the same.

"What are we supposed to use it on? We got any idea who it is we're even following?" Rook did his best to ignore his growing list of concerns about the evening.

"Well, not exactly, now that you mention it." The subject of the night's work brought Critter back to the present. "I can tell you it's not The Agency. Case in point, 'cause they're leaving a trail for us to follow, and it's not just ghosts and ashes."

"The Agency, that's the same thing as The Primal Bureaucracy, right?" Rook wondered how long it would take to memorize all the new places and organizations he needed to know. None of which he had heard of before two months ago.

"Yeppers, the goddamn boogeymen themselves. Worst shit you can run into, in my opinion." Critter cleared his throat with a nauseating croak. "Hand to God, we run into those fellas tonight, I'm just turning the car around and we're going home."

"Heh, yeah, like we would get that lucky." Rook didn't care that Critter was probably joking. He knew in his stomach that the unknown on The Nightroad was just as deadly as any clandestine organization they might run across. And if they had to take an off-ramp? Who could say what might lie waiting for them on the other end?

Critter seemed to sense his companion's thoughts drifting away. "So yeah, it's probably some cult bullshit. *The Screaming Eye* or *The Ghosts*

Of The Broken Dawn, I would guess. Those weirdos always seem to find their way onto The Nightroad, and they love nothing more than causing trouble."

"Okay, so then tell me this: Why did we let them get away from us?" Rook was never quite sure if Critter was secretly a genius or just incredibly lucky.

"That's just it. I let them get away. Way I see it, the longer we race after 'em out here, better the chance we run into something nasty. 'Gaunts, Roadogs, the ay-for-mentioned Agency; the list is about endless. Then, who knows what kind of mess we have to deal with? We let 'em go. Hopefully, they stop in another mile or two, and we can get the drop on 'em. Pop the mine, clean up the bodies, then go home. Easy peasy, right?" Critter was used to working alone and resented having to explain himself.

"I suppose so," Rook said. The tacit confirmation of his fears did little to ease his mind. He looked out the window of the passenger's side of the car. If he focused on the horizon for too long, the scenes silhouetted against the starry backdrop seemed to shift and change. Near the road, the ground looked solid, just as if they were back on Highway 61 in Hueta County. The ground and sparse shrubs looked purple and blue in the strange starlit glow, but solid at least. Was it? Rook wondered. He never liked the answers to his questions.

"So let me ask you something." Rook turned his gaze away from their surroundings. "How long have you been at this? The whole Exodos Omnis thing?"

"Hell, since the 90s, sometime. My old lady got axed by a yeti when we were out camping up north." Critter lit a cigarette. "I say we were camping, but the truth is we were hiding out. Should have known better than to go outside to investigate the weird shit we heard. But we didn't know anything. Shocked the hell out of both us and that yeti when our lights fell on it. Made short work of Sheila, but I managed to stick it with my boot knife and it ran off. After that, I was just about hunting the bastards. Got pretty good at it too, 'til Ex-O came calling. 'Hunt even stranger game, save more people from your miserable fate.' Same bullshit they feed you. Who says 'no' at that point? I didn't have anything to go back to." Critter shook his head. "Didn't help that I pretty much extinct-ified them yeti to boot." He seemed to beam with something akin to pride.

The sedan crested a hill and began a slow descent. In the distance, headlights could be seen off to the side of the road. Critter shut off the headlights and pulled the car over to the shoulder. "Best to keep it running," he said as he popped the car into park.

Rook grabbed the binoculars from the console and opened his door. "Guess we go take a look then," he said.

"That's the spirit," Critter grinned.

The ground Rook stood on was indeed as solid as it had looked. He followed Critter for a way before the former ducked behind a larger outcropping of bushes.

"Hand me the binoculars," Critter said. After a moment focusing the device, Critter silently scanned their intended destination. "Well, shit," he finally concluded.

"What is it?" Rook asked, more nervously than he intended.

"See for yourself," Critter said, handing the binoculars back to Rook.

Rook put the binoculars to his eyes and focused them on the headlights before them. He had expected to see people (some variety of cultists, if Critter was correct) camping out or otherwise getting their bearings. Instead, he saw only gore. Rook stifled most of a gasp. What remained of the occupants of the vehicle they had been chasing lay strewn about the area. There was little left other than chunks of meat and bone. Amidst the carnage, a tremendous black beast prowled. Its head was immense and clearly canine, though its body was more extensive and more muscular than any wolf or dog Rook had ever heard of. It was casually munching on an arm when it looked in Rook's direction. Rook's blood froze.

"See, I told ya—Roadogs. Spend long enough on The Nightroad, and something's gonna eat ya." Critter chuckled. "Let's head back to the car."

"So that's it then?" Rook dared to hope.

"Nah, not by a long shot. The night is still young, and we've got our friend in the backseat still. I figure we head back to where these guys came from. What was it—twenty, thirty miles back? That was a new ramp, right?" Critter was all business.

"Um, yeah, it was a little over twenty miles back. And that exit wasn't on the map." Rook didn't like where this conversation was headed.

"Awesome. See? This is turning into a great teaching opportunity." Critter loved nothing more than rubbing Rook's nose in his lack of experience.

"Our real job out here is cataloging new exits from The Nightroad. Reeves needs the stories for The Book, and keeping The Nightroad safe is our half of the accord that keeps our little corner of Eagle Creek hidden. So let's see where our fine friends, the puppy chow, came from. If we're lucky, we still get to fry a bunch of cultists." Critter said. It was clear he enjoyed his work.

"Yeah, I guess so. Don't expect you'd care much if I objected anyway," Rook said.

"Indeed I would not," Critter replied as he slid back into the driver's seat of the dark blue sedan.

Rook hurried into the passenger's seat. There was no sense in giving Critter a chance to leave him behind for a laugh.

As the car turned around, he felt a pang of nervousness at turning their backs on the Roadog. Had there been more of them lurking in the darkness? Then he remembered that there were any number of equally awful things all about them in that darkness, and somehow, the nervousness subsided. This was his life now, like it or not, and while he certainly wasn't ready for whatever lay beyond the off-ramp they now raced toward, he was determined to face it, whatever might come.

The Final Case of Marion Hollister

I.

On the morning of September 28, 2015, Mac woke with a start. Some terrible dream had haunted his sleep, vanishing more and more with each passing minute that his eyes remained open. He was drenched in sweat and paused before rising, sinking into the surreal air around him.

Professor Marion Hollister, "Mac" to his few friends, was an exceptionally average man. Quiet since childhood and with a generally amiable personality, Marion Hollister always managed to be the most easily forgettable person in any situation. Once, while on a school trip when he was ten, he was left behind at an art museum. A mistake that was only noticed once Mac's parents arrived at the school to pick him up. Unflappable as he generally was, Mac had managed to slip past the notice of the security guards as they closed the museum for the day. Needless to say, there was some commotion once school officials and Mac's parents returned to the museum to fetch him, but Mac was no worse for wear. He had been looking at the paintings and minding his own business and had yet to notice that the museum had emptied. His parents would credit the extended stay in that museum as the catalyst for his lifelong love of the institutions and his eventual career choice. However, they still worried that the mild-mannered Mac would have trouble with the complexities of life as he grew.

Mac never minded, however, and had managed to settle into a quiet life as the curator of the Eagle Creek Natural History Museum, a small adjunct museum attached to the local Eagle Creek Grand University, located in the eponymous town of Eagle Creek in Hueta County, NY. He looked the part as well, standing five foot, ten inches tall, with thinning hair of a typical brown coloring that matched his eyes. He wore traditional tweed jackets and a pocket protector, perhaps his only notable accessory.

The Eagle Creek Natural History Museum was something of an oddity in contrast. It had been endowed at its inception with a vast fund that had ensured the museum's continued operation for the intervening two hundred years. This fund was a point of contention at the university, as their bylaws had been amended to prevent the museum's closure or the re-appropriation of said funds. The university was compelled, by access to another similar endowment, to leave well enough alone and to allow the museum to operate as it saw fit, which was what it did. However, the decision never sat right with the succession of administrators that moved through the university over the years. In time, the museum faded into just another neglected department of the sprawling Eagle Creek Grand University, or ECGU, as its constituency called it.

None of this mattered to Professor Hollister, who was entirely content to tend to a small, quiet museum. As part of the arrangement between the two institutions, he was required to teach two classes at the university proper, but this, too, was of little consequence to the easygoing Mac. Instead, Mac used the opportunity to inject his pet passion, forensic anthropology, into the university curriculum.

It was this class, *An Introduction to Forensic Anthropology*, which Mac taught with uncharacteristic zeal that had earned him the campus nickname of "The Bone Doctor" and eventually attracted the attention of the local authorities.

While the city of Eagle Creek was notable for its university, among other things, it severely lacked many of the municipal facilities that one generally associates with a city of its size. Characteristically, it needed a proper coroner's office. So it was that Mac was put into contact with one deputy, Matt Hughes, of the local Hueta County Sheriff's Department. Deputy Hughes would, on occasion, bring remains into Mac's office at the museum for identification and requests for other assistance from Mac that often fell outside of the usual mortuary services that the sheriff's office contracted for. This was the highlight of Mac's existence, and he drew tremendous pride from his contributions. In truth, Mac's average contribution was to rule out a set of remains as being human. Usually, the remains were of swine from one of the local farms or coyote, but he had been instrumental in helping to close a tragic missing person case that had gone cold a few years earlier.

That cold case cemented the friendship between Mac and Deputy Hughes and earned each some notoriety. The local paper even ran a piece on Mac, lauding him as a local hero. The attention was not necessarily welcome to either man, as each tended to be something of a loner, but instead, had provided yet more common ground between them. They kept similar hours and were cut from similar cloth, and in a relatively short time, Deputy Hughes had become entirely trusting of Mac and his assistance. Then came the case of university student Heather Gomez.

Heather Gomez was a junior at ECGU. An honor student and, by all accounts, a generally well-liked person, the tall, long-haired former dancer disappeared one night in the late spring after an evening tutoring session. No trace of Ms. Gomez was discovered over the course of a two-month manhunt conducted by the Hueta County Sheriff's Office. Then, in the early summer, when unidentified but recent remains were found, Mac was almost inevitably called in. The remains turned out to be from a missing persons case a few counties over, but it was of little consequence. Mac was involved now and seemed to take it personally that such a thing could happen on campus under his watch.

Hughes and the sheriff's department didn't know that Heather's disappearance was personal to Mac. Two springs prior, when she was a freshman, Heather had enrolled in Mac's sparsely attended *Museum Studies* class. Owing in part to the small class size, only three students at the start of the semester, Heather and Mac quickly got to know one another. Heather was older than her contemporaries, 28 as opposed to the customary 18, and had spent the early part of her twenties as a student at the prestigious Marnse Academy of Dance. A devastating ankle injury ended that part of her life at 26, and she was now in school working on a degree in social work. Clever and hardworking, Heather quickly earned Mac's respect in the classroom, and it wasn't long before a genuine friendship blossomed between the two.

The following fall, she enrolled in "Introduction to Forensic Anthropology" and finally saw Mac in all his glory. This, much to Mac's surprise, was the catalyst for newfound feelings of affection from the much younger Heather. At first, he played it off, a hazard of teaching adult humans in their prime; Mac was sure that soon enough, Heather would find greener pastures to move onto and leave a silly crush on her teacher behind. Some of his charm was in Mac's obliviousness.

In his office on campus, Mac could still feel the confrontation they'd had in early November of that year, as though it hung forever suspended in the air about the place.

"You know how I feel, how I've felt for a long time now. You can't tell me there isn't something here." Heather had straightened her dark, wavy hair and had a glamorous look that stilled Mac's heart. "I've seen how you look at me, Mac; you aren't as sly as you think." She smiled then, and Mac returned the gesture, feeling that the jig was up.

"Fine. I won't lie about it. I think there could be something between us, but it simply isn't possible while you are my student. I won't risk both my career and your future here on a fling." Mac had regretted saying it the moment it was out of his mouth.

"Is that all I would be to you, Mac, a fling?" The hurt on her face was plain.

"No. I didn't mean it like that. I wouldn't want to have a fling. That's what I'm saying. I do have feelings for you, Heather; I just can't act on them at present." He remembered blushing at the admission and her kind laughter at his expense.

Then came a fateful party on New Year's Eve, thrown by Mac's longtime friend and former student, Anderson. Under the mutual influence of too much alcohol, the pair's affections finally became physical, but it proved a bridge too far for the mild-mannered Mac.

Everything had gone bad then, eventually ending in Mac arranging for rides home for himself and Heather. He spent the remainder of the school year avoiding her and much of anything happening on campus. This behavior continued into the next school year. Confined as he was to his museum, Mac was unaware of Heather's disappearance before Deputy Hughes contacted him about the case.

Though he was worried it would preclude him from helping, Mac decided to inform Hughes of his connection to Heather after the initial remains were determined to be from another individual. He pleaded with Hughes to look past his close connection with the victim and allow him to continue to aid in the investigation.

Deputy Hughes welcomed the assistance, and throughout the summer, he and Mac poured everything they could into the investigation. Nothing ever turned up. By the season's end, Deputy Hughes was being pressured by the sheriff's department to declare the case cold so as to free himself up for other duties. Hughes resisted for a time but, by the end of September, had to relent. Disheartened, he broke the news to Mac. Mac was determined to press on but was quite crestfallen at their apparent failure.

Now, the easygoing Mac had always had one particular vice, as it were, psychedelics. He had been turned on to LSD as a college student in the 90s and had since developed a taste for psilocybin, the active chemical in the aptly named "magic mushrooms." Though he used them primarily to relax, Mac had been abstaining over the summer due to his nearly daily contact with Hughes. He had even considered letting the sheriff's deputy in on his little secret. However, he decided against it in the end, citing the still considerable stigma associated with such drugs among law enforcement. Besides, Mac reasoned, it wasn't like he was doing anything particularly dangerous or uncommon among his contemporaries.

Mac's close friend, the aforementioned Anderson, happened to be something of a local legend with regard to the production and procurement of such things. With the case indefinitely closed, Mac was quick to dial him up and arrange a meeting.

Mac headed out to meet Anderson, who never seemed to sleep or be unavailable, at his residence about a half-hour's drive from Eagle Creek.

Though it had been unseasonably warm of late, a cold air blew on that gray and ominous evening, and storm clouds could be seen on the horizon. Anderson lived among the vast stretches of farmlands and woods that made up Hueta County, outside of the city of Eagle Creek.

Though he was over a decade younger than Mac, the brilliant and driven Anderson Peate had already acquired more degrees than his former teacher. With bachelor's degrees in Philosophy and Mycology, an MBA, and a Master's in Botany, plus being well-versed in any number of other subjects, it was reasonably easy to see how Anderson came by his legendary reputation, at least among local academics.

Once he had arrived, Mac promptly made his way inside through the always-open side door. Anderson was seated on his decades-old couch in the larger of two downstairs living rooms and greeted his friend as he entered. Arrayed about him on the nearby coffee table was a bewildering collection of jars and containers of all sorts and sizes. Mac could see mushrooms in some, weed, lavender, camphor, and several other, stranger-looking plants he couldn't readily identify in others.

Anderson was busily sorting through the jars, seemingly intent on finding something particular.

"Ah, The esteemed Professor Hollister, welcome. It has been far too long since we've seen you around these parts," Anderson smiled as he looked up to his approaching friend. The lights in Anderson's house were customarily low, but Mac thought the place looked darker than usual for some reason. Intermittently, a blue light bulb in a tall corner lamp buzzed on and off. The noise was grating on Mac's nerves, and he sighed. He was more stressed over everything than he wanted to admit.

"It's been a busy few months, that's for sure." Mac tried to seem more upbeat than he was feeling but imagined that he was doing a relatively poor job. The pair had been friends since Anderson had enrolled in Mac's "Introduction to Forensic Anthropology" class at ECGU some years prior. After graduating with his second degree, Anderson had suddenly moved off campus to a large farmhouse he had inherited from some distant relative. Thus began his career in "pharmacological distribution," as he called it, and the advent of his now considerable venture into herbal remedies and medications of all sorts. His fields grew the raw materials he used to brew all manner of essential oils, herbal salves, custom herbal teas, and other naturally derived, healing, and wellness products.

That he included the sale of marijuana and magic mushrooms to his repertoire and looked like a character from 'The Big Lebowski' only made him more impressive to the droves of college students who visited Anderson regularly. He enforced a strict "no driving" policy to his guests who partook of those wares and, as such, was almost constantly surrounded by visitors. That night, however, only he and Mac seemed to be in the massive farmhouse.

"I'm sure it has been; there was little doubt after hearing you on the phone. You're still working on the Heather Gomez missing person case, right?" Mac was only mildly surprised that the well-connected Anderson already knew of his current preoccupation.

"Yeah, I am, or at least I was until today. The higher-ups are declaring the case cold and moving Hughes on to something else. It all just sort of leaves me flapping in the wind now, and there's still no trace of Heather."

"I remember her from that New Year's Eve party. What was it two years ago? She certainly knew how to make an impression on people. Though, if my memory serves, she only had eyes for you," Anderson looked up from his jars to meet Mac's gaze. "How did you swing stodgy, old Hughes, into agreeing to your participation in the investigation?" Anderson seemed quite ready to converse with his former teacher about the case.

"Um, I was just upfront with him. Nothing ever really happened between me and Heather. I kind of blew it in classic Mac fashion," Mac smiled sheepishly. "Besides, Hughes isn't that bad of a guy."

"Hughes is a dinosaur. His views on modern society are laughable at best and borderline authoritarian at worst. I won't argue that the man has a knack for sorting out the trouble the county gets now and again, but he oversteps his station. Not everyone who exists within the gray parts of our society is a bad guy." A student of Timothy Leary and

Hunter S. Thomson, Anderson was a counterculture persona, a half-century or so removed from the actual events that inspired his work.

Hughes was also the only member of the local law enforcement cadre that ever hassled him over his various quasi-legal dealings, an act which added no love for the former in Anderson's heart.

"Yeah, he can be a little dated sometimes. They call him "By the Book Hughes" down at the station, but, like you said, he's a good cop. He was our best chance at finding Heather if they would just give us more time." Mac fell quickly into talking about the case, though he worried about exposing anything more than he needed to.

"So then, why haven't you found her yet?" Anderson asked, prodding Mac to tell him more.

"Well, that's just it, though; there's nothing to find. We've been over everything: security camera recordings, local canvassing, forensic examinations of the scene, everything. There's no trace of Heather anywhere. One minute, she was on campus, and the next, she was just gone."

Anderson looked up suddenly from the table with a jar in hand. "Huzzah! Found it!" He exclaimed. In the jar was a collection of small canvas bags about an inch long on each side. "This is an exceptional tea; I concocted it a few months ago with mushrooms and kava root, a dash of grass, and a few other miscellaneous things. It should be right up your alley if I know anything about your tastes in these matters. And believe me, I do." The sometimes cheeky Anderson smiled again at Mac, determined to lift his friend's spirits.

Just then, there was the sound of a car pulling into the long driveway of the farmhouse. "And that would be VanCamp," Anderson said as he disappeared into the kitchen, "he's just back from Europe and said something about a 180-year-old bottle of scotch if you're interested," he called back to Mac.

Mac had always enjoyed the company of Ethan VanCamp, a local real estate magnate and head of a ridiculously profitable construction company. The worldly VanCamp was a little barrel of a man, no taller than Mac, but with the look of someone who could, and likely had, wrestle a bear into submission. Widely known for his flamboyant, over-the-top personality, VanCamp was someone the anthropologist in Mac loved listening to and the stories of his travels were the best tales of the bunch.

VanCamp entered with his usual pomp and bombast. "Greetings from the Emerald Isles and all points adjacent!" he called to Anderson as he walked into the living room. His longtime girlfriend, Debra, was close on his heels. "Well, what do we have here? Good to see ya, Mac!" He offered a hearty handshake to the much milder-mannered Mac.

Anderson had returned to the living room by then, hot cups of tea in hand. He handed one to Mac and placed the other near where he had been sitting.

"What's all this?" VanCamp asked immediately upon seeing the mess on the table and the steaming cups Mac and Anderson held.

"You don't have to know everything about everything, honey," Debra added. She always seemed mildly embarrassed by her counterpart, though they were otherwise inseparable. Debra was in her thirties, with short brown hair and dark green eyes. She had known Heather as well; the two worked together in the university administration office, and Mac felt a pang of guilt at not being able to offer news or hope of Heather's eminent rescue.

"It's my special concoction," Anderson beamed proudly in answer to VanCamp, "designed to relax you, lift your spirits, and possibly show you strange and fascinating hallucinations. Though it is a milder effect, it only lasts a few hours."

"Sign me up!" VanCamp enthusiastically added as he produced the scotch from a bag he was carrying. "Plus, we'll need to get into this."

"As you wish, though, I expect a grand tale of how you came by this bottle," Anderson said, examining the surprisingly ancient-looking vessel. "You too, Debra?"

"Not tonight, Anderson; someone has to keep an eye on this one." She motioned toward VanCamp, who was busying himself, opening the bottle of scotch.

"Um, I'd love to hear about your trip as well," added Mac. He was about halfway through his cup of tea and was already feeling the effects.

The lights seemed to dance slightly, and an overwhelming sense of calm and peacefulness took over his body.

Soon, the four settled into a friendly conversation. VanCamp was only too eager to regale his comrades with stories from his most recent trip, and before long, all present were involved in deep discussions and generally enjoying the effects of Anderson's tea. Several joints were passed around, and though Mac typically tried to show restraint when visiting with Anderson that night, he felt compelled to go along with the flow and attempt to unwind.

"So let's have it then," Anderson said to VanCamp as the former returned from another trip to the kitchen with a stack of glasses in hand.

VanCamp handed the bottle of scotch to Anderson, who began filling the glasses for those present. "Well, I tell ya, it isn't as grand of a tale as I'm normally used to. No royalty involved or famous folk, you understand. We bought it in an old Scottish manor. Apparently, a cask and several bottles were found in the ruins of an old burned-down manor not far from where we were. Our gracious host had purchased the land that said manor was on and had commissioned an archaeology team to excavate the ruins before he had them turned into a tennis court. Inside, they found the bottle we are now enjoying, along with several others, and the cask, as I mentioned." VanCamp was taking his time as if savoring the memory as much as the drink. "See, that's where things got weird. I asked why he bothered with the excavation in the first place; that sort of shit isn't cheap. The old chap told us that it was on account of the cannibals."

"Wait, what?! Did you say cannibals?" Anderson almost choked on the stiff drink as VanCamp left the exclamation hanging in the air.

"My thoughts exactly!" VanCamp was clearly enjoying the attention his story was getting. "You see, the previous owners of the manor, the one that burned down, they were something of local pariahs. Shunned for any number of superstitious, nonsensical reasons, they were the first suspects whenever something strange happened. Time passes, and all of a sudden, locals start disappearing. We're talking about the early nineteenth century here. Some questionable evidence was produced, and constables were called to search the manor grounds. It seems they interrupted some sort of clandestine feast attended by the family and several people from out of town. In the back kitchen, they discovered several of the missing people, butchered as one would a large hog."

"It's giving me goose bumps listening to this again. There was something truly creepy about that place," Debra interjected, looking mildly lost in the memory herself.

"I couldn't agree more," VanCamp continued. "Well, you can probably imagine what happened next. It wasn't more than a few hours, by our host's account, before news of the scene had reached the local population. By the end of the day, a mob of "concerned locals" had gathered around the manor, torches and pitchforks in hand. They burned the place to the ground and thought everything was destroyed. And everything was, essentially, except this one cask and several bottles of scotch. You can understand that I had to have it. Shame he wouldn't sell me all of them and the cask, but what can you do." VanCamp looked mildly dejected.

"Lord knows you certainly tried," Debra chuckled, and the brief levity lifted the gloom beginning to gather.

"That is, of course, assuming any of it was true," Mac said, only catching too late that he was thinking aloud.

"Always the skeptic, eh Mac?" Anderson smiled.

"Yeah, Debs was skeptical, too, when I bought it. But I know a good story when I hear one. Who even cares if it's true, right?" And VanCamp gave off a hearty laugh.

"Let's talk about something else, please, Ethan. This story is giving me the creeps all over again. There was something about that old man; he wasn't right." Debra looked at VanCamp pleadingly.

VanCamp smiled and relented. "Don't get all worried, babe; like Mac said, it was probably all just bullshit." And he turned and gave a telling wink to Mac.

Hours passed, and Mac enjoyed true relief from the stress of the past few months. Though he had hoped to talk more to Anderson about the case, he was more than content to listen to the strange tales VanCamp was full of that evening. Long into the night, the four spoke on many topics, and Mac almost forgot everything back in the real world.

Around 2 a.m., mildly bleary-eyed still, Mac headed back home. There is a deep darkness to the back roads of Hueta County. Very few street lights exist outside the cities, and the homes are spaced considerably apart, most of them being farms. It is surprisingly easy, among such a deep gloom, to lose one's bearings and become hopelessly lost among the turns and twists of the roads only locals tread. Anderson's home sat comfortably at the bottom of a steep hill, nestled away from the sight of passing traffic.

As Mac's light blue sedan crested the hill rising south of Anderson's place, he noticed how clear and crisp of a night it had become. The storm clouds of the early evening seemed to have passed by without so much as a drop. Instead, a slight crescent moon painted the landscape a faint blue-gray. Atop the hill, the vast expanse of the night sky lay bare before Mac's eyes in all of its terrible grandeur, and Mac worried that the effects of Anderson's mysterious tea were not entirely behind him.

There were several paths one could take to return to Eagle Creek from Anderson's country home, and Mac chose the more rural and winding option. He wished not to encounter any traffic on his drive, and though it was longer overall, Mac felt no need to rush in returning home.

Several miles from Anderson's home, as he turned onto a cross street that would eventually lead him back to a main thoroughfare, the lights of Mac's car panned across a farmhouse opposite where he was stopped. There, in the window on the second floor of what looked to be an ancillary building on the farm, stood unmistakably Heather Gomez. Mac slammed on the brakes of his turning vehicle and sat stunned for a moment. How could this be? Quickly, he pulled his car over to the side of the road and burst from the driver's seat, flashlight in hand, ready to investigate this new lead.

When he again illuminated the window, it was empty, and Mac paused. Could he have been mistaken? Coming to his senses, he realized regardless of what he saw, there was little he could do half baked and at two in the morning. Still, he hesitated. Was that indeed Heather? He almost called Hughes and wavered on the edge of action, paralyzed for a moment. After a few minutes, the adrenaline rush passed, and Mac decided to head home before he drew any unwanted attention.

On the drive home, Mac's mind reeled at the possibility of a break in the case. There were more questions now than he was entirely comfortable with. What mad chain of events could have led him to stumble onto such a clue? But he was confident that the tea had passed his system. And he was sure he saw Heather in that window. He would know Heather anywhere. No, this was serendipity beyond explanation, Mac thought. What else could explain it? In the morning, he would contact Deputy Hughes, and finally, they would put the business of Heather Gomez behind them. Mac was sure of that as well. They were going to save her.

II.

Several things occurred to Mac once he had sufficiently awakened and rose the following morning. The first was that, in all likelihood, he was mistaken. There was, right as he was thinking of it, likely some terrified young woman living at that address whom he had scared senseless. Who wouldn't be afraid of the deranged madman clamoring from his vehicle in the dead of night, chasing after women in windows? There was something unspeakable in the back of Mac's mind, but he couldn't yet come to terms with it.

His second thought was that Hughes would never listen to him without proof. The gruff deputy was known for many things, but skipping on the details was not one of them. Nor was he likely to be overly forgiving of Mac's choice to drive himself home after the night he'd had at Anderson's. A decision Mac now questioned himself in light of sobriety. Could it all have just been some lingering hallucination? Though he would have liked the simple explanation, Mac's recognition of Heather was hard to shake. And there was something else, something in his gut telling him to press on.

This led to the third thought: Mac needed to figure out some connection between Heather's case and that strange old farm before he brought anything to Hughes. This would mean actual investigation on his own, and Mac openly questioned if he had it in him. Wasn't this more the sheriff's department's business than it was his? Again, the unspeakable thought danced at the corner of his mind. Though he could not explain why, Mac felt he needed to continue on this course with a conviction he had seldom known.

One thing Mac knew he could do was to dig a little into the location, that strange farm where he had seen Heather the night before. At least potentially, this path could concretely solve the identity issue if he was lucky. Mac resolved to reach out to VanCamp, partly due to how recently he had seen the local realtor but also because he knew there was very little the deeply involved VanCamp didn't know about the county at large. Of course, VanCamp was unavailable when Mac phoned, but he left a message with the polite secretary who answered and was sure he would hear back soon enough.

By that afternoon, Mac did indeed hear back from VanCamp, and he learned that the location in question was known as the Alsop Farm, which was owned and operated by Herman and Peggy Alsop. It was common knowledge, VanCamp claimed, that the farm had fallen on hard times. However, it wasn't for sale as far as he could tell. Then, the always inquisitive VanCamp asked why Mac was interested in the first place, offering that he had some properties available in the area if the latter was looking for something in particular. At this first sign of suspicion, Mac decided to end the call.

A brief search into the public records showed Mac that the Alsops had no children. Further, it appeared that the building was likely an additional house on the property, perhaps for the housing of the seasonal workers common throughout the county, in which he had seen Heather. It could easily have been someone else. Stymied by this new information, Mac devised a plan to dig deeper.

One of his duties at the museum was to search out potential new exhibits for display. The university was always looking to drum up good press and loved nothing more than an insular, self-aggrandizing puff piece. Projects focused on the surrounding localities within Hueta County were consumed with almost equal voracity.

Mac spent the remainder of the day in his office at the university. He gathered pamphlets and some of the media about the museum that he had and genuinely prepared a presentation for the Alsops. VanCamp had let slip that the farm was almost as old as the university, so it was a relatively simple thing for Mac to develop a pitch about local contemporary history and the Alsop Farm.

That evening, Mac spent time contemplating his plan. Again, he considered involving Deputy Hughes, and again, he forestalled the coming revelation to his companion in deference to finding actual evidence. What kept circling his mind? A vague thought, some faint half-remembered thing that seemed so vitally important. Mac lay down to another night of restless and fitful sleep, unable to escape the haunting sensation that there was more to this situation than he was aware of.

The next day was Wednesday, and free of his teaching obligations, Mac spent the morning finalizing his pitch for the Alsops. After arranging for coverage at the museum and a brief lunch, Mac headed out to the Alsop Farm.

With the paperwork in tow, he planned to approach the situation as genuinely as possible. There was tangible potential danger if these people had kidnapped and were holding Heather. Mac had trouble at first controlling the nervous energy that pervaded his body.

The maroon university van Mac drove pulled onto the Alsop Farm nearly thirty minutes after leaving the school. Mac had decided at the last moment to take the museum's "official" transport—not so much to add to his ploy, but more so if, by chance, his sedan had been seen when he first happened upon the farm. The van was slow and uncomfortable, but he was confident that the added caution would only work in his favor.

Pulling up to the main house, Mac noticed the farm seemed abandoned. A single dilapidated pickup truck in the driveway was the only evidence of any other people from the outside. Mac parked behind the truck and headed up the porch to the front door.

Before he could knock on the large wooden door, it swung open wide, and an irate elderly man dressed in overalls and a flannel shirt was on the other side.

"Whatever it is, we don't want any!" The man insisted as he stepped onto the porch.

"I'm sorry, um, you must have mistaken ..." Mac stammered, but it was clear his counterpart was in no mood to listen to any explanation.

"I told you, boy, I don't care what it is or why you're here. If you got any sense you'll turn around right now and get out of here! If you know what's good for you!" The man practically fumed.

The last part caught Mac off guard. Was that an actual threat from this ancient human being? He hesitated for a moment, caught by the unexpected nature of everything unfolding. Then, a call came from inside the house.

"Who's here, Herman? Why haven't you let them in?" Mac presumed the female voice to be that of Peggy Alsop.

"They were just leaving, got the wrong address. " Herman called back as he glared at Mac.

"But sir," Mac protested, "if I can just talk to you and your wife for a moment, I promise I'm not trying to sell anything." Mac did his best to seem genuine and not as nervous and trembling as he felt.

The call from inside came again, more forcefully this time. "Let them in, Herman! Don't be inhospitable!"

The old man sighed and shook his head. "This is on you now, boy; I tried to warn ya," he turned and walked back into the house, beckoning Mac to follow.

For a moment, terror gripped Mac's heart. What was he getting himself into here? He considered his continued decision not to involve his friend Deputy Hughes in his investigation. Steeling himself against this new apprehension, he stepped across the threshold.

Inside, the door opened onto a hallway with a set of stairs directly ahead on the right. Herman had moved into a living room on the left, and a dining room could be seen through an archway on the right.

As Mac's view came around to the stairs again, almost suddenly, Peggy Alsop appeared. The elderly woman looked small and frail but moved down the stairs with a powerful grace. Inexplicably, Mac's body resisted moving any further into the strange home.

"Come in, come in, dear," Mrs. Alsop chimed. "Don't let my grumpy old husband give you a hard time. He's just never been the friendliest of sorts. So you're from the university, I take it? I saw the van outside. Whatsoever can we do for someone like you?"

Mac exhaled and fell into the pitch he had practiced. It primarily explained the university anthropological research initiatives and architectural archives, which Mac felt sounded obtuse enough to be believable.

The Alsops listened politely, now all three of them sitting in the living room. They seemed surprisingly amenable to Mac's proposed project for the farm. Though he had hoped for such a turnout, Mac couldn't help but feel this was too easy. It was far too willing on the part of the Alsops. Indeed, no kidnapper would willingly invite strangers into their midst like this. It had almost seemed that the mention of students and people from the university regularly visiting the farm palpably excited Mrs. Alsop. Herman had changed his mood considerably, too, now seeming to be a doting husband and thoughtful man, nothing like the firebrand from the porch.

There was something else as well, something Mac was barely conscious of. Faintly and seemingly from somewhere above him, a peculiar sound was emanating. It sounded like metal being dragged across concrete but delicate and almost oddly musical. Or was it outside? Perhaps some piece of farm equipment that was running? It was hard to focus on the sound, and it was barely audible, but something in it chilled Mac to his core. Chalking it up to his nerves and the pressure of what he was undertaking, he decided to ignore this strange new factor and continue with his questioning.

Then came the big part, digging into the events from several nights before. Mac found it difficult to believe these people had anything to do with Heather's disappearance. Still, he had not come this far only to back out at the crucial moment.

"Were both houses on the property from the original construction in the 1800s?" Mac started, hoping to turn the discussion to the other house on the property, where he had seen Heather.

"No, that other house was built in the '40s by my grandfather's father," Herman replied. "Used it to house workers, at least we used to."

"So, no one lives there now?" Mac pressed, trying his best to hide his true intentions.

"What's that matter?" Herman replied, and Mac began to think he was on to something meaningful.

"Um, nothing, I suppose," Mac answered, trying to seem surprised at the elder Alsop's reaction. He knew better, of course; now, a picture of what was occurring was beginning to form in his mind. Mac was sure he had seen someone in the window of that second house several nights before; there was no doubt in his mind of that. He took the reaction from Herman Alsop as more confirmation of his beliefs.

For his part, Herman, too, seemed to notice a change in the nature of the conversation. "I think we've answered enough of your questions for today, Professor Hollister. You'll have to excuse us; there's work to be done around the farm," and he motioned for Mac to leave.

Peggy Alsop again chimed up. "Not very hospitable," practically spitting out the last words.

Mac hesitated but decided there was likely little more he would get through this manner of questioning, so he rose to leave. In the hallway before the front door, Mac paused and turned toward the living room to offer a final thanks and goodbye to the Alsops. For the briefest moment, he swore he saw something atop the steps to the second floor, but it was gone before his mind had a chance to decipher the strange image it was receiving. Mac shook his head and headed outside, beginning to fear that the stress of the endeavor was getting to him.

Back in the university van, Mac discreetly spied the second house as he headed back down the driveway. Did he actually believe that the elderly Herman Alsop had managed to kidnap and detain Heather Gomez? He wondered. But what other explanation could there be? Mac had witnessed a wide range of behaviors from Herman during their relatively brief encounter, and he certainly imagined the possibility of madness from the elderly couple.

Mac drove back to the university and pondered the situation he had found himself in. He decided patience was his best approach and resolved to head home and try to rest on the knowledge he had gained. He was going to have to involve Deputy Hughes at some point. Exactly when that was going to happen needed to be settled.

That evening, after a meal and some needed busywork from the university, Mac settled into another fitful night of sleep. In his dreams, he was haunted by the image of Heather Gomez in that old farmhouse window, crying out silently for him to save her.

III.

The following day was Thursday, and Mac headed to the university proper to teach his two obligatory classes, as he did every Tuesday and Thursday from 10 a.m. to 2 p.m., including his on-campus office hours. Mac relished the opportunity to get his mind off the terrible dreams and ever more sinister implications at that lonely farmhouse in the sticks. Still, it was hard to shake, and a terrible foreboding fear permeated Mac's thoughts. There was something at work on the Alsop Farm; he was sure of it.

The further he moved away from the encounter, the more he became unsettled by Peggy Alsop. Something in her behavior had seemed off, but it was her voice, in those moments she seemed upset, that had begun to stoke fear in Mac's heart. Was there some connection between his awful dreams and Mrs. Alsop's distorted call, or was that just Mac's imagination? Mac's body involuntarily shivered; whatever was going on, he couldn't deny his composure had been weakened due to everything over the past days.

By the time Mac had finished his stint at the university, he had decided on a course of action. Though he could not explain why, he felt that he needed to return to the Alsop Farm. There was an urgency to this thought that had not been present before, but Mac worried that his meddling would spell disaster for Heather. He needed to act. He knew he had nothing to take to Deputy Hughes but could desperately use the experienced sheriff's deputy's assistance. Mac spent the next hour crafting a letter to Hughes explaining his suspicions about the Alsops and detailing this intention to return to the farm to get into the second house and either rescue or gain evidence of the whereabouts of Heather Gomez.

Though both of his suspects were elderly and, on the surface, physically no match for Mac, he felt a great fear for his safety on this chosen path. He was determined to follow through on the desperate rescue mission his mind had concocted despite his fears, goaded on by a growing sense of courage that burned in his chest.

His letter was completed, and Mac headed for the university post office box to mail it. He figured that given his choice to use "snail mail," he would have roughly two days to see his plan unfold before Deputy Hughes was alerted to it. What Mac could never know was that the local postman was on campus just minutes after his letter was in the box. It was the postman's last stop of the day before returning to the Eagle Creek post office, conveniently located next door to the Hueta County Sheriff's Department. Mac's letter would end up on the desk of Deputy Hughes a scant hour after it was mailed.

Mac returned to the maroon university van and headed toward the Alsop Farm. He was prepared for anything but imagined some variety of talking the Alsops into giving him a tour of the premises. Though by now, with even the thought of her mildly unnerving him, Mac figured Peggy Alsop was the most amenable of the pair and his likely ticket to viewing the property. To this end, he brought along two rather large volumes of architectural history books he had grabbed while on campus. He reasoned that his best chance at finding anything was to appear as believable as possible.

A half-hour later, Mac arrived at the Alsop Farm. As he approached, he noticed how starkly illuminated the farm was in the afternoon light. Herman Alsop was sitting atop a small tractor near the barn when Mac arrived, and he motioned for Mac to come over to him.

Mac exited the van and walked over to Herman, who remained atop his tractor though it was shut off. "I know why you're here, Professor Hollister; we ain't got much time."

Mac made to interject, but Herman continued.

"You're here about that Gomez girl. I recognized your name when you came around yesterday. The paper ran a couple stories on you and that deputy last year when that old case got finished. You're right to have questions, but for now, you just gotta trust me and listen."

The old man's eyes kept darting between Mac and the farmhouse behind him. Herman was yet again completely different in character. Urgent almost to the point of pleading, Herman seemed far more the frail elderly farmer Mac had initially expected to encounter the day before.

"There's something in that other house, not ours, mind you, but the old workers' house. It came here a few years back, came from the stars. I don't understand how or really why, but it can speak, and it has power over people's minds. Once you've seen it, it can wrap itself up into your thinking. It's allergic to the sun, so it says, and it sleeps around now. It's the only reason I can talk to you like this. Normally I can't say nothing about it. Not that I don't want to, you understand, but I can't. It won't let me. Even now, with it asleep, I can feel it behind the back of my eyes." Herman trembled slightly and looked, for all the world, as if he might keel over. "Peggy, my poor sweet Peggy, is too far gone now. She sleeps when it does, doesn't even think for herself anymore. The thing is flat, you see, two-dimensional, like some sick ribbon with terrible eyes. It eats folk by squashing 'em down to be like it is; it takes months. It needs us to keep itself hidden and won't let us go no matter what. There's nothing you can do to stop it, and you can't come by here and bring them students and all that. It'll take 'em all! Every last one of 'em!!"

Herman Alsop shook with rage, fear, and desperation. His eyes were wild with madness and terror, and Mac was visibly stunned at the turn of events. Had this man just admitted to knowledge about Heather Gomez and then blamed an alien for it? Nothing Mac had prepared for had been enough for this. His mind reeled. He made to walk toward the house, but the surprisingly agile Herman Alsop was off the tractor in a blink and blocked his path.

"No! You've gotta go now, Hollister. You ain't getting in the house. It'll be up any minute now! Don't make me stop you!"

Mac was so unprepared for this line of events that he caught himself believing the old man's wild story. What was it that Herman had said? A ribbon with eyes. The image made Mac's blood freeze. There was something evil on that old farm, and Mac faltered. He rushed back to the van, his heart in his throat, and headed frantically away from the farm.

Shock and terror clawed at Mac's mind as he raced away from that cursed old farm. Something drove his fears, but he struggled to comprehend it. It was right there, in Peggy's voice and in the odd scraping sound he had heard in the Alsop's home, but somehow, it was still out of his grasp.

Adrenaline was coursing through his veins, and Mac nearly drove headlong into an oncoming delivery truck. He swerved at the last moment and pulled his car over to the side of the road. He was still close enough to the Alsop Farm to see its barn on the horizon, far too close for Mac's comfort at the moment.

Mac was unsure how to proceed but was sure that continuing to drive in his current state was dangerous, not only to himself but also to anyone who happened across his path. He reasoned that he needed time to think and desperately sought a place to cool his heels. Then, a thought occurred: Anderson's house was only a few miles away.

With renewed urgency, Mac made quickly for Anderson's home at the bottom of the nearby hills. He pulled into the drive and saw that, indeed, Anderson's SUV was parked there, and it looked as though the entrepreneurial botanist was home.

Mac entered the farmhouse by the usual means but could not immediately locate Anderson. The larger living room and kitchen were devoid of life, and inside, the house was dark with curtains drawn and no lights on. Mac paused for a moment near the side door he had entered through. Where could Anderson have gotten to? His logic told him Anderson was likely somewhere amidst his various fields tending his crops. Though they were in late September, Mac knew that Anderson would have things growing up until the first snow was on the ground.

Heading back outside, Mac made his way into the backyard. Both before him and to the right of the small yard, Anderson's fields of wild plants stretched out as far as the eye could see. To the left, the area was hemmed in by the neighboring hills. Though an impressive sight, there was still no sign of Anderson or anything that led Mac to think someone was working outside. The afternoon light cast strange shadows from the hillside, and Mac felt compelled to move back indoors.

Inside, Mac stopped in the entryway of the side door. Nothing had changed in the farmhouse, and sadly, Mac began to think that his trip to safer and saner surroundings had been in vain. Then suddenly, and giving Mac something of a shock, a call came from below him. "Is someone up there?" came Anderson's familiar voice.

"Hey Anderson, it's Mac," Mac replied, relieved that the sound had been familiar.

"I'm in the basement. Come on down! You remember the way?" The last part was added as almost an afterthought.

"I think so," Mac managed to reply, though he doubted that Anderson heard him. This was not precisely the situation he had expected to encounter, and his nerves were frayed enough as they were. He made his way into the second smaller living room, in the back of which there was a door leading to the basement. The door was open, and light could be seen shining from below.

Mac made his way down the rickety stairs as carefully as he could. An earthy, musty aroma greeted his nostrils as he descended. Rounding a sharp corner at the base of the stairs, he came upon an even more unexpected sight. Aligned over a dozen long tables were tray after tray of mushrooms of every shape and variety, as could be easily imagined. The sight was the farthest thing from Mac's mind and shook him from his panic-stricken state.

"Well, um, this sure is a sight," was the best thing Mac could manage in spite of himself. Anderson was sitting on a tall stool in the approximate center of the tables. He wore a dirty apron and a pair of enormous yellow gloves over his usual hippie attire. He seemed to be tending to one of the trays, which contained a strange bright red fungus Mac had never seen before.

"Yes, yes, welcome to the grotto, as I call it." Anderson had pet names for almost everything. This is where I cultivate my shrooms, though I imagine you gathered that much already." He put the tray back among its fellows with a concerned look. You aren't one to show up unannounced, Mac. Is everything alright?" Some would say Anderson was almost prescient at times.

"Yes ... no ... sort of, I guess. I don't know," Mac smiled weakly. He had been so near the brink of madness just minutes before, and now, as he stood amongst the almost surreal sight of Anderson's grotto, he was unsure exactly what to think. Did he believe everything that crazy old farmer had told him? Maybe that was it; maybe Herman was crazy, driven mad by some kidnapping scheme gone wrong. Maybe he was going crazy, Mac thought.

"Kind of feels like we're losing you here, Mac; maybe you should come upstairs and sit down," Anderson said, looking at Mac with equal measures of concern and suspicion.

Mac nodded in agreement, and the two headed back upstairs the way Mac had initially come. Once in the smaller second living room, Anderson led Mac back into the kitchen and a waiting seat at the spacious table that dominated the area. Once Mac was seated, Anderson put on a kettle for tea and passed his unexpected companion a lit joint he had produced from seemingly somewhere on his person.

"I don't usually partake during the week," Mac stammered, still mildly in a daze.

"It'll help you calm down, trust me," Anderson smiled as he blew out a smoke ring.

Mac relented, not knowing what else to do and needing to take Anderson's advice regardless of his ego. He took a long drag from the joint and coughed.

"Now, don't go and get into a coughing fit; that won't do. 'Mr. I don't want any,'" Anderson chuckled at his friend. Mac felt some of the tension in his mind beginning to ease.

"So, can I ask you a strange question?" Mac looked expectantly at Anderson. He wasn't exactly sure where he was going with this, but he needed to get some sense of himself again, and this seemed to be the easiest path.

"Not that this entire meeting hasn't been a bit strange, my good man, but sure, ask away." Anderson had always been fond of listening to anything and everything people chose to tell him with complete and rapt attention.

"Do you believe in aliens?" Mac asked, though he felt foolish once the words were out of his mouth.

"Like little green men from Mars? or, like, 'Do you believe life exists somewhere out in the universe?'" If it's the latter, that's an easy 'yes,' based solely on statistics. But this doesn't feel like you are having some existential crisis here. What's really going on?" Anderson was always perceptive, but at the moment, Mac needed a little more disbelief and a little less of Anderson's withering intellect.

"I honestly don't know. It's just, um, a story I heard," Mac hesitated, as unsure about what he felt as he was about overly involving Anderson in a potential investigation. "You talk to a ton of people, right? I've had experience canvassing and taking surveys during grad school. You get used to how people talk about things. You can tell pretty easily when someone is lying or if someone's holding something back, that sort of thing. But sometimes, you get these people and the things they say, they say them with such authenticity, such urgency, that you can't doubt what it is they're telling you." Mac paused and let out a deep breath. Things were working themselves out in his mind that his consciousness was unprepared for. "I just heard a story like that. Not really that far from here. And, well, I guess it's gotten me sort of rattled."

"Well, that certainly does explain some of it, I think." Anderson looked again, concerned for his friend's well-being. "One would think your background in anthropology would have given you some experience with the odd tale or two. Hell, you barely blinked at VanCamp's sordid drama about the cannibals the other night." Anderson was already working on a theory of his own regarding his friend Mac. "But, like you said, I do indeed talk to plenty of people, and I am sure there is more to this story." He paused and looked directly at Mac, seeming to gauge something in his mind. "I don't entirely imagine I am going to convince you to tell me that story you heard, but all the same, there seems to be something else to all of this."

"I suppose there is," Mac said. "You see, this story could explain what happened to Heather." Mac swallowed hard and suddenly felt a lump in his throat at the thought of Heather's fate.

"And that would explain the rest." Anderson had an understanding look on his face. I always thought there was something between the two of you. Not just some schoolgirl fling, you understand, or vice versa for her. It seemed like there was a genuine connection."

"I'm, um, not really in the practice of admitting to this stuff if you follow." Mac seemed almost worried over what he was revealing to himself, Anderson notwithstanding. "And there's nothing to admit to; it wasn't like that. Maybe after she had graduated, but now we may never know." That last thought stung Mac's mind worse than he had intended.

"You're going to find her Mac. Just keep believing that and keep working. Can you call in Hughes?" Anderson was doing his best to comfort his troubled friend.

"Wouldn't expect you to suggest that," Mac shrugged, "but we are supposed to be off the case. Remember? I did leave him a message, but I don't know when exactly he will get it. I may need to act on my own." Mac was steeling himself to eventually return to the farm.

"Now that sounds unexpected, Professor Hollister," Anderson only ever used Mac's official title when he wanted to make sure Mac was listening. "I don't know what you're thinking of, but you've got a kind of mad glint in your eyes, Mac. I think you should maybe cool your jets here for a moment. You aren't acting like yourself."

"Ah, maybe you're right, what the fuck am I thinking?" Mac sighed. He only ever cursed when he was extremely stressed. "This is a lot, not being able to find Heather. I can't really tell up from down anymore." Mac gathered himself and took a deep breath. "I probably should just call Hughes, but I'm unsure if that will help. I can't imagine he'll be interested in reopening the case so soon, especially with my laughable evidence."

"Which I would still love to hear about sometime, mind you, maybe after everything has sorted itself out," Anderson added with his characteristic broad smile.

"Maybe someday," Mac smiled again, at ease from his friend's kindly demeanor.

"In the meantime, I have an answer to your earlier query," Anderson began. "I've been thinking about it since you asked it, and my answer is yes, I believe in aliens." He paused there and gave Mac a concerned look.

"That said, it is entirely something else to believe aliens had anything to do with the disappearance of your lady friend."

Mac wasn't sure entirely how to take what Anderson was telling him.

"But I could be convinced to believe that, too, given the right circumstances." Anderson seemed to sense Mac's growing confusion. "From what you told me the other night, it seems like you've exhausted the normal options for finding her, right? So now your mind grapples with things outside the normal to explain it. That is sound reasoning, as far as I'm concerned. My issue is with the evidence you claim to have gained. You were one of the people who taught me to value hard facts and scientific evidence when I was in school. This would lead me to think you have something incredible as proof. But that doesn't seem to be the case." Anderson paused, not wanting to come down too hard on his friend.

"You aren't wrong," Mac conceded. "I don't have anything to go on here besides my gut reaction. But I can't shake it all the same." A chill passed through Mac, and he began to worry again about the toll everything was taking on him.

"Now, don't get too far ahead of yourself, though remember I said I believe you. Abduction stories are pervasive, and I would be the first to admit I've seen some strange things here in the wilds at night. Who's to say something like that couldn't have grabbed Heather? Maybe you just aren't looking for the right evidence."

This thought hadn't occurred to Mac. Suddenly, he felt heartened by his friend's support.

"You said the last place she was seen was on campus, correct? Maybe there is something there that could corroborate this story of yours. Something that wasn't part of what you had been looking for before but is now. Of course, figuring out what that *is,* is an entirely different chestnut." Anderson smirked and thought about this new problem he had concocted.

Still, Mac felt great relief that Anderson had believed him. Somewhere in his consciousness, he knew he would need to return to the farm. He was determined to be ready for it this time. He would need the evening to make more preparations, but he had considered this and given himself enough time. What drove this determination to save Heather single-handedly, he could not say, as never before had such behavior been part of who he was.

Eventually, Mac rose from the table and, after offering his apologies for the interruption and his heartfelt thanks, made his way back to the maroon university van, parked haphazardly in the driveway. The afternoon was getting on, and Mac had no desire to stay out past dark with everything he had heard that day.

Now calmed but cautious, Mac drove back home. He reasoned that if he took a different route, stopping at his office in the museum rather than going directly home, he could avoid driving past the Alsop Farm again. While he needed no such justification to take a different path home, Mac headed on a slight detour. Nearly forty-five minutes later, Mac concluded his drive at a loss as to how he should proceed but was determined to continue to act. The presence of Deputy Hughes' cruiser outside of his office at the museum was almost not a surprise.

IV.

Mac parked and exited the van as the sun was making its final pass toward the horizon. The day was rapidly turning to night, and Mac couldn't help but feel that time had been slipping away from him all week. As he walked to the museum and his apparent pending encounter with Hughes, Mac's nerves began to take hold. Was he ready to tell Hughes everything he had seen, everything he had heard? Did he even believe it? All Mac knew for sure was that he needed to act.

Mac walked into the museum to see Hughes standing at the reception desk. The tall, muscular sheriff's deputy was the epitome of the image of a cop. "Was wondering when you were gonna get back," Hughes said in his usual placid manner. Mac wondered how long the sheriff's deputy had been waiting for him.

"Come to my office. We, um, need to talk about a few things." Mac tried his best not to let his nerves overwhelm him.

"I should think so," Hughes replied, following Mac deeper into the museum.

It took Mac twenty minutes to calm down enough to begin explaining what had just occurred and another half hour for the actual telling. Deputy Hughes listened quietly and even took several notes over the course of the story. When Mac finished, he looked pleadingly to Hughes for guidance.

"And you mean to tell me you believe all of this?" Deputy Hughes began. "I've got to ask Mac, are you high?"

Mac was noticeably taken aback at the question. "How, um, what are you even talking about?" he stammered.

"Oh, come off it, Mac, I'm a cop. I've always known about your friendship with our dear Anderson Peate, and you practically reek of pot at the moment. It's not really a big deal, especially these days, but this. If you aren't high, I might start to be a little worried about you."

Mac stared blankly at Hughes. "Okay, fine, yes, I smoked a little pot with Anderson an hour ago or so; it's not like I'm fucked up here or something." He was mildly offended that Hughes couldn't see that he was sincere.

"Alright," Hughes continued, "so you want to know what I think? I think you came across a bored, unpleasant, and possibly senile old curmudgeon. He recognized you from the paper, and since you bothered him the previous day, he decided to take you for a ride. He fed you a frankly ridiculous story, which you ate up and probably spent the afternoon having a laugh at your expense."

"Then, just to make sure your important new information for our investigation was promptly reported, you rushed over to the house of the local drug kingpin and got a good buzz on. And now, probably addled by drugs and inane banter, you hurry back to the university to continue into the night with your unsanctioned investigation," he paused, "Did I get everything?"

"And I suppose it means nothing to you that I saw Heather on those premises?" Mac protested, determined to make Deputy Hughes believe him.

"About that, what exactly were you doing out there so late at night? I'd guess at the involvement of ol' Anderson again." The smug look on Hughes' face irritated Mac. "You do realize you aren't an actual part of the Hueta County Sheriff's Department. You can't start an investigation into someone because of something you think you glimpsed at the moment. Or for any reason, while we're on the subject," Hughes paused and gave Mac a concerned look.

"Look, Hughes, this is serious." Mac tried to hide the fear and doubt in his voice. "I know how this sounds. I feel crazy even telling you about it, but there's something to this; I can feel it. There was something about how Herman spoke. I know he wasn't lying. At least come out to the farm with me and have a look around. Something ... we have to do something." Mac noticed a desperation in his voice and actions he had not entirely intended.

Hughes stared at Mac. The deputy had come to trust him over their time working together and had never known the mild-mannered museum curator to embellish on much. Still, believing such a tale was a tall order, as was his "official" involvement should he comply with Mac's request. As much as he wished it otherwise, Deputy Hughes had no real reason to doubt Mac's story, content notwithstanding. His pivot practically knocked Mac over.

"Okay, let's go out there and talk to this Herman Alsop then."

"You have to listen ... wait ... what?" Mac stumbled over his words. His mind was not fully capable of accepting his companion's radical change in course.

"Well, you said yourself, Mr. Alsop admitted to involvement in the Gomez case unprompted, right? At the very least, it's culpable under filing a false police report. If this will put you at ease about everything, then so be it. I'm not terribly busy at the moment," Hughes said.

Mac blinked, still stunned by the change in Hughes' attitude. He realized, too, that there was a fear over returning now, in the early evening, to the farm. Mac knew it was madness to believe Herman's story, but he couldn't get past the earnest plea from the elderly farmer. "It'll take 'em all!" The words echoed in Mac's mind.

"You okay, Mac? You're turning white," Hughes' concern for his friend's well-being was as much a practical necessity as anything else.

"Yeah, um, I can manage. We'd better be prepared, though; I don't think this is going to go well." Mac tried his best to act as calm and collected as he could.

"You really believe all this, hunh? That we're about to meet E.T.? I've never seen you like this; I have, honestly, been waiting the last five minutes for you to tell me you're putting me on. Now what? Do you want a gun? Should I call for backup?"

Mac was stung by Hughes' apparent condescension, but the upset deputy continued.

"We'll go out there, interrupt those people's night, and then you and I are going to have a long talk about wasting police time and the boundaries of civilian investigations." Hughes still expected Mac to break and admit to some ruse or poorly thought-out joke.

Mac swallowed hard. "I didn't mean anything like that, just to be ready for something. You don't have to believe me; we just need to do something." He was stunned that his courage had chosen this moment to draw a line in the sand.

"Alright then," Hughes concluded, "I'll follow you out there in the cruiser. Let's go."

V.

Mac tried desperately to make sense of everything as he drove his light blue sedan out to the Alsop Farm. From the outside, he imagined it looked like he was in some sort of trouble, what with the Hueta County Sheriff's Department cruiser close on his heels. The reality was far worse, he worried. Everything in his instincts told him that something was rotten at the Alsop Farm. He was sure he had seen Heather in that window four nights prior. Mac's thoughts broke away. Had it only been four days? So much had happened in that time that Mac struggled with its enormity.

Then, there were the questions surrounding Herman Alsop. Was an elderly man of his condition even able to carry out such a kidnapping? Herman's behavior had varied wildly every time Mac had met him.

Further, Mac didn't want to admit how concerned he was over Herman's "explanation" of everything. What was it, just in the corner of his mind? Some realization that his sanity simply refused to acknowledge. The description Herman had made, "a ribbon with eyes," had stirred some sick recognition inside of Mac. He shuddered and felt momentarily ill, enough that he nearly missed the farm's driveway.

As the two vehicles pulled up the drive to the main house, Mac wondered if he had the will to see everything through. He had never been much on heroics, but some previously unheralded reserve of courage pushed him on.

Mac and Deputy Hughes exited their vehicles and walked up to the porch. Though it was still early in the evening and relatively light out, the porch light was on, and the whole area was lit with an orange glow.

"Let me do the talking, okay?" Hughes said to Mac as he knocked on the door.

There was no response.

After a minute, Hughes knocked again, more forcefully, in the classic "this is the police" fashion. Still, no response came from the old farmhouse.

There were lights on in the lower floor of the house. This and the bright porch light all spoke to the elderly couple being home, as did the pickup truck in the driveway.

"They were quick to answer previously?" Hughes asked almost absentmindedly. "I'm gonna walk over to the barn, see if anyone is out back. Wait here and keep knocking. Give a holler if anyone comes to the door. I'll be quick," he added, and in a flash, was on his way around the right side of the house toward the barn.

Mac noticed his hand was shaking as he went to knock again. Distracted, he almost struck Peggy Alsop as she opened the door.

"Oh! Professor Hollister, what brings you back out here tonight?" Peggy smiled, but Mac couldn't help but feel she had been expecting him.

"I, we, need to, um, talk to your husband, Mrs. Alsop." At that moment, Mac remembered he was alone and gave a sharp call over his shoulder for Hughes.

"What's wrong, dear? Is that a sheriff's car? What's going on?" Peggy seemed to be rapidly losing her pleasant demeanor.

"It's important, Mrs. Alsop. Is Herman available? We just need to talk to him," Mac continued as forcefully as he could. He could feel his pulse quicken with each passing moment as he stood on that oddly illuminated porch. Deputy Hughes was still nowhere to be seen, and gravely, Mac worried for his friend.

"My associate, Deputy Hughes, just went to check if anyone was in the barn. He'll be back any moment. Could you get Herman for us?" Mac pressed the issue even though he had no real plan of where to go next.

Peggy Alsop seemed to have recovered from her initial shock. "Yes, of course, dear. I'll get Herman. Why don't you come in and have a seat in the living room? We'll leave the door open for your sheriff friend." Peggy turned back into the house and motioned for Mac to follow.

Reluctantly, Mac followed. He didn't want to be alone in the farmhouse, and further, he had no reason to trust Peggy any more than Herman. He relented for reasons he could not properly articulate.

Inside, Mac sat uneasily on the oversized couch. There was a terrible stillness all around him, as if the house itself was afraid to make any sound. It was also terribly dark, though clearly, lights were on somewhere downstairs. The orange glow of the porch light crept in from the hallway, and Mac thought again of his erstwhile companion. Could something have happened to Hughes? What exactly was his next move, Mac wondered.

When Mac heard it again, it was subtle, hanging just at the edge of audible sound—this vile scraping sound that managed to repulse and horrify with equal measure. He had heard it before when he was in this very living room but had discounted it as the sounds of an old house or his madness from the stress. Now, there was something else to the sound, something that made it sound organic. Additionally, its location seemed different, outside the house rather than above it.

Mac stifled the urge to vomit. There was also the realization that the sound had been present that first night as Mac had scanned the adjacent building looking for Heather Gomez. The knowledge almost kindled some more profound understanding in Mac, and for a moment, he swooned upon the edge of madness.

"Mac! You in there!" The call came from the porch and broke Mac from his stupor. "I'm here, Hughes!" Mac replied. He then got up and went to the hallway to meet the deputy. He hadn't expected Hughes' weapon to be drawn when he entered the entryway.

"Thank god. We got trouble, Mac," Hughes lowered his weapon. The experienced sheriff's deputy was shaken.

"The barn's full of bodies ... remains, but something's wrong with them. They're all smashed and thin, like paper; I've never seen anything like it," Hughes shook his head as if trying to shake the image from his mind.

"I've called for backup. We're gonna wait for them; then we're taking this place by force; no way two old people did all of this. Something bad is happening here, Mac. How'd you get inside?"

"Peggy let me in. She went to get Herman," Mac answered, not entirely following Hughes' line of thinking.

"Herman's dead, Mac. His body is in the barn. It looked like a shotgun blast, close range. His was the only normal body I found," Hughes stated as matter-of-fact.

Mac reeled at the news, and a deep fear rose in his stomach.

"Where'd she go, Mac?" Hughes' eyes flashed wildly, and Mac pointed up the stairs they were standing next to.

"Okay, new plan," Hughes continued a grim determination growing in his voice. "You head out to the cars and wait for backup. Tell them where I went when they get here and watch for anything suspicious," Hughes paused, "I'm going to go upstairs and see what's become of Mrs. Alsop."

Deputy Hughes switched on his flashlight and grimaced. "Doesn't look to be any light up there."

Mac stood stunned, barely hanging onto his consciousness. Although he did not want to abandon his friend, even more so, he didn't want to head up the shadowed stairs to the second floor. Mac managed a quick "Okay, good luck" as Hughes began his ascent and made his way back outside.

The cool night air seemed to relieve the tension and ongoing horror of the night. Mac looked up to a star-filled night sky and wondered how long they had been indoors. As he waited nervously by the car, Mac's vision returned to the smaller second building on the farm. In the window of the second floor stood Heather Gomez, just as she had four nights prior when Mac first stumbled upon the farm.

A sense of delirium took Mac's mind, and he walked toward the second house. When he arrived, he found the front door open. For a moment, Mac thought he heard gunfire somewhere behind him, but the sound and accompanying thought left him as quickly as they had arisen.

Inside the auxiliary house, Mac could see little else save for the dimly illuminated stairs to the waiting second floor. How similar this place looked to the Alsop's home. Mac could scarcely tell he was in a different building.

Mac wavered at the foot of the stairs. He was sure now that he had heard gunfire, but he lacked the will to turn around. By the time Mac decided to go back the way he had come, he was atop the stairs looking into a black and foreboding doorway.

Mac walked through the doorway into a scene no sane person could have handled. What was left of Heather Gomez lay bloody and half crushed beneath a horror Mac's mind struggled to comprehend.

It (whatever It was) indeed looked something like a piece of black ribbon. It was suspended in the center by unknown means, and two terrible, sharp eyes flanked the writhing arch it created. Each eye was easily the size of a human head and contained within its gaze, an intelligence both awesome and terrible in equal measure. Beneath its ribbon-like body, thousands of smaller translucent tentacles stretched down and encompassed Heather Gomez's remains. Mac thought they looked like the tendrils of a jellyfish, and again, he had to fight the urge to vomit.

As the creature moved, it seemed to pass back and forth between visible and invisible. Mac found this sight strangely and deeply terrifying. Then, unbidden, the whole thing began to vibrate, and that vile, familiar scraping sound rose to meet Mac's ears.

Suddenly, the awful thing spoke, its entire form shaking and buzzing sickeningly. It produced sounds unlike anything Mac could have imagined, and he was overcome immediately. Though not traditional audible speech, the assault of sounds and tones conveyed the thoughts and intentions of the thing Mac now knew was known as a Thleem. It, and others like it, had come to our world from a place beyond, where things were more like them. They had intended to feast on the energy of forms, on the power intrinsic to the extra dimensionality of our reality. Something had gone wrong, though; the Thleem had run afoul of some great and terrible power in our world and were being hunted to extinction. They had miscalculated how harmful our sun would be to their strange forms and now were trapped. Hiding from both the sunlight and the feared hunters, the Thleem pleaded its case.

Mac wavered as the world outside of the terrible bubble of sound seemed to fade away. What point was there to any of this? Was this thing truly attempting to drum up sympathy in Mac's heart?

In response, another sonic assault bombarded Mac's senses. It was safety the Thleem sought—human minds to mask their existence from the dreaded hunter and access to a food source. Mac began to feel his grip on the world fading while the mind-boggling Thleem continued to urge him into action, into saving it. There was something else Mac feared he was missing, but the extended contact with the Thleem was having a substantial and deleterious effect on Mac's sanity.

Suddenly, Mac remembered Hughes and instinctively turned toward the exit.

Again, the Thleem's mind-speak overwhelmed him, and Mac saw, with eyes not his own, the broken bodies of Deputy Hughes and Peggy Alsop. Hughes had a gaping wound in his side while three bullet holes smoked on Peggy's chest, clustered around her heart. The rage of the Thleem at Peggy's demise was palpable, and Mac caught himself feeling sorry for this awful, unimaginable thing. The revulsion Mac felt at the sight of his dying friend was too much, however, and frayed the contact between him and the Thleem.

The world swam around Mac, and a merciful blackness rose in his mind. Under a wave of blessed silence, the night faded away.

VI.

Mac woke to the bright morning sun on his face. He was in his car, seated in the driver's seat, and parked on the side of the road leading away from the Alsop Farm. There was no sign of Deputy Hughes' cruiser or the promised backup.

How he had come to be there escaped him, and Mac's blood froze as he thought back to the night before. Nothing in his recollection made sense. Where was Hughes? How could he even be here, on the side of the road, in his car? Rapidly, concerned thoughts bombarded Mac, and he struggled to maintain his consciousness and sanity.

For a time, Mac simply sat in his car, unable to act. Nothing made sense to his fragile mind; even the most superficial thought turned grave and terrible. It occurred to Mac that there was one sure way that he could discern the status of things at the farm, which was simply by getting out of his car and walking up to the house. Here, Mac's natural tendencies finally took over, those recently obscured by his newfound courage, and he fled in horror.

Mac drove back to the university at top speed. Why he neglected to go home, he could not say, but once he was on campus, Mac made directly for the museum. At his office in the museum, he paused and steeled himself for his next move.

Mac called the Hueta County Sheriff's Department and asked to speak with Deputy Hughes. The dispatch operator kindly informed him that Hughes was on vacation and wouldn't be back for another week. When he inquired if anyone had seen Hughes the day before, the confused dispatcher simply reiterated that Deputy Hughes was on vacation. Then Mac tried Hughes's personal number, but there was no answer, much as he had feared.

With his efforts to assess Hughes's whereabouts and well-being reaching a dead end, Mac decided to move on. Reasoning that there was likely little he could do for Hughes, Mac figured the police would eventually be alerted to his absence. There was something else driving Mac's urgency now, survival instinct, and there was little that occurred to him that was not laced with fear over the threat of his demise. Mac collected together some of his personal belongings from his various offices and beat a hasty retreat for his home.

Once home, Mac rushed inside. Something about being outdoors was making him nervous, and he desperately wanted some calm and peace. Inside the cool house, Mac breathed a moment of relief before his mind again began to swim with myriad thoughts, both strange and terrible.

Every time his thinking drifted back to the night before, a new sharp terror gripped his heart. It was madness even to attempt to rationalize what he had seen, what he had felt. Mac lamented the fate of his friend Hughes but realized, as well, that something must have happened after he lost consciousness. Shouldn't the dispatcher have been waiting for his call? How could he not have been alerted to Hughes' condition if the deputy had survived and gone for help as Mac sincerely hoped? He could always make his way down to the Sheriff's office and check on Hughes' cruiser, but something about the certainty of such an act turned his mind against it.

Then Mac's thoughts drifted to Heather, and sorrow overtook his heart. He could still see her there, strangely mutilated beneath that terrible horror from beyond the stars. If only he could have done something more, but he had failed to save her, failed to care for her, failed to be there when she needed him most. The grief was nearly more than Mac could bear, and for a time, he simply sat in his home and wept.

As Mac's sorrow began to abate, his survival instinct again raised its head and urged him into action. That awful thing had spoken to him the night before, and though it was all strangely distant in his mind, a new fear began to take hold in his heart. Hadn't there been something the Thleem had wanted from him? Though he could not recall, an urge to get farther away from his perceived adversary still arose.

It was then Mac decided to flee altogether, and to that end, he now worked frantically. His parents, dead five years now after a tragic plane crash, had left him their Florida home in their will. Mac had been using the house as a vacation home for a few years and felt it would be far enough away from the horrors he had endured to give him some peace.

Gripped by madness and fear, Mac arranged a one-way flight to Florida and rushed to the Eagle Creek Intercontinental Airport. Once there, he boarded the flight and felt a mild sense of relief as the plane took off and started to put distance between him and that blasted farm.

When Mac arrived, the Florida house was quiet and dark. It was just as he had left it the year before when he vacationed there during spring recess. No outward sign of occupation existed, and Mac finally began to feel a sense of relief and safety.

Inside, Mac settled onto the oversized couch that dominated the expansive living room that comprised most of the ground floor. For the first time since waking in his car, he finally stopped running. Seated there on that couch, in that empty house, a plain and terrible thought occurred in the dark recesses of his mind. It was the Thleem that Mac thought of. He had seen it once before, that very first night. It had been floating behind the image of Heather all along, but his mind had refused to acknowledge it. And what was it that old Herman Alsop had said, "Once you see it, it'll hold sway over your thoughts."

Mac looked up at the ceiling and began to tremble with uncontrolled fear. Faintly, just at the edge of hearing but emanating from the second story of the house, a singular and terrible scraping sound could be heard.

Joyride

I.

A bright summer sun shined above the shallow creek. Birds and frogs could be heard in the woodlands behind them, but Gabriel Veetch and Beauregard Remmington Willis III were far more concerned with their fishing prospects that sunny afternoon. The youths, both aged 16, were standing in a small tributary creek in water up to just below their knees, watching their bobbers intently. So far, nothing was biting.

"So anyways, like I was saying, they call it The Nightroad because you can only find it at night," Gabe said. "Apparently, the sunlight drives it away or something. I don't know; Marcy's aunt was kind of vague about it all. She said it was like it was haunted, but worse." Gabe stood a head taller than Beau and was the more handsome of the two, with a chiseled jawline and flowing blonde hair offset by deep blue eyes.

"Yeah, sounds like bullshit to me, that's for sure," Beau chuckled. Short and stocky, with a crew cut and broad shoulders, Beau looked much more comfortable in the creek than his counterpart. He reeled in his line, the juicy worm still dangling from its hook. "Man, fish really ain't biting today."

"No, I don't think it was. You weren't there. Marcy's aunt made a convincing point," Gabe continued.

"About a haunted ghost road?" Beau raised an eyebrow. "You do hear yourself, right? Sounds like run-of-the-mill, campfire ghost story nonsense. How do you go about thinkin' anything like that could be true?" The heavy-set Beau was accustomed to a particularly easy life, coming as he did from a family of wealthy landowners from down south. He had developed into something of a realist as a result.

A fish jumped out of the water some hundred yards away from the boys.

"Well, at least there's hope," Beau said. "Maybe we should move a little downstream."

"You really aren't as excited about all of this as I imagined you'd be. Like real ghosts and monsters and shit. On a road that comes out in the sticks, right around here. Like, close enough for us to go and check it out." Gabe reeled his line in as well and made to move downstream.

A cool summer breeze blew through the undergrowth as the boys reached the shore. "You aren't *scared*, are you?" Gabe prodded.

"Not likely," Beau replied. "'Specially since this shit's all make-believe. But, whatever. It's not like we have a ton of stuff to do tonight."

The boys walked a short way south along the creek. This time, they tried their luck casting from the shore.

"So what exactly are you plannin' at then?" Beau had been more moved by the attempt to slight his courage than had been outwardly apparent.

"So you're in?" Gabe asked.

"Yeah, whatever, I'm in. Are we gonna ride our bikes out during the daytime and stake the place out, or what? How far away is it?" Beau wouldn't admit it, but there was a sense of excitement and anticipation building in his heart.

Gabe smiled broadly. "Oh, don't you worry about that; I've got a plan. See, my mom is going to be out all weekend with Derrick—some concert bullshit. I don't know. Anyway, the car will be right there, and I have the keys already. I say we just borrow it and go for a little drive."

"Ha, you sneaky bastard. I knew you were gonna be trouble with that fake ID. I dunno how you get away with this shit," Beau chuckled.

"Well, at least we won't have to ride bikes in the dark again, that sucks," Gabe added.

For a time, the pair continued to fish at the creek shore. Despite their best efforts, their dogged adversary seemed unwilling to cooperate. Eventually, the sun began to hang low in the sky.

"Alright, we better pack up 'fore it gets dark. So you want me just to follow you back to your mom's house?" After the quiet and uneventful day fishing, Beau was ready for an adventure.

"Yeah, they left this morning in Derrick's jeep; the place is all ours for the time being," a devilish look crossed Gabe's face.

The two friends walked through the woods to where they had stashed their bikes.

"Race you there!" Gabe called as he took off ahead of the unsuspecting Beau.

There was no way they could have known what would come, but that afternoon would be the last time either of them would be fishing near Eagle Creek for the foreseeable future.

II.

Gabe was sitting at the kitchen island drinking a glass of water when Beau entered the residence. The small white and brown-sided ranch house was in the poorest part of town, and Beau always felt out of place when he was over. Gabe did his best to pretend he didn't notice.

"Ya only won 'cause ya cheated. Just so we're clear," Beau said. He was sweating and had obviously been trying quite hard to catch Gabe during their impromptu race.

"If you say so," Gabe replied. "It's not really important; we've got bigger fish to fry tonight."

"Sadly, we have no fish to fry tonight. Not with our luck at the creek. 'Cause I could use a bite," Beau smiled wryly. He knew precisely what Gabe was talking about.

"You know that's not what I mean. Just make yourself a sandwich or something if you're hungry. You know where the fridge is," Gabe was unamused.

"Now we're talking," Beau smiled. He busied himself at the fridge, assembling a massive sandwich, which he then proceeded to consume with frightening speed and efficiency.

"If you're finished, we should talk about our plan." Gabe looked out the window at the growing darkness as dusk encroached upon them.

"Your plan, you mean. I'm just coming along to laugh at your ass when this all turns out to be nonsense." Beau wasn't interested in letting on that he was as excited as Gabe was about the night's prospects.

"Fine. My plan. Whatever. Look, we don't know what we're going to run into. We should at least talk about it a bit before we head out. And it's getting dark. It's probably better if we get started as soon as we can." Gabe was still looking out the window and seemed to be growing more anxious by the minute.

"Okay, okay. Calm down. What do you want to talk about? We already have the keys to your mom's station wagon, which you're driving since you're the one with the fake driver's license. And, you know where we're going? I'm just gonna assume that part cause this would all be for nothing otherwise. What else is there? Let's just get a move on." Beau had always been a doer more than a planner.

"That's not everything!" Gabe practically shouted. "You weren't there. When Marcy's aunt was telling us about it, she just kept going on about how dangerous it was; it was chilling. I think there has to be something to this. I just don't know what."

"Fine, then. We should bring a couple of flashlights and a baseball bat with us, too," Beau stood up and stretched in preparation.

"You can't solve all your problems by clubbing them with a bat, dude," Gabe said.

"Heh, shows what you know, pretty boy," Beau smiled at his friend.

The levity brought with it a shared laugh and palpable relief from the gathering stress. The boys were really going to do this. There was no time like the present.

It only took another minute for Gabe to toss two flashlights, a map, and a couple of bottles of water into a backpack. Beau went out back to grab the baseball bat. Scant time had passed, and the boys were sitting in the front two seats of Gabe's mother's sea foam green, paneled station wagon. Their supplies were haphazardly piled in the back, along with their fishing gear from earlier. It certainly wasn't the type of conveyance one would typically associate with a wild night of teenage debauchery, and perhaps that helped to hide it from those eyes that are always watching places where strange and unexplainable things gather.

The engine came to life with a roar, and just like that, they were off. Interestingly, to Beau, at least, they turned to head downtown rather than out into the countryside once they came to the end of Gabe's street.

After a few minutes, Beau spoke up. "So ... where we going?"

"We're going to check out the haunted Nightroad place. Why?" Gabe replied.

"Cause it kinda seems like we're heading to your girlfriend Marcy's house," Beau gave his friend a stern look.

"Look, I know you two don't really get along, but she's the one who knows where we're going," Gabe was matter-of-fact about everything.

"You said you knew where we were going!" Beau was incredulous.

"I never said that; you just figured I did. And in a way, I know how to get there; I know Marcy is coming with us and that she knows the way. I know by association," Gabe was ready for this argument.

"Whatever, dude, this is bullshit. You didn't tell me the eco-terrorist was coming." Beau despised Marcy, mainly for taking away his time with his best friend Gabe, but on the surface, the two were ideologically opposed. Marcy was deeply involved in the local environmental movement and took the conservation of their world to be of the utmost importance. Beau, in contrast, was the epitome of excess. Driven around in big, gas-guzzling SUVs and bragging about taking his uncle's private jet for ski weekends in Colorado, he was everything that Marcy took to be wrong with society.

"Don't call her that, dude. She hates it. Just be cool; this is a once-in-a-lifetime night we're about to have. Isn't that worth more to you than having to put up with my girlfriend for a few hours?" Gabe pressed on as they neared their destination.

"Alright, fine. You know me, I can go along quietly. I just don't see why you couldn't tell me this upfront. But no sense lingerin' on it. These ghosts ain't gonna bust themselves, right?" Beau hated to admit it, but Gabe was right. Putting up with Marcy was a relatively small price to pay if they really got to see something supernatural. He still didn't want to make it too easy on Gabe, though.

After another minute, they pulled onto Marcy's street. Gabe pulled the car over to the side of the road at the hill overlooking Marcy's cul-de-sac.

"Why we stopping?" Beau asked.

"You know how it is. Marcy's parents aren't really my biggest fans. Plus, she's grounded after that party we went to last weekend. She's going to sneak out. Don't worry, she'll be here." Gabe gave his best convincing smile.

"Man, this just keeps getting better," Beau laughed.

For ten minutes, the pair sat in silence along the side of the road. Then, with little warning, Marcy Capella-Burini approached from the east. She wore a denim jacket over a tee shirt and jeans, with a backpack over her shoulder. Her short brown hair was usually up in a pair of pigtails, but tonight hung down to just below her ears. She smiled when she saw the pair waiting for her, her magnificent green eyes flashing in the glow of a streetlight. Nearing the station wagon, she stood expectantly at the passenger side front door.

"Oh, you've gotta be shitting me," Beau couldn't believe what was happening.

"C'mon dude, just be cool. You'll have more room in the back anyways," Gabe felt that the night was slipping through their hands.

"Fine, asshole, but I'm not gonna forget this," Beau said as he got out of the car. "'Evening, Your Majesty," He said to Marcy as he passed her and got into the back seat.

"Thank you, Beau," Marcy replied, smiling ear to ear. She was a year younger than the boys, but you would never have known it from her appearance. Classically beautiful with striking deep green eyes, Marcy had developed faster than her peers and had earned a place among the most coveted girls at the local high school—a fact Gabe was exceptionally proud of. "So, are you boys ready for a night of ghost hunting!" Apparently, Gabe had been planning this with Marcy for far longer than Beau had been aware.

"Yeah, let's get on with it," at least Beau could agree with Marcy on that.

"Alright, alright. Onward and upward," Gabe said as he pulled back onto the street and performed a U-turn. They weaved their way across the main thoroughfares of Eagle Creek, staying off the main roads as much as possible. After another five minutes, they were nearing the southeastern edge of the city and the night that lay beyond.

III.

The night was clear and mild, moonlight and a vast array of stars now visible at the edge of the city's poisonous light. The collected passengers of the sea foam green station wagon sat upon the precipice with bated breath. Something wild and new was about to befall them, and one could practically taste it on the breeze.

"So my aunt says that The Nightroad is attracted to supernatural stuff and stuff that is out of the ordinary, right? There's an old house out in the swamp south of town. It's supposedly haunted, and I guess it totally is 'cause it's what we're looking for. It's on a dead-end street that stops just before the swamp becomes impassable. The road will be connected there somehow. I guess we'll see when we get there," Marcy explained. She seemed equally confident and unsure about everything she said, though they all went along with it regardless.

With little more discussion, they were off toward the swamp. Technically known as the Hueta County Wetland Conservatory, the sprawling swampland covered an area of approximately fifty square miles in southeastern Hueta County, fifteen miles south of the city of Eagle Creek. Within its borders, several well-established walking trails and bird-watching posts were frequently used by the population at large.

"Turn here," Marcy directed. They left the main road and headed into the confines of the swamp. Having turned away from the more populated areas, the sky began to take on a strange quality. Clouds seemed to ripple into existence just above the road, only to vanish once the car drew near. The deep darkness of the evening seemed almost to lighten. The group drove on, turning down several more seldom-used roads, always headed deeper and deeper into the swamp.

"There should be another turn-off up here in a mile or two," Marcy said. "It's a dirt road, the dead-end road we're looking for. But slow down; this place is really giving me the creeps." She reached out and held onto Gabe's shoulder.

"Yeah, whatever's going on with the sky right now, I've never seen anything like it before. This is wild." Gabe was having trouble focusing on driving.

Beau sat, speechless for once, in the back seat, his eyes scanning their surroundings as fast as they could.

After another minute of driving beneath the flickering almost-clouds, they reached their turn-off. The dirt road looked barely big enough for one car, let alone two. A large rusty sign sat askew upon a pole to their right. "Dead End," it read. This was the place.

Slowly, Gabe pulled onto the dirt road and headed further into the maddening display that the swamp was becoming. The road was rough, jostling the occupants of the station wagon, which was not designed for these sorts of excursions.

Everything around them took on strange new qualities. Thick, rope-like moss hung from the trees like some arboreal spider webs had been strung about by creatures whose size was not something one wanted to linger upon. The trees loomed, more knotted and writhing with every hundred yards the car traveled. They crowded the sky and obscured the spectacle that the strange cloud formations had become. Deep, cold gloom surrounded them.

The headlights of the car fell onto the facade of a house off to the left, a few hundred yards in the distance. As there had been no other signs of habitation up to this point, the teens took this to be the place. Gabe slowed the car to a stop with the headlights fixed on the building.

"This has gotta be the place, right?" Beau was looking out the open back driver's side window.

"I'd say so," Gabe said. He looked over to Marcy and Beau. "So, are we going to check it out?"

"Hell, yes! This place is damn freaky, you were right about that much." Beau fished their flashlights out of the backpack.

"I don't know, maybe this was a bad idea," Marcy looked about to panic. Her great big eyes darted about frantically as if her mind was struggling to keep up.

"Calm down, babe, it's alright," Gabe tried to calm her.

"Oh, come on! Listen, sugar tits, ghosts aren't real. None of this is anything more than some weird weather and an abandoned house. Get your shit together." Beau's attitude could sometimes be called combative.

"Ugh, you're such a pig!" Marcy spat back. "Why do you even hang out with him?" She said to Gabe.

"Alright, alright, shit, cool it, you two. This place is so strange. Maybe something's out here, maybe not. But if you two are just going to bicker and call each other names, we might as well just bail."

"Yeah, alright, sorry, Marcy," Beau was quick to step up, his tough guy act beginning to falter in the growing gloom.

"Whatever," Marcy scoffed. "At least being pissed at you makes me less scared about this place. Okay, I'm ready. Let's go."

With no more conversation, they were outside of the car. Gabe had stopped the engine and turned off the lights, and now, two long rays of white light cut through the darkness from the boys' flashlights. Marcy carried a small camping lantern she had produced from her backpack, which illuminated their immediate surroundings.

"C'mon, let's see what there is to see," Beau said as he started down the road toward the house, baseball bat comfortably slung over his shoulder. They were about fifty yards away from what looked to be an old, overgrown driveway.

"Seems like the road keeps going for a ways. Are we sure this is the place?" Gabe said as they approached.

"Well, one way to find out," Beau said. He headed up the driveway. While it was overgrown, the old driveway was also much easier going than the wild and unkempt lawn that surrounded the building. Gabe and Marcy followed close behind.

Strange noises assaulted their ears as they neared the house itself: animal cries that couldn't be clearly identified, the sounds of storms in the distance, and a deep moaning rumble that seemed to rise from the earth itself. Each step brought more sensations. Was that movement up-stairs? Had something run off into the swamp? Were they alone out here?

Finally, Beau reached the front door. It was boarded up, but the job was done poorly, and the door within was not secured. Several hard swings of his bat brought the intervening two-by-fours down with a discordant crash, and the group gained entry to the building.

Beau burst through the opening with Gabe close on his heels. Once inside, they stopped with a start at the unexpected sight they encountered. Simply put, there was nothing there. With no furniture, walls, or even flooring, the house was more of a shell than an actual dwelling. Strange echoes bounced off the walls as the teens gathered themselves from the anticlimax.

"Fuckin' told you!" Beau's voice rang about in the void.

"I can't believe it! There's nothing here. I was sure we were going to see something. It was so creepy walking up here," Gabe said.

"It's alright, bro; happens to the best of us. You just got swept up in some nonsense 'cause of a chick," Beau chuckled. He was clearly enjoying the outcome so far.

By then, Marcy had made her way into the building and stood just behind where the boys were.

"Well, this certainly is disappointing. I wanted to see a ghost or two for sure. Who even leaves a house frame up like this?" Marcy was observant, if nothing else.

"Okay, look, I'll give you guys that it's creepy and weird out here. But that's all it is. There's no spooks or specters that are gonna come and get us. This was mostly just a good excuse to steal Gabe's mom's car."

"I mean, it is still early. Maybe this just isn't the right place. We could go further down the road if you guys want," Gabe wasn't ready to give up on their night at the first sign of difficulty. "We still need to see if we can find that Nightroad place."

"I'm still pretty spooked, but I'll go if you want to. Maybe there isn't anything to this like Beau says." Marcy seemed unsure of herself and kept looking around as though she expected to see something erupt from the shadows.

"Alright, fine. But we gotta stop at the car for a minute first. I need something." Beau went back outside and headed back toward the car.

Gabe walked up to Marcy and took her hand. "C'mon babe, more adventure awaits," he smiled and hoped his efforts would ease her worry.

They exited the abandoned house and began to follow Beau back to the car. The sky had returned to its typical star-filled brilliance, and the cool air of the evening brought with it calm. Had it ever been anything else?

By the time Gabe and Marcy reached the car, Beau had retrieved the item he needed. The joint in question was about twice the length of his finger. Everything in excess had always been one of Beau's signature beliefs.

"If there ain't no spooks, might as well spark up," he smiled, knowing full well how this turn of events would affect Marcy.

"Ew! Keep that away from me! I can't smell like weed when I go back home. You know I hate this stuff, Gabe," Marcy was furious.

"Yeah, and you know Beau smokes. But he was just about to step off into the brush there to keep it away from you. Weren't you, buddy?" Gabe shot an imploring look at Beau.

"Yeah, yeah. Wouldn't want to upset you, your highness. I'll just go off behind those trees over there," Beau pointed to a small copse of trees not far from the roadway they now stood upon. "I'm sure nothing scary is waiting out in the dark," he said, primarily to himself. The baseball bat remained resting on his shoulder, all the same.

After a few moments, Beau had disappeared behind the trees, an intermittent cloud of smoke the only indicator of his location.

The winds shifted and blew strange smells from the surrounding swamplands. Gabe stood by the car while Marcy busied herself with her backpack from the front passenger seat.

"You know, maybe I should go keep an eye on Beau," Gabe said, almost absentmindedly.

"And leave your girlfriend in the car while you go to smoke weed with your buddy? On a haunted road, in the dark nonetheless," Marcy teased. "It's fine, just be quick about it. I think I might have had enough adventure for tonight."

"Alright, babe. And don't quit on this just yet; you never know what we might find if we stick to it. I still want to see this Nightroad place your aunt was talking about," Gabe smiled his charismatic best, and Marcy blushed slightly in response.

"Okay, fine. Just get going. I don't want to wait for you too long out here." Marcy settled into the passenger seat and tried not to think too hard about what might be waiting in the darkness.

Gabe walked over to the trees that hid Beau from view. He could smell the acrid smoke and smiled in response to its familiarity. Beau always had the best weed.

"Hey, just coming to check on you," Gabe called as he neared his friend.

"Thought I heard something," Beau said as Gabe rounded the trees and moved into view. He puffed out a large ring of smoke. "Surprised you were able to get away from the missus."

"Marcy isn't some crazy chick that wants to control me. Which you might realize if you bothered to give her the time of day," Gabe said.

"You come out here to lecture me or smoke?" Beau raised a curious eyebrow.

"Fine, whatever. Pass it here," Gabe relented.

For a few minutes, the pair smoked in relative silence. The marijuana helped to ease the stress that their minds had been under and brought with it a relaxed calm that made everything around them seem surreal.

A crow cried out in the distance, some ways above them. The sudden sound roused the pair from their light stupor.

"Alright, that's enough. Let's head back. No sense gettin' all freaked out before we go see where this road leads too." Beau tossed the remains of the still-burning joint into the brush. After a moment, smoke started to rise.

"Good one, asshole. A forest fire is just what we need right now." Gabe was mostly just giving his friend a hard time.

"How'm I gonna burn down a swamp?" Beau stated as he moved past Gabe, heading back the way they came.

Gabe walked toward the smoke and stomped with his foot to put out the smoldering embers. The fire had spread more than expected, and it took several well-placed stomps to put out the burgeoning blaze.

As his foot found the earth for its final time, a strange noise rose around them. It was the moaning, creaking noise they had heard earlier, walking up to the abandoned house. Now, however, it was louder and all around them.

The boys froze, held in place by some unseen force in the sound that enveloped them. The area Beau had chosen for a smoke spot was a small, clear place behind the copse that could be seen from the road but before the more giant trees and undergrowth that denoted the swamp proper. Past them, heading into the swamp, great trees had grown up from the muddy ground, and old rotted stumps littered the landscape.

Approximately thirty yards from their clearing, six such trees were clumped close together. Initially, it had seemed that these trees held aloft a trio of older, slimmer dead trunks that likely fell during a storm. Though it was impossible, these tree trunks rose of their own accord, with the accompanying creaking sound, and moved from behind the closely knotted group of trees.

As they rounded the trees, great black hooves could be seen at the base of the trunks. Could they somehow be legs? The answer was soon enough apparent.

Held between the two more prominent and leading legs (for it was abundantly clear now that that was what they were), a sleek equine head moaned out its terrible call. Upon its skull, where one would have expected ears, instead, two large muscular shoulders connected to the head and came together below it to form the basis of a truncated body. The thick, hairy body was supported by the third trunk-leg, creating a hideous tripod of unspeakable horror.

Upon the long equine head, four glowing eyes opened up. Again, it called out its moaning cry to the two boys, now paralyzed with fright as much as any harmonic spell. For a moment, it seemed as though the world stood still.

Suddenly, the horse-headed demon sprung forth, propelled by its central leg, and roared, revealing a hideous collection of rotten square teeth that champed as the beast slobbered.

Instinctively, the boys leaped back, but Gabe stumbled and fell to the ground. With a resounding thud, one of the beast's front legs came down on the middle of Gabe's back, pinning him to the swamp floor.

Its eyes clicked open and closed with a horrid sound as they painted the surrounding area in a strobe of greenish glow. Beau felt his consciousness begin to swoon.

The beast huffed, and a foul-smelling air suffused around them. It gave out its terrible call one final time, almost imploringly, and then everything went sideways.

As the massive equine head descended for what looked to be a killing blow, Beau sprang into action. Propelled by instinct and fear for his friend's safety, he swung the bat as hard as he could toward the head of the vile thing pinning Gabe to the ground. The bat shattered with a resounding "thwack" on the beast's snout, and it staggered back. It seemed as much in shock at the turn of events as it was injured by the assault, but its movement served to free Gabe from its grasp.

Wasting no time, the boys turned and fled. Half mad, they ran as fast as their legs could carry them out from behind the copse of trees and back toward the station wagon. Their conscious minds struggled to keep up with everything that was happening.

The commotion had drawn Marcy's attention, and though she only heard the moaning cry faintly from where she was seated in the vehicle, something deep within her stirred as she turned her gaze upon the approach of her two friends. She had meant to chastise them for taking so long, but whatever it was she shouted was drowned out by the crash of trees.

From behind the copse of trees, tearing them from the ground as it charged through, the horse-headed demon emerged enraged. It bellowed after the boys as they fled, then horribly gave chase with a staggering galloping motion. Marcy screamed from her seat in the station wagon but could not turn away from the approach.

A moment later, the boys reached the vehicle. Beau tore the backseat door open and dove inside while Gabe slid across the hood of the station wagon toward the front driver's seat. Had either had the time to admire it, the move had a certain "Dukes of Hazard" quality they would have both admired. All there was time for instead was to run.

Gabe slammed the keys into the ignition and turned them with a silent prayer. As before, the engine roared to life, and Gabe floored it. Not thinking to turn around, they plunged into the darkness and the impending dead end with the beast hot on their heels. Every time it gave out its terrible cry, Marcy shuddered and began to weep. Beau watched from out the back of the vehicle, unable to move his gaze from the ever-encroaching monstrosity.

"Where. Where are we going?" Marcy finally managed to get out.

"It's not important. We gotta get out of here first!" Beau was at a loss.

"Where the fuck are we going!?" This time, she was shouting.

"I don't know," Gabe finally spoke, "we just have to get away from that thing! Oh God, why did we ever come out here?"

Marcy broke down, sobbing and trembling. The horse-headed demon gained on them with every step. A second later, it was practically in the back seat. With a resounding thud, the terrible beast smashed its head into the rear of the vehicle, causing the back end to swing out to the left. Gabe wrestled with the wheel in an attempt to regain control. The station wagon shook terribly as the quality of the road began to deteriorate, dirt and rocks spraying into the air around them.

Gabe fought back control of the station wagon and again gunned the engine. Already going at a considerable speed, the small six-cylinder engine whined back in response. Still, it managed a few more miles per hour and pulled them away from their pursuer, if only slightly.

The horse-headed demon seemed worse for the exchange as well; its pace slackened, and a bright green substance (perhaps blood?) was running down the side of its head where it had impacted the station wagon.

The road narrowed as they sped along. It looked as though they had come to the dead end at last. "I don't really know what we're going to do here. We're running out of road," Gabe said.

Beau's heart was racing, "this is bad."

"Just keep going. Don't let that thing catch us," Marcy said, her voice dripping with fear.

Behind them, the horse-headed demon also slowed in response to the deteriorating conditions. Their slight lead on it was maintained, but for how long was unclear.

"I guess a car crash is better than gettin' caught by that thing," Beau chuckled. What else could they do? He swallowed hard as Gabe floored the pedal. The swamp raced up to meet them.

IV.

Beau closed his eyes in anticipation of their cataclysmic end. He could still hear Marcy crying. Gabe was silent. Then again, as though they had just burst through the door of the abandoned house, nothing happened. The car stopped shaking. It seemed as though they were again on pavement. Beau opened his eyes and gasped.

They were still in the sea foam green station wagon on a large black-surfaced road with strange, though familiar, road markings. Above them, the sky was clear and filled with more stars than Beau had ever seen. Though their approach was now veiled in fog, the horse-headed demon no longer seemed to be in pursuit.

"You guys seeing this?" Beau said.

"What?! How ..." was all that Gabe could get out.

"Are we dead?" Marcy sniffed.

"Sure don't feel like it," Beau was beginning to come back to his senses. "Besides, you're still here. Sure ain't my Heaven," he said.

"Oh fuck you, fat ass," Marcy responded.

Then, all three exchanged a glance and began laughing. Somehow, they were alive. They had escaped from something beyond imagining. Whether by luck or fate mattered little. They were alive, and all three rejoiced in their own way.

"Okay, so now, where are we?" Marcy was the first to break the spell of their miraculous survival.

"This has got to be it, right? The Nightroad. Just like your aunt was telling us, it's real. And somehow, we made it," Gabe was still smiling. He slowed the station wagon to barely a crawl but resisted the urge to stop outright and pull over.

"Can't be. All that stuff you were talkin' about was nonsense. This can't be real, can it?" Beau was having issues reconciling things in his mind. Everything he believed told him that what he was now experiencing was impossible. That those beliefs must be, in fact, wrong was more than he was prepared for.

All about them, the scenery had taken on a blue-purple sheen. It was dark, but not, and the surrounding area could be seen clearly, up until it reached a thick layer of fog about 200 yards off either shoulder. Beyond the fog, the horizon cut strange alien shapes upon the sky. The character of the ground had changed as well, seeming now to be arid or desert-like and far removed from both the swamp they had previously been in and also the general topography of Hueta County at large. Where were they now, indeed?

Finally, Gabe pulled the station wagon over to the shoulder and stopped. Too much had happened, and they needed to get their bearings.

"So, what now?" Gabe said.

"This is so unbelievable," Marcy started, staring out the window.

"You're not wrong about that," Beau was in rare agreement with Marcy. "You think we could just turn around and go home?"

"It couldn't be that easy, could it?" Gabe was puzzled as to how to proceed.

"But what about that thing? Are we even sure it's not still chasing us?" Marcy still seemed on edge.

"You'd think it woulda caught up by now," Beau said, looking out the back of the station wagon. Were those lights in the distance?

"Yeah, I think we're safe and all, but like, how do we even go back?" Gabe seemed to be getting nervous. "I had my eyes closed when everything happened; I'm not going to lie."

"Same, bro. It's alright. I mean, we turn around and go the other direction; maybe we'll see something we recognize or some shit," Beau said.

"So then you guys didn't see it?" Marcy said. She stared out the front of the car into the darkness, and the light in her eyes seemed to diminish.

"See what?" The boys responded in unison.

"Just before we ran off the road into the swamp, everything started to change. It was awful. Like the world was being ripped apart and put back together all around us, it all rose to a terrible climax, and then we were just here. Like someone flipped a switch and turned on a new reality," tears were running down Marcy's cheeks, "I don't want to go back."

"Well, what else are we gonna do?" Beau raised an eyebrow.

"Yeah, Beau kind of has a point. We can't really just keep going. Who knows where this could lead to," Gabe tried to smile to reassure Marcy, but it was becoming difficult to hide his concerns. "We have to try to get home," determination was building in Gabe.

"I don't want to alarm anyone," Beau said, "but somebody is coming up on us. Looks like they're moving pretty quick, too."

"Another car? Out here? What do we do?" Gabe hadn't started up the station wagon yet.

"Man, we don't wait around to find out who they are," Beau shouted, "get us moving!"

Gabe started the engine with haste. It whined and stalled in response. It seemed that the extended chase with the horse-headed demon had taken a toll on the sea foam green station wagon. The lights on the dash flickered and went dead. No further response emanated from under the hood. They were dead in the water.

"What are we going to do now?" Gabe said, the unknown vehicle steadily gaining on their position. It looked like a sedan of some kind.

"We're going to get help," Marcy said, and without a word more, she opened the door and stepped out of the car.

The approaching sedan slowed as it neared their position, pulling to a stop behind them, its lights still hiding most of it from view.

"We need help!" Marcy called as she waved to the driver of the unidentified vehicle. Gabe recovered from his shock at Marcy's exit and hurried to catch up with her. Not entirely comfortable being left behind, Beau followed a moment later.

Outside of the car, the three teens stood in the headlights of the unidentified vehicle. Suddenly, its lights shut off, and the car could be clearly made out in the strange blue-purple light. It was a ramshackle of a vehicle and looked to be assembled from parts of several different cars. In shape, it looked closest to a Chevelle, but one that had clearly been put together in a junkyard. An odd collection of antennas decorated its roof and hood.

Out of the front driver's side door stepped a tall man wearing glasses. He was thin and dressed in a mechanic's shirt and blue jeans. He approached the kids and waved. "Hey there. Wow, you guys are just kids. Did you say you needed help?" He smiled but stayed at a distance from the teens.

"Yes, please. Our car broke down, and we are a little lost," Marcy smiled and put on her most innocent expression. "Do you know where we are?" She asked.

"Hmm. I suppose I do, as much as anyone does. I'd wager you do, too. Most people out here don't get here by chance," The tall man inspected the teens with an all-encompassing gaze.

"Look, mister, we're just trying to get home. My car stalled; maybe you could give us a jump?" Gabe took over, hoping to shield Marcy from the potential danger of the unknown.

"Yeah, what are you doing out here anyways? If you don't wanna answer the lady's questions, maybe we don't need your help," Beau, too, stepped between Marcy and their new acquaintance.

"Calm down, kids," the tall man chuckled. "I wasn't trying to give you a hard time. You can never be too careful out here, eh? The name's Reeves," he smiled at the teens. Something about his behavior seemed to put the trio at ease.

"Beau," Beau replied, "and this is Gabe and Marcy. I gotta say, running into someone out here was the last thing I was expecting," he reached out a hand to their newly arrived rescuer.

Reeves shook Beau's hand as he moved closer to the teens. "So how'd you even get out here, kids, that on-ramp a mile back?" The group moved closer to the station wagon.

"To be honest, we're not really sure. One moment, we were in the swamps outside of Eagle Creek; the next, we were here," Marcy said. It was strange that all three of them were so trusting of their new companion.

"Makes sense; the county is full of trouble these days," Reeves looked to be thinking about something the teens knew nothing about. "Regardless, let's take a look at your car. Pop the hood; I'll go grab my tools," he said as he rushed off to his strange-looking vehicle.

"We're sure about this?" Gabe asked as Reeves moved out of earshot.

"What else can we do?" Beau said, "He seems on the level."

"I hate to admit it, but I agree with Beau," Marcy said, "What other chance do we have to get out of here? You two didn't bring any tools, did you?" Her expression was both reticent and mocking.

By then, Reeves had returned to the station wagon. Gabe opened the hood, and the two of them were soon busy looking over the contents of the interior.

Beau returned to the backseat to fetch a bottle of water. Marcy lingered in the strange twilight, standing in between.

After a short time and some rather hurried repairs, Reeves closed the hood and instructed Gabe to try to start the car again. This time, the engine roared to life, and it seemed that disaster had been averted.

"I don't know how to thank you," Gabe said as the group stood outside of the now-running station wagon. "We would have been in a lot of trouble if you hadn't shown up."

"It's nothing. My civic duty, we'll call it." Reeves smiled.

"You never did answer how it was you came to be out here or where we are and all that," Beau said, still not sure of his intuition's guidance.

"Let's call it a shortcut. It makes my work commute easier, ya know. As for where we are, it's best just that you know not to come back. This place is dangerous, even when you're prepared like I am. Nothing good usually haunts these roads." Reeves' look was stern.

"Except for you, that is," Marcy said.

"Yeah, let's go with that," Reeves was quick to change the subject. "Turn your car around, head back the way you came. Go about a mile or so, and you should see an off-ramp, just like on any other highway. Take it. Get yourselves home and forget how to get here. This way will be closed soon enough, I assure you."

Reeves looked over the collected teens and couldn't help but feel a pang of guilt that he couldn't lead them safely to their destination. Still, matters were afoot, and business called; he needed to be off.

"I've gotta motor. You kids be safe, and get your asses home. Resist the urge to go exploring, okay?" He waved to them and got back into his strange car. Just as quickly as he had arrived, Reeves drove off into the distance.

Beau, Marcy, and Gabe got back into the sea foam green station wagon. The night had been a rollercoaster, but at least they might have an idea of how to get home now. Just drive off the exit and go home. It could be that easy.

"What are we going to do about that thing in the swamp?" Marcy asked, her voice quivering.

"Let's just beat feet and hope it's gone by the time we get there," Beau said, eager to get on the move again.

"Yeah, babe, we'll just take it easy. We should be able to get back off that dirt road before anything comes after us. I hope anyways." Gabe had meant to be more reassuring.

"I don't like this, but I guess we don't have any other choice." Marcy seemed to be steeling herself for a coming confrontation.

"Right then, let's go," Gabe said as he turned the station wagon around on the wide road and headed back the way they had come. "Just like a mile to go, nothing to it. Onward and upward," He said.

After just a minute of driving, headlights could again be seen coming up from behind them.

"Again? What's this now," Gabe said, nervousness rising in his voice.

"It's gotta be Reeves, right? No way we run into two different cars out here in this place." Beau was watching out the back window as the car came ever closer.

"Let's just stop and see what he wants," Marcy said. She, too, was looking behind them and seemed nervous.

"Alright, hold on." Gabe pulled the station wagon over to the side of the road.

The approaching car did not seem to be slowing down. It was upon them in an instant, a sleek black sedan that appeared to eat up the surrounding light. It slammed its brakes and skidded to a stop, blocking the escape of the sea foam green station wagon. From within, three armed men emerged, all dressed in black. The doors to the station wagon swung open, and the teens were dragged, kicking and screaming, from the confines of the vehicle.

Held at gunpoint now, on their knees in the strange purple-blue sand, all seemed lost. Marcy was crying again. All of this, everything had been too much.

A fourth individual exited the car and walked in front of the terrified friends.

"Teenagers!? Really!? God hates me." He pulled out a pack of cigarettes and lit one. The cloud of smoke he emitted seemed profuse. "What are you idiots going to do? Neutralize them all? Do you have any idea how much paperwork that is for me?" He paced as he addressed the other men.

"Just let us go, mister. We didn't do nothin'," Beau tried his best to sound confident.

"Who the fuck was talking to you!" The smoking man turned on Beau. "Stupid fucking kids, what are you even doing out in a place like this. No, something here isn't right. Where's Reeves?" He stood towering over Beau, though the latter refused to shrink from his gaze.

"We don't know no Reeves." Beau was resolute. Reeves had helped them; no way was Beau ratting him out. Gabe's eyes darted back and forth between Beau and their mystery assailants. Marcy wept softly.

The smoking man just let out a low growl. "Fine. Take the blonde one for questioning. Leave the other two to the mercy of The Nightroad; I don't have the time to clean up the extra bodies." He let out a final cloud of smoke and tossed his cigarette into the darkness.

"What?" Beau managed to get out before the butt of a sidearm knocked him out.

Marcy screamed but was knocked unconscious a moment later.

A close-range taser put Gabe under and he was dragged into the back seat of the black sedan. Then, with a squeal of the tires, the black sedan took off into the darkness, leaving Beau and Marcy unceremoniously crumpled along the shoulder.

Beau was unsure of how long it had been when he woke. Marcy was still out cold and seemed to have taken quite the blow to the head. He gathered himself and went to wake her as gently as he could.

"Hey, you alright?" He said as he rubbed her shoulder.

"Ow. My head …" Marcy seemed to be coming around. "What just happened?"

"I don't have a clue. I'm guessing they took Gabe. Who the hell were those guys?" Beau was nursing a sore jaw as well from where he had fallen. "We have to go after them!" Marcy said. Her eyes blazed with a fire Beau had not seen before.

"Yeah, I get that; we can't leave Gabe like that. But where did they go? Maybe we should turn back the other way and try to find Reeves. Maybe he knows who took Gabe? I don't know how long it's been," Beau got to his feet and walked over to the station wagon. "You comin'?" he called back to Marcy.

"Okay, let's go save my boyfriend." She said as she got back into the station wagon. "We can't go back without him." Marcy was resolute and commanding, possessed of a strength that Beau had both never seen and couldn't help admiring.

"Right. One way or the other, we gotta save him." Beau nodded. This night certainly hadn't gone as he had expected.

In the end, they agreed to go looking for Reeves, as he was their best lead on the mystery assailants who had taken Gabe. Beau turned the station wagon for a final time and headed off in the direction they had seen Reeves last. With luck, they would find something that could lead them back to Gabe. They were the only chance he had and they weren't going to fail him. "Onward and upward, as Gabe would say," Beau tried his best to stay strong.

The sea foam green station wagon moved back onto The Nightroad and headed out into the darkness.

V.

Unbeknownst to Marcy Capella-Burini, an experimental radio transmitter tag had been secretly placed into the lining of her backpack. Her parents had tired of trusting the troublesome teen and her equally problematic boyfriend. So Marcy's father had borrowed the device from his employer, Hastings Global, to keep tabs on his reckless daughter. Upon discovering Marcy missing from her bedroom on the night of August 16, 1994, Mr. and Mrs. Capella-Burini were quick to fall back on the electronic device to determine their daughter's whereabouts. The readings weren't promising; for some reason, the transmitter was unresponsive, its last ping occurring deep within the Hueta County Wetlands Conservatory.

The local police were called and dispatched to locate the erstwhile teens. By the morning, they were still unable to locate the teens but had seen evidence of their passing. Near the last known location of the radio transmitter tag, fresh tire tracks were found heading down a dirt road. At the end of the dead-end street, they found evidence of something approximately the size of a station wagon barreling off into the depths of the swamp.

It was not common, but still not unheard of, that cars and people sometimes got swallowed up by that old swamp. It was too complicated and too expensive for the county sheriffs to bother dredging for the vehicle. It was a terrible tragedy, but sometimes these things happen. Nothing more could be done.

Officially, Gabriel Veetch and Marcy Capella-Burini were listed as missing and presumed deceased. No mention was made of Beauregard Remmington Willis III, and if his family missed him or otherwise cared about his disappearance, it was unapparent. A small memorial now sits at the entrance to the dirt road to ward away others who might be callous to the dangers within the swamp. No further incidents have occurred.

The 6th Wall

I.

The following document is protected by the authority of the Primal Bureaucracy (The Agency, Command). The Primal Bureaucracy is the foundation of all ordered life. The Primal Bureaucracy guides the future to protect the present. Our authority is absolute. Any attempts at misuse or proliferation of this document are ill-advised.

Contained below is the account of Agent In Charge (AIC) Angela Jefferies. It was initially submitted as part of the final report concerning the week of 12-12-22, a week culminating with The Primal Bureaucracy taking active and complete control of Cosmic Variable designated CV0735 - The House Of Walls, on 16-12-22. Agent Jefferies was placed in charge of the operation in specific response to the events of 16-12-22 and was tasked with assessing whether the actions of our agents had directly led to the cataclysmic events of that day. Opinions contained herein are those of AIC Jefferies alone and do not represent the opinion of The Primal Bureaucracy. Proceed with caution.

II.

Cosmic Variables (CV), entities or places whose properties cannot be adequately explained by the common understanding of science, exist everywhere, right before our eyes. Sometimes these things are so well hidden and so innocuous looking that they exist for ages, undisturbed by humans or other living things. Some even exist within the milieu of modern life and manage not to harm or interfere with the living world for remarkable amounts of time.

So it is with a simple-looking, two-story house in a sleepy little suburb that could pass for almost anywhere. It's probably best that the specifics remain obscured but know that if you have ever traveled through any of the numerous towns that sprout up in the vicinity of the larger cities of man, then you have seen houses that look just like the houses in question, and have similarly paid them all little attention. No records exist concerning the house's construction. No one alive in its proximity can recall when it wasn't around. The earliest known records of CV 0735 (The House Of Walls) are from the original seizure of the property in 1854 by agents of The Ghosts Of The Broken Dawn. Records indicate that this seizure on the part of The Ghosts was orchestrated in response to several contemporary news reports associating a recent string of missing persons cases with the house in question. At that time, it was summarily sanitized and believed to be rendered inert. This record exists, as that understanding of The House Of Walls has proven faulty, and further observation and/or sanitization may be required. Complete control of this CV now rests with The Agency.

Included below are the results of several months of recon, by both physical and metaphysical means, into the events surrounding the week of 12-12-22, wherein the status of The House Of Walls changed from dormant to active, resulting in a direct action taken by The Agency. They are presented as a chronological study for ease of communication.

Following the original sanitization of the home in 1854, the location was sold back to the general population and has been used as a residential home consistently through to modern times. At the time of the event, the house was owned by Mrs. Abigail Bertram, whose family had owned the location since the late 1960s. The aged Mrs. Bertram was an absentee landlord living far away in warmer climes, and she used a local management agency to administer to the needs of the home's residents, which were commonly of the minor maintenance variety. This management company was found to be a front for the Ghosts, and their records indicate a continual monitoring program existing from 1854 until modern times. No irregular or aberrant activity was recorded during the subsequent 168 years.

In the late fall of 2022, a new tenant moved into The House Of Walls. Stacy Fontaine (Subject) is, by all outward appearances, a relatively common young professional. Standing five foot two inches tall, with curly orange hair, she exudes the stereotypical "girl next door" appearance. Outwardly, she is friendly, if somewhat reserved. Her propensity to be preoccupied with her work and absent from the active world around her had made her few friends, leading to a relatively insular home life. One that likely added an element to the eventual course that her existence took. Her work, the rigorous programming and testing of cutting-edge AI technology, took up almost all of her active time and was all she ever wished to discuss with anyone. Her only other interests were her small, black and orange cat, Jinx, the general mayhem that came along with him, and her main hobby, videogame entertainment - specifically her PS4. Her life, in all other facets, had never developed. Still, she was very good at what she did, a genius, some would say, and was at least financially comfortable. The Subject reports she was happy with where she was overall.

The recent high point in her life had been the rental of an entire home, with a rent-to-own plan in place, and the end of a decade of living with a steady stream of new roommates. Though she was alone in the reasonably large house save for her cat, she had always been comfortable with her own company and was eager to take complete control of her life and new home. Perhaps that makes this record all the more sad, given its almost forgone conclusion. As with all such CVs, the best that we can hope to do, in the end, may be to shield humanity from their existence and keep our kith and kin safe through the world's shared ignorance.

Stacy had been living in The House Of Walls for one month without incident when an event caused the trajectory of her life to change. It is salient here to know the specifics of The House Of Walls. The house itself is primarily benign and seems constructed from contemporaneous materials commensurate with its original acquisition in 1854. The angle and pitch of the walls within are slightly askew from what should be expected from both its outside dimensions and recorded blueprints. It is unknown how this construction was completed, and all attempts by The Agency to replicate it have been unsuccessful. Overall, however, this strange construction has little effect on the structure, save that it creates a small space, a closet in the farthest back corner of the centermost room, that precisely aligns with the dimensions of several overlapping instances of reality. What this means, in layman's terms, is that inside this closet, potentially, one could manage to travel into other instances of reality.

The original records concerning the building, gained by our personnel after the capture of a Ghosts cell in the northeast, indicate that their concern was regarding the seemingly inert space inside the closet. Specifically, Unidentified Entities (UE) could use the area as a means of egress into our reality. It was theorized that the reports from the period of individuals disappearing after entering the premises were explained as those individuals entering the closet and somehow managing to transition into another version of reality. Initial attempts to destroy the home were unsuccessful. Instead, monitoring and recording equipment were placed within the confines of the closet by the Ghosts, a Class-5 metaphysical tripwire and associated recorder, and the interior of the home was remodeled to remove the erroneous angles. Access to the closet was obscured behind a false wall.

This was the state of the home, monitored and secured by The Ghosts Of The Broken Dawn when Ms. Fontaine rented the premises. What the Ghosts had failed to ever determine was how the missing individuals from the 1850s had disappeared. They had simply made the irregularity safe in their limited view and moved on. Perhaps other considerations were taken into account, but such is not evident from our current records.

Routine scouting, performed in the aftermath of 16-12-22, revealed a nearby (.36 km) connection to The Nightroad (see CV0011 The Nightroad). This would seem the most likely cause for the Ghosts to maintain The House Of Walls secretly, but their records indicate no knowledge of the on-ramp. Instead, the information gathered from the Ghosts was mundane and perfunctory at best, as perhaps should be expected from the group.

All current signs indicate that The House Of Walls is an anchoring point for The Nightroad, regardless of the location's active or dormant status. Extreme caution should be taken when interacting with the house directly. To reduce foot traffic, it is suggested that the area be made into a historical landmark or other easily ignored public building. The following clearly indicates that the house should no longer be used as a residential home.

On the morning of 12-12-22, Stacy Fontaine was safely within the house at the beginning of a much-needed bit of time off from her job due to the coming holidays. At some time between 08:30 and 09:00, she completed the deployment of a state-of-the-art monitoring system designed to safeguard the sensitive intellectual property contained within her many electronic devices. Foremost among the features of the monitoring system was an infrared laser scanner that covered the length and breadth of the interior of the building in its electronic gaze. Though it directly led to the reoccurrence of the house's aberrant properties, this monitoring system provided a wealth of information and full video recording of the events in question until its destruction on 16-12-22.

The monitoring program took approximately fourteen hours to detect an error in its records. The monitored space within the home, that is, the entirety of the home, was just slightly smaller than it should have been, given the stated dimensions of the house. The machine learning program Stacy had designed to monitor the space suggested a simple culprit, sub-par remodeling efforts by previous tenants, and a simple solution. While she possessed the contact information for the local management agency that had always overseen the repairs of the home, Stacy decided she would perform the necessary maintenance herself. It is reasonable that she considered the management company culpable for the current state of the house and that, given her designs on eventually purchasing the residence, she would accept the responsibility of seeing the repairs appropriately completed. It is also worth noting that the move to "jump right in" and address the problem hands-on is a characteristic behavior of Ms. Fontaine, as will become apparent.

Using the data from the monitoring system, Stacy located the walls of the home that were most likely causing the strange readings. These walls would need to be removed, and after another hour's work, she had a plan to begin the remodeling effort.

Stacy went to sleep that evening, convinced she was starting on a grand new adventure. She was not incorrect, though it would take a genuinely twisted psyche to reason that what she eventually endured was anything someone would hope for.

Biometric readings from the monitoring system indicate fluctuations in Stacy's sleep patterns, consistent with highly active dreaming. Dreaming periods lasted far longer than commonly seen in individuals under normal conditions. There is no current explanation for this phenomenon, and the Subject reports no memory of any dreams on the night in question.

At 08:41, on 13-12-22, Stacy woke to a chilly winter morning. Despite the readings from the previous night, she seemed unaffected by any troubled sleep. After a small breakfast, she moved into the house's living room to begin the impromptu remodeling. From the information she had gathered with her monitoring system, she reasoned that all of the house's interior walls were potential targets for her sledgehammer and crowbar.

Indeed, she found that the current interior walls of the home were all overlaying older parts of the structure. During the course of the day, Stacy removed five walls, all overlaying older sections of the interior walls of the house. The removed sections were practically unnoticeable in several spaces, seemingly small and insignificant.

Content with a day's hard work, Stacy retired to an early dinner. The first recorded extra-dimensional activity occurred at 18:23. Voices, specifically distant whimpering cries, were detected by the monitoring devices Stacy installed. The decibel level recorded indicates these cries would have been easily audible to anyone within the structure. At this point, neither the monitoring devices of the Ghosts nor our local agents had detected any irregular activity.

That Stacy heard the cry was abundantly apparent, given the behavior recorded by the monitoring system. For just over one hour, she searched the house for the source of the cry but seemed unable to locate it. Indeed, the recorded audio is detected throughout the home, often appearing to be moving away from Stacy's contemporaneous location.

At approximately 19:45, she ceased her search. Unable to locate the sound, she again turned to her monitoring system and its live data collection, culled from the air around her, for answers. Here, she encountered something she had not expected. The monitoring system had detected movement within the home other than hers and the cat's. Sure that she was alone but for her feline friend, Stacy renewed her search to ensure she hadn't missed something.

From the recorded video, it seemed that Stacy began to panic. Indeed, the thought of an unknown intruder in one's home is cause for serious concern and potentially overwhelming fear. There seemed to be something else to Stacy's growing erratic behavior, however, and the video recorded that she appeared to be talking to someone throughout the time she searched for the unidentified intruder. No audio of this conversation was recorded and the Subject reports no memory of anything specifically said during the time in question.

Stacy hurried through The House Of Walls, stopping her search when she arrived in the centermost room. Again, the extradimensional cry was heard at increased volume, and Stacy stopped cold. After a moment's recovery, she returned to her computer and focused the program on looking for measurement errors in the centermost room.

While it had initially seemed that all of the interior discrepancies had been corrected, upon further examination, Stacy discovered a

6th wall. This was the back wall of the centermost room that was only slightly askew from what should have been expected.

With haste, Stacy removed this 6th wall with her trusty crowbar and sledgehammer. Behind it, she discovered the door to the closet, boarded closed with the words "Do Not Open" written across it in rough white paint. The warning was scrolled in several languages that Stacy recognized. Undaunted and propelled by both the cry and her frantic search for an intruder, Stacy proceeded to tear down the boarding and open the door. The records of the Ghosts do not indicate any warning being placed on the door, as such, at the time of its initial boarding-up in 1854. According to Ghosts records, the wall hiding the closet was in place continually, with minimal repair and maintenance during the entire time of their stewardship.

At this moment, 20:03 on 13-12-22, a magnitude 6.8 psionic tremor was detected by our agents operating out of the ███████████ listening post. Personnel were dispatched to the location and live Agency monitoring was established at 20:36. It was determined then that the local Ghosts cell was also alerted to the irregular activity. On-site agents were directed to eliminate the cell, and at 21:45, reported all members of the Ghosts cell neutralized.

Video recording from the intervening time indicates that Stacy did not enter the closet but instead closed the aperture after a short time and returned to the living room, shaken. Here, she remained for several hours, seemingly in deep thought. At 22:00, Agency personnel were ordered to allow the events unfolding in The House Of Walls to transpire along the path they were currently on. At 22:16, silent observation protocol was ordered, and agents were moved to a staging area to prepare to secure the location.

Given the events that would eventually transpire, it is this Agent's opinion that something of tangible importance occurred in the thirty-seven approximate seconds that the closet door remained open and that the agency should take more drastic measures to determine the specifics of any information that may have been transmitted during this period.

After remaining in the living room in silence for over two hours, Stacy eventually retired to her upstairs bedroom at 22:23. The Subject was recorded as sleeping at 23:06. At 23:08, agents infiltrated the location to place Agency monitoring devices at several critical junctures within the premises, and to make observational contact with the interior of the closet.

Recorded audio from on-site agents, herein referred to as Agents A and B, is transcribed below.

23:34, 13-12-22, The House Of Walls:

Agent A: The fifth monitoring device is mounted and engaged. [Agent B], are you in place to breach the closet?

Agent B: Roger. Preparing to open the closet now; there doesn't seem to be anything here that would impede me.

Static interference

Agent B: Oh God! What the hell is that! ... No! How is it moving?! *Indeterminate screaming*

Sound of door slamming closed

Agent A: [Agent B] Status? Report! Are you still there?

Static

Agent A: Moving to [Agent B]'s last known location. Command, requesting immediate backup.

Command: Request denied. Follow protocol agent, determine the status of [Agent B].

Agent A: Acknowledged. I'm in the central room now. [Agent B] is not here. No signs of a struggle; the room looks otherwise empty. There are a few construction items stacked along the eastern wall. How should I proceed?

Command: Open the closet and determine the whereabouts of [Agent B].

Agent A: Acknowledged. Opening closet now .... The closet seems empty; there's nothing here, no [Agent B]. Correction: there appears to be a large crack in the back wall. Moving in to investigate further.

Brief pause

Agent A: There's a noise emanating from the crack, not the crying we were told about, and it sounds far off; it's hard to make out. It's too narrow widthwise to fit [Agent B] through .... What was that? There's movement behind the crack. There's something in here on the other side of the wall.

Command: That is not possible [Agent A]. Between the closet's back wall and the laundry room's wall, there should only be room for insulation or pipe work. Monitoring indicates the laundry room is clear.

Agent A: Forget what the plans say; there's a whole space back behind this wall. It's dark and I can't see anything from this distance. Should I breach the back wall?

Command: Hold position [Agent A]

Brief pause

Command: [Agent A] Recall from the present location. [Agent B] to be logged as lost. Secure the closet door and vacate the premises.

Agent A: Acknowledged.

As was necessary, per the events of 16-12-22, [Agent A] was neutralized on 17-12-22 by acting AIC.

After successfully implanting Agency listening devices at The House Of Walls, all active agents were moved to a safe observational distance, and silent observation protocol was enacted at 23:47 on 13-12-22.

The following morning, at 08:41 on 14-12-22, Stacy awoke, clearly still shaken. She ate a minimal breakfast and spent most of the morning absently playing video games or seemingly going about her normal daily activities. At two separate times, 09:04 and 11:16, she returned to the centermost room and opened the closet. Both times, she remained outside the closet and was clearly recorded speaking to something within. Strangely, with Agency recording equipment in place by this time, no audio was collected of the Unidentified Entity (designated UE0735), which was the other half of these conversations. The Subject is either unable or unwilling, at present, to relay the information from these contacts.

The content of Stacy's half of the conversations is transcribed below.

09:04, 14-12-2022, centermost room of The House Of Walls:

Stacy Fontaine (SF): You ... you have to stop talking in my head. I can barely think straight. I don't care about your prophecy. I don't understand what you want.

Unknown Entity (UE0735): *inaudible*

SF: That doesn't make any sense. How are you trapped in my closet? There's nothing in there.

UE0735: *inaudible*

SF: You don't scare me. You're just a voice in my head, not this thing you claim to be. I don't care what you showed me last night.

UE0735: *inaudible* (Stacy reflexively cringes and seems momentarily in pain.)

SF: STOP! Oh god, what the hell was that?

UE0735: *inaudible*

SF: Okay, okay, just don't do that again, please. What ... what even are you? Why me?

UE0735: *inaudible*

SF: I don't want to. Please don't make me.

UE0735: *inaudible*

SF: I still don't understand. What do you mean by "sustain us?"

UE0735: *inaudible*

SF: I won't. I can't. Just leave me alone!

Stacy exits the room and returns to her earlier activities.

11:16, 14-12-2022, centermost room of The House Of Walls:

Stacy Fontaine (SF): You have to stop. I don't want to remember these things anymore; those aren't my memories. I can't do this. You're making me go insane.

Unknown Entity (UE0735): *inaudible*

SF: NO! No more! Please! I'll do what you want; just make it stop. Please. *Sobbing*

UE0735: *inaudible*

SF: How will I know when it's been enough?

UE0735: *inaudible*

SF: Okay! Okay! Just give me a little time.

UE0735: *inaudible*

SF: I won't, I promise. Just make it stop, and I'll get you what you want.

Stacy exits the centermost room again.

For the remainder of the afternoon, Stacy spent all her time with her cat, Jinx. At the time of recording, the significance of this was missed, and it was assumed to be a coping mechanism for Ms. Fontaine. Had this cue not been missed, it is possible that direct Agency intervention could have been enacted to prevent the coming calamity. As it was, events were allowed to proceed without hindrance.

At 18:13, Stacy entered the kitchen of The House Of Walls and procured a kitchen towel. She wet the towel, then returned to the living room where the cat, Jinx, was sleeping on the back of the couch. With frightening efficiency, Stacy clasped down on the animal's mouth and nose with the towel while her other hand wound around the throat of the tiny creature. The cat thrashed at its unexpected aggressor in a desperate play for salvation, but Stacy's strength and will proved superior. After a brief struggle, it expired. The altercation had produced several cuts on Stacy's arm, and she was bleeding rather significantly. With haste, she ran to the bathroom and bandaged up her arm, staunching the flow of blood.

Stacy then took the remains of the animal to the centermost room. She opened the door and placed the carcass just outside of the closet. Video equipment records something dragging the corpse into the confines of the closet and then the door abruptly slamming shut.

Stacy remained in the centermost room for several minutes afterward, overcome with emotion. She eventually left and returned to cleaning up after the small feline's slaughter. She was shaken but still clearly spoke to something as she moved about the house. Frustratingly, no audio of these conversations was captured.

After completing the cleanup, Stacy prepared herself as though she would leave the house. At 19:00, she exited The House Of Walls and headed east along the sidewalk. Agents were dispatched to maintain observational contact with the Subject. Stacy walked at a moderate pace to the nearby convenience store, where she purchased a bottle of liquor and a pack of cigarettes. Prior to this, no use of any drugs, legal or otherwise, had been observed by our agents.

By 19:14, Stacy had returned home. Again inside The House Of Walls, she prepared a strong drink and proceeded to consume it while sitting at the table in the kitchen. She was clearly avoiding returning to the living room and, by 19:54, had finished a majority of the liquor, remaining within the kitchen throughout. At 20:04, Stacy stepped outside to her back porch to have one of the purchased cigarettes.

Coincidentally, as she stood on the porch in the haze of the gathering smoke, Rusty, the neighbor's aged golden retriever, ambled through her backyard. The elderly dog had a knack for escaping his relatively confined yard and the often absent supervision of his equally elderly owner, Mrs. Gretchen Ponce. Rusty settled beneath the bush near the base of Stacy's porch.

Here, something clearly changed. The Subject reports that at that moment, inebriated as she was, she considered a different path forward for herself, one of compliance. She returned to the interior of the house and made her way to the centermost room without delay. Her path took her through the living room for the first time since the incident with Jinx, but her previous reticence seemed no longer an issue.

She did not open the closet but instead stood before the door and conversed implicitly with UE0735 within the closet. Though she can clearly be seen speaking on the recording equipment, both her own and that of the Agency, no audio of this conversation was captured. Our research suggests this is likely due to an inter-dimensional connection between the Subject and UE0735 on the other side of the breach within the closet. The Subject is reluctant to go into detail concerning this conversation, other than to say that she attempted to gain her freedom through willing compliance with the demands of UE0735.

After completing this conversation, Stacy returned to the kitchen. She gathered some leftover scraps from a dinner earlier in the week and, with little effort, managed to coax Rusty into the kitchen. The friendly old dog was all too happy to gobble up the unexpected treats and did not seem to notice as Stacy moved into position near his head, a butcher's knife in hand. After a brief pet behind the ears, Stacy managed to deftly slit the throat of the unsuspecting animal. The deep and clean cut severed any chance the creature had at calling out its death knell, and it fell, twitching, to the floor. Wrapping the wound as well as she could with a nearby towel, Stacy hauled the dying animal to the centermost room. She placed it, as before, in front of the opened door, where it was summarily dragged off into the depths of that hellish portal.

Again, back in the kitchen, Stacy set about cleaning the mess from her endeavor. Prepared as she was this time, the work was quicker and the process was completed in a cold mechanical manner. Once she had finished, Stacy immediately retired to her upstairs bedroom. Despite the traumatic events of the evening, she was asleep only minutes later, recorded unconscious by the monitoring system at 20:56.

At 01:16 on 15-12-22, Agency monitoring devices detected a Class-3 inter-dimensional contact. Two apparitions manifested on the lower floor of The House Of Walls—small opaque worms held aloft on arachnid-esque legs, each measuring approximately one meter in length (designated UE0735a and UE0735b, Worms). The creatures glowed with a faint green light and skittered about the ground floor in much the same manner as a dog would when entering a new location. Particular attention was paid to the areas in the living room and kitchen where Stacy had earlier killed the two animals.

During the initial contact, Stacy was securely in the upstairs bathroom. Monitoring agents had assumed that the Subject was on a routine overnight bathroom break, but the Subject's behavior afterward suggests she was sleepwalking.

Exiting the bathroom, Stacy stopped at the top of the stairs to the first floor. One of the Worms, as they would come to be colloquially called, was clearly visible at the foot of the stairway. The second entered the scene moments later. Ms. Fontaine did not react to the sight of the apparitions, but instead remained at the top of the stairs, watching the creatures for several minutes. After remaining together at the bottom of the stairs for approximately thirty seconds, the Worms returned to their previous activities.

By 01:32, Stacy had returned to her bedroom and was again recorded as sleeping.

The inter-dimensional contact stopped abruptly at 01:34, with both apparitions spontaneously vanishing from all collected recording equipment. Stacy remained sleeping without apparent disturbance until 08:41.

After waking properly on Thursday morning, Stacy hurriedly went about her routine morning tasks. By 09:30, she was again in the center room, fed and seemingly ready for a busy day's work. Stacy silently opened the closet door where she stood transfixed, just outside the aperture, for fifty-three seconds.

While the Subject claims no memory of this incident or the content of any communication therein, evidence from the resulting events clearly contradicts this. It is implied by her actions that Stacy did indeed expect to receive some communication from UE0735 that day and, in fact, did.

Though we have no leads as to how this was possible, at that moment, on 15-12-22, Stacy Fontaine was given explicit, detailed information regarding CV1746 (Elixir Of Ueblp), specifically how to procure the necessary reagents to produce the elixir with readily available, modern household materials; rather than the organic components to whit all previous information claimed were essential for creation. This information is now cataloged as CV1746b and is available through proper sources. For obvious reasons, it will not be repeated here. Suffice it to say that the substance in question is a highly potent paralytic agent that, upon injection, produces complete conscious paralysis within five seconds, with variance seen due to age and overall mass of subjects.

Shortly after her contact with UE0735, Stacy again left the confines of The House Of Walls. She walked to the local bus stop, about a half mile away, and took the bus into the business district of the suburban sprawl she called home. Agents followed at a safe distance while the Subject proceeded to shop in three local stores. Again, security demands some vagueness be allowed in this instance, as even knowing the locations Stacy visited could potentially lead to the general discovery of CV1746.

Regardless of where she visited, after nearly two hours of shopping, Stacy again boarded the bus and returned home. By 11:46, Stacy had returned to The House Of Walls. Within minutes, she was busily at work in the kitchen. Standing at the stove, she was cooking several concoctions composed of elements of the items she had purchased and was occupied beyond anything we had previously witnessed. At 11:58, observing agents identified the substance Stacy was making as CV1746. A call was sent to Command to request permission to move in.

Again, The Agency refused to intervene, even though Stacy was now in possession of heretofore unknown information (CV1746b) and a substance (CV1746) typically considered sufficient to warrant immediate neutralization. Why this decision was made has not been forthcoming from Command and a definitive answer is not expected. Regardless, in this Agent's opinion, preemptive action on our part was called for, and it was negligent that we allowed what would eventually happen to occur when we were entirely capable of at least attempting to prevent it.

With Command's order to allow events to proceed unhindered, agents resumed silent observation. Stacy completed her work in the kitchen at 12:48 and produced 15 ml of the elixir, filling three syringes. The process that had created the elixir was surprisingly caustic to her pots. Stacy deposited them into a large garbage bag after cleaning up the rest of the operation.

Stacy exited the kitchen through the back door and was distractedly placing the garbage bag in her outside garbage can when she was accosted by her neighbor Gretchen Ponce, owner of the recently deceased golden retriever, Rusty. The two spoke briefly outside, and Stacy was seen hugging her distraught neighbor. The two then entered the kitchen of The House Of Walls through the back door and Stacy proceeded to make a pot of coffee. Their conversation is effectively benign and omitted for brevity's sake. It's main concern was Mrs. Ponce's search for her missing dog.

The escalation was reportedly unexpected by agents on hand. After making reassuring small talk with her elderly neighbor, Stacy suggested that they move into a different room in the house, promising to help Gretchen by printing "Missing" posters for her. It was subtle, but Stacy seamlessly slid a filled syringe into her pocket as she tidied up the coffee cups. She then led Gretchen into the centermost room. The elderly woman had time enough to question why they had gone into a room without a computer or printer in it before Stacy stuck her with the elixir-filled syringe. In three seconds, Gretchen Ponce was paralyzed, prostrate on the floor of the centermost room. Stacy dragged her body to the closet and opened the door. Here, another psionic tremor was detected and Stacy can be seen arguing with something on video. The lack of audio indicates that the conversation is with UE0735. Eventually, she props up Mrs. Ponce and dumps her, face-first, into the closet. The door promptly shuts and Stacy hurriedly exits the room.

Ms. Fontaine had, at this point, done numerous things that would generally initiate intervention protocols on the part of The Agency. Given Command's reluctance to take measures up to this point, the acting AIC ordered that no further intervention requests be posted to Command until such time, if any, that an extinction-level threat was detected. This order was seen by agents on-hand as confirmation that both no intervention was going to be forthcoming and that it was most likely a Terminal Event that was being witnessed. That detail is essential, as the nature of Terminal Events—things out of synch with the universe that simply burn themselves out before they cause any harm—was a guiding force in the lowered urgency that the case was given at the time.

In the meantime, Stacy returned to her routine daily tasks. She spent several hours on her primary PC, reasonably doing work, or at least appearing to, and then transitioned to the living room to stream some of the more popular current offerings available through Netflix. No longer did Stacy seem bothered by being in the living room, and in character, something in Stacy's nature seemed to be changing. Such can often be the case when someone is exposed, at length, to things beyond our ordinary world.

After a light dinner prepared on the stove that just recently helped her concoct her murder weapon, Stacy made another unexpected move. She retrieved her cell phone and contacted a male co-worker, Curtis Schultz, who answered after only a few rings. The two had a past, as reported by the Subject, and it was not uncommon for the pair to use each other for physical relief without the burdens of emotional entanglement.

At 18:23, Mr. Schultz arrived at The House Of Walls and promptly made his way to the front door. Stacy met him there and motioned from the nearby window for Curtis to come to the back of the house. He complied, and she let him into the house through the back door, just as she had with Mrs. Ponce.

Further evidence occurred here that speaks to the deteriorating condition of Ms. Fontaine's mental state. Foremost of which is that she threw herself at Curtis Schultz with reckless abandon. The poor sod barely had time to object before she had both of them half naked and was rapidly making for the master bedroom.

Upstairs, Stacy put phase two of her plan into action. Mr. Schultz was considerably larger than Stacy, both in height and overall girth; he had a predilection toward spending time in the gym, attempting to "cultivate mass." Through the use of her not-insignificant feminine wiles, Stacy convinced Mr. Schultz to partake in some light domination, namely that he allow her to cuff him to the large four-poster bed in the main chamber. Mr. Schultz would likely have agreed to anything, given the situation Stacy had put him in. Still, his complicity was not lost on Stacy, who shows little reticence for her actions throughout this event. The fact that the Subject already possessed the fluffy pink-furred handcuffs suggests that this was not the first time something like this had come up between the pair.

Cuffed and tied to the bed, Stacy spent the next forty-five minutes having her way with Mr. Schultz. For the sake of the Subject's privacy, further details concerning this interaction are omitted. After finishing with him, Stacy retired to the upstairs bathroom, leaving her captive still chained to the bed. When she returned, after a brief trip downstairs to the kitchen, she had one of the elixir syringes in her hands. A short conversation between Stacy and Curtis is included below as it reveals frightening details concerning UE0735 and further illustrates the depth of madness into which Stacy had fallen.

19:20, 15-12-22, the master bedroom of The House Of Walls:

Curtis Schultz (CS): Hey babe. That took longer than usual. You wanna untie me?

Stacy Fontaine (SF): No, not really. At least not yet.

CS: Heh, yeah, I appreciate your enthusiasm and all, but I'm gonna need a minute to recover here. C'mon.

SF: No, you really don't understand. It's hungry now; I need to give It more. To sustain It through the transition.

Stacy injects Curtis with the syringe

CS: Ow! Did you just stick me with something? Is that a needle? Oh, my head is spinning. You crazy bi ... *Paralysis sets in*

SF: That's better. You never did have anything interesting to say, did you? Poor stupid Curt, at least you were a good fuck. You know, I didn't think I could do it at first. Not with Jinx or even that old dog, but it was easy. And freeing. Maybe it's my new friend in the closet, but every time it goes further, it gets better. This time, I think I'm ready for what It really wants, though I guess I should have warned you first that this would be our final night together.

Stacy chuckles and begins to undo the restraints holding Mr. Schultz.

SF: I really never liked Gretchen; she was a nosy old coot. And that insufferable dog, always hiding out in my backyard. And soon, everything will be finished. Then the real fun starts if anything I've been shown is any indication. And let me tell you, Curt, I've seen some shit. HA! So apparently, the stuff I injected you with leaves you wholly conscious and feeling but completely paralyzed. Let's test it out.

With a heave, Stacy shoves Curtis' body off the side of the bed. There is an audible groan from Curtis.

SF: Awesome! Let go, Bucko; best not to keep the devil waiting, they say.

With that, Stacy proceeded to drag Mr. Schultz downstairs. She seemed to take a twisted glee at the rough handling she was delivering to her disoriented charge. It was quite a racket, however, and it took a decent amount of time for her to get the larger man down and into the centermost room.

Observing agents were expecting Mr. Schultz to be left before the closet door for whatever was inside. Stacy, however, had different plans and left the paralyzed Curtis Schultz in the middle of the centermost room, a reasonable distance from the closet door.

Stacy returned to the kitchen of The House Of Walls and retrieved her butcher's knife. The large blade, designed for carving meat, had already tasted the throat of one unsuspecting animal, but human life was something else. Stacy was practically skipping on her way back to the centermost room.

Again, in the centermost room, Stacy dragged Curtis toward the closet door. She propped him up in a slouched sitting position before the closet. The door opened itself in response. Standing behind Mr. Schultz, Stacy pulled his head up by the hair and cut a deep gash through his exposed throat. At 20:07, another massive psionic tremor was detected as glowing, spindly legs, much like those of the Worms, reached out to encompass Mr. Schultz, who was then dragged into the closet.

The door slammed shut with considerable force and Stacy fell backward onto the floor. Here she remained, transfixed by some unseen and undetected force. Stacy's body writhed and thrashed about the floor in a bizarre fashion, and biometric readings indicate Stacy experienced multiple orgasms during this time. After several minutes of this behavior, Stacy fell unconscious and remained sleeping on the floor of the centermost room for three hours.

At 23:12, another inter-dimensional contact was recorded. The Worms had returned, though each was closer to four meters long now. They materialized in the centermost room and proceeded to gather up Ms. Fontaine and carry her unconscious form upstairs to her bedroom. There, they left her unceremoniously on the still-disheveled bed. The Worms had spent what would turn out to be the majority of their time on our side of the breach, caring for the transport of Stacy Fontaine. At 23:55, the contact was again broken, and both apparitions disappeared. It is theorized that the killings, which were now taking on a ritual appearance, were leading to an increase in the stress upon the active breach in the closet, thus allowing a more and more accurate projection of the Worms to manifest. Though they could move Ms. Fontaine, it was a laborious and slow affair, accomplished with much apparent difficulty. Why it was necessary to move Stacy to her bed is not readily apparent.

Safely in her bed, Stacy slept undisturbed until 08:41 on 16-12-22. When she woke, it was clear that the stress was beginning to affect her. Frantic in her actions throughout the morning, several times, Stacy simply broke down sobbing for minutes on end.

Then, without warning, at 09:43, she tore out the monitoring system that she had installed on Monday. Though a salient detail to have considered if one premeditates murder, it was a relatively moot gesture by this time.

At 10:56, she returned to the centermost room and conversed silently with the closed closet door again. At 11:04, the door suddenly swung open, and Stacy stood transfixed for one minute and thirty-seven seconds in the doorway. At 11:06, the closet door slammed shut, and Stacy swiftly turned and exited the room.

Something had occurred when the door was open and its effect on Stacy was nauseating to behold. Her movement was now changed, her gait unrecognizable from before, as if unseen hands pushed along her legs, her movements inorganic and wrong.

Then, abruptly, everything changed. At 11:09, there was the sound of someone on the front porch. On-site Agency recording equipment documented the arrival of the mailman. Stacy's movement suddenly returned to normal and she rushed toward the front door. She whipped the door open and startled the postal carrier. After apologizing for scaring him, Stacy pleaded for assistance. Observing agents thought this was perhaps the culmination of the Terminal Event they were witnessing, but such was not to be. Stacy implored the mailman to assist her with remodeling, in progress, claiming to need another set of hands to hold one last joist so she could set it in place and complete her work.

The mailman, to his fault, was kind, and with a little prodding, agreed to assist. At 11:10, the postal worker, one Garret Fife, entered The House Of Walls through the front door. He removed his mailbag, placed it near the door, and followed Stacy into the living room, which incidentally had seen the majority of the remodeling work over the last few days. There, Stacy instructed him to hold up a piece of wood for her to nail into place. Holding the material and facing away from Stacy, he never suspected as she crept up behind him and drove the syringe she was secretly carrying into the side of his throat. The attack was not entirely successful. Mr. Fife dropped the board and thrashed wildly at his unseen assailant. Stacy was thrown to the ground before she could administer the full dose of the elixir properly. She clamored to her feet and rushed off toward the centermost room.

Despite being an incomplete dose, it was significant enough to severely impair Mr. Fife's attempt at an escape. He had barely staggered to the center of the living room before Stacy had returned, butcher knife in hand. She tore at him with incredible speed and drove the blade deep into his chest in the blink of an eye. Holding him then by the head much as one would a lover, she effortlessly snapped his neck, and he fell to the floor dead.

Wasting no time, Stacy hauled the body off to the centermost room and the awaiting, open aperture. She seemed to have none of the issues moving Mr. Fife she had encountered with Mr. Schultz. The consumption of Mr. Fife, within the closed confines of the closet, was audible for the first time. Several observing agents became physically ill at the onset. It was subsequently classed as a Level-4 biohazard.

Stacy returned to the kitchen, acquired cleaning supplies, and returned to the living room. In place of the gore-covered, disheveled mess, Stacy found the Worms, busy tiding the room and consuming the errant blood, now each nearly six meters long. Rather than react, Stacy simply stated, "It was about time you did something to help." She then returned her tools to the kitchen.

It is significant that the Worms' appearance had not initiated an interdimensional contact and that they were likely fully manifest into our reality at this point. They were clearly not the entities with which Stacy had been communicating and were, in practice, treated much as one would a canine. After cleaning the room, the Worms retired to the upstairs, where they congregated in the main bedroom and settled on the floor.

In the kitchen, Stacy was startled by the sound of tapping on the back door glass. At 11:38, Cheryl Alma, one of Stacy's few close friends, entered The House Of Walls through the back door. Stacy was visibly relieved to see her close friend and embraced her moments after she entered the house. She then broke down sobbing and the two retired to the living room to talk.

Their conversation is transcribed below.

11:43, 16-12-22, living room of The House Of Walls:

Stacy Fontaine (SF): Thanks for coming over, Cher; I really don't want to be alone right now. (AIC's note: it is unclear when or how Stacy contacted Ms. Alma. No such communication has been recovered.)

Cheryl Alma (CA): It's no biggie; I only live a block away now; it was barely a short walk. *Cheryl smiles at her friend* So what's wrong? You kinda look like shit, sweetie.

SF: Well, thanks. *Stacy chuckles* I don't know how long it's been anymore. What day is it?

CA: It's Friday, sweetie. You're starting to worry me. What happened? Also, where's that crazy little cat of yours?

SF: *Sobs* He's gone, Cher, I don't know what to do. * Stacy again embraces Ms. Alma*

CA: It's okay, let it out. These things happen sometimes. Did he get hit by a car or something?

SF: No, *sobs* it was me; it's all my fault.

CA: What do you mean, sweetie? Does this have something to do with that bandage on your arm?

SF: I ... I can't say. It's not safe, and it's far, far too late. Oh God, what am I doing? *Stacy begins shaking uncontrollably.*

CA: Okay, okay, just try to calm down. Everything will be alright. But you're gonna have to explain this to me, okay, if I'm gonna help. What happened to your cat, Stacy? What's going on here?

SF: I couldn't explain it if I tried Cher, but I think I can show you if you let me. Everything is in the center room; once you see it, you'll understand.

CA: I can't say I'm excited about this, but okay. Lead on, show me what's going on, and maybe we can figure something out.

Stacy and Cheryl rose from the couch and walked the short distance to the centermost room. Every indication was that Ms. Alma was in considerable danger at this point. In the centermost room, Stacy led Cheryl to the closet, its painted white warning not lost on Ms. Alma. As they stopped before the closet, the door slowly swung open.

What Ms. Alma saw is unknown. She stood transfixed and in awe of whatever it was she saw in that closet. Stacy slid her foot in front of Cheryl's leg and, with a barely audible "I'm sorry," toppled her friend into the waiting oblivion beyond the breach. The door slammed shut, and Stacy let out a large sigh. Audio of Ms. Alma's demise was again present and is currently classed as a Level-2 biohazard.

Stacy then retired to the kitchen for a haphazardly prepared lunch. It was strange that Stacy kept so rigorously to her routines in response to the trauma she had so far endured. That she was no longer of her sane mind was apparent.

The remainder of the afternoon was remarkably quiet. Stacy spent most of the time seated on the floor of the centermost room, surrounded by the Worms, swollen to lengths close to eight meters. There is no recorded conversation or video of Stacy communicating with anything. Six hours transpired in this manner, Stacy leaving the centermost room only twice, both times to use the restroom.

At 18:32, Stacy was roused from her seated stupor by another knock at the front door. Much more gingerly now, Stacy made her way to the front door and opened it to a sight she, perhaps, should have expected sooner. Two patrol officers from the local police department stood waiting on the porch in the diminishing light of the day.

Stacy was clearly startled by their appearance and seemed to instantly become nervous. The officers, Trent Lane and John Rimes, were on a routine canvassing patrol looking for information concerning Mr. Garret Fife, the local mail carrier who had not returned from his route. His abandoned postal car was found a block away, but all signs indicated that he was simply out on his route. Stacy was erratic at best, attempting to convince the officers that she had no idea whatsoever as to the whereabouts of Mr. Fife. Officer Lane, who paced the porch looking through the windows as his partner spoke with Ms. Fontaine, spotted the mailbag still sitting near the front door.

Less than thirty seconds later, at 18:41, the officers were both within The House Of Walls. Stacy had beat an expeditious retreat just before they had entered the house and now led them headfirst toward the centermost room.

The Worms crashed past Stacy as the group made its way through the living room. Officer Rimes, in the lead, was torn to pieces by the giant glowing horrors before managing to draw his weapon. Officer Lane was not caught as unprepared as his partner and managed to let off a series of shots before the Worms set upon him. One found purchase in Stacy's shoulder, and she fell against the wall, tumbling into the centermost room.

The Worms made quick work gathering up the corpses of the fallen police officers and dragging them into the closet. The Worms went with them, through to whatever terrible end was in store on the other side, it seemed.

Then it happened. At 19:01, a magnitude 9.2 psionic tremor was recorded, and potential dimensional failure was detected. In the centermost room of The House Of Walls, a terrible, scratchy voice rang out. "Now is the dawn of ████████████████!! Weep mortals, for the path to oblivion opens!!"

At the mention of ██████████, Extinction Protocol was enacted per general standing orders. Information was sent to Command and a Blackout Team (BXT) was dispatched to the location. The BXT was expressly instructed to recover Ms. Fontaine and not to neutralize her.

At 19:03, BXT members arrived on the scene and entered the location. Moving directly through to the centermost room, two agents secured

Ms. Fontaine and removed her from the premises. Outside, Ms. Fontaine was given over to medical personnel for treatment of her injuries.

Inside, agents moved in and prepared to breach the closet. Moments after Ms. Fontaine was safely removed from the house, and perhaps in response to it, the Worms burst forth from the closet, destroying the intervening door. Agents were quick to deploy canister-bound ionizers, which had a severely deleterious effect on the lead Worm. The second Worm managed to dodge the majority of the ionizing blast and, incidentally, ended up practically on top of BXT Agent Mendez. Mendez was torn apart in moments despite polycarbonate Kevlar armor. The remaining BXT members trained their canister launchers on the gore-riddled scene and obliterated the second Worm. They had, however, failed to properly dispose of the first Worm and, injured, it lashed out at nearby BXT Agent Smith. A long, sharp leg took Agent Smith's head clean off his body. There was no ammunition left for the canister launchers at that point, so agents resorted to the application of terminal heat through standard-issue Inferno Guns. It took three minutes to reduce the lead Worm to ash.

Throughout the interaction, the deep, scratchy voice of UE0735 continued to threaten and taunt the BXT agents. On-site communications agents deployed noise-canceling software within agency monitoring devices to prevent audible transmission of the profane and madness-inducing babble spewing forth from UE0735. It was clear that all UE0735 was capable of at this point was bluster and threats. That its transition into our reality must have been, in fact, incomplete was confirmed by agents on-site.

With the Worms disposed of and UE0735 still transitioning into our reality, the remainder of the securing action was relatively trivial. Surviving BXT agents brought in and deployed a Class-1 Heavy Marigold Device (HMD). The HMD established harmonic equilibrium and separated the overlapping instances of reality, physically sealing the breach. It was evident from the ensuing sounds within The House Of Walls that this process was terminal to UE0735. Beyond our abilities to counter at close range, the sounds were extremely hazardous to anyone capable of hearing them, classed as a Level-1 biohazard, and one BXT agent, acting AIC Agent Mullens, turned his service pistol on himself and self-neutralized.

At 19:27, The House Of Walls and Ms. Stacy Fontaine were secured. The HMD would hold the dimensional breach inert and prevent further incursion. Though the location could not be destroyed, now that it is under Agency control, any additional risk is minimal.

Though UE0735 invoked ▮▮▮▮▮▮▮▮▮▮ during its attempted incursion into our reality, it is unlikely that UE0735 was, in fact, ▮▮▮▮ ▮▮▮▮▮▮▮▮▮. The most convincing evidence to this end is that some members of the BXT survived and managed to eliminate UE0735. It is unclear from our records if destroying ▮▮▮▮▮▮▮▮▮ would be possible. It is ironic that The Ghosts Of The Broken Dawn held the location for 168 years and never detected its potential connection to ▮▮▮▮▮▮▮, given the links between the two.

Further neutralization was ordered as part of the Extinction Protocol, specifically the potential connection of this site to ▮▮▮▮▮▮▮ ▮▮▮▮. The entire extended family of the previous property owner, Mrs. Abigail Bertram, was neutralized as of 20-12-22. Agent A, as previously reported, was neutralized on 17-12-22. Surviving members of the BXT were all prescribed medication to eradicate the memories of the event.

Ms. Fontaine was placed into Agency custody. Though Stacy Fontaine committed multiple instances that would have normally necessitated neutralization, her safety was ordered to be of paramount importance. She was offered a deal: work for the Agency, turn her gifts with computers to our advantage, and be allowed to live. Unsurprisingly, she accepted.

Subject reports regularly for psych evaluation and has proved invaluable to Research & Development. That she might be contaminated by an interdimensional presence only further cements the need to keep her close at hand.

In five days, what looked, at first, to be an ordinary house, rented by a typical tenant, turned into a potential reality failure and the need to invoke Extinction Protocol to prevent our mutual demise. It is the opinion of this Agent that the course of events that transpired within

The House Of Walls was intentionally allowed to progress to some unseen end, known only by Command. Does it have something to do with the nearby connection to The Nightroad? Only Command truly knows the answer, and none should be expected.

The ramifications of our actions are often hard for those of us on the ground to understand. Equally, the orders we receive, the actions taken by Command, and everything we deal with on a daily basis are shrouded in mystery. That doesn't excuse the careless waste of a total of ten lives, but in the end, they are of little consequence when weighed against the good of all mankind. Command's duty is to see what we cannot and instruct us accordingly. Ours is the burden to follow those orders, and in this case, that is precisely what our agents did. There are forces at play here beyond what any one person can comprehend. As long as we are able to keep the rest of the world safe, it is a price I, for one, am more than willing to pay.

End report.

Interlude: Rook's Story, Part 2

There was very little time left to act. The creature, which had been human just minutes before, had Critter pinned to the hood of the car. Its now distended arms and legs gave it the edge it needed to best Critter, and while he fought furiously, it would only be a matter of time before the fang-filled mouth of the vile thing tore his throat out.

Rook's gun was empty and clicked away impotently as he raced from the shadow of the burning house behind him and toward the car. What the hell was he going to do? He leaped over the corpse of a Screaming Eye cultist and only barely managed to keep his footing upon landing.

The creature tightened its grip on Critter's arm, piercing into his flesh, and he let out a howl in response.

Then, a thought occurred to Rook. They had gotten the drop on the Screaming Eye cultists and had taken out the two lookouts stationed outside with little trouble. Then, inside, everything went sideways, and Critter decided to burn the place down. They had never used the mine, which was conveniently still sitting in the back seat.

Rook's pace quickened, now only a few steps from the commotion on the hood. He tore past Critter, an anguished look of abandonment etched on his companion's bruised face.

Rook swung the back door of the sedan open and dove inside. The infamous device needed no priming or prep time, "just push the big red button," he had been told. Rook pressed the button, and a deep rumbling noise began to rise from the hypersonic mine. Then, a hazy white wave of distortion burst forth from the device, knocking Rook into the seat behind him. As the wave passed through the creature, it burst in spectacular fashion, covering Critter in a shower of blood and viscera.

"Well, God Damn!!" Critter shouted in triumph. "Thought you were about to leave me there for a second, Rook. See, you got some stones after all." He chuckled. You couldn't tell that he was inches from death only moments before from his attitude.

Rook was breathing hard, but at least it was over. "Yeah, I guess you owe me one now." He crawled out of the back seat and stood before the cultist hideout as it was fully engulfed in flames. In the distance, sirens could be heard.

Critter was already in the trunk, at the first aid kit, bandaging up his arm. He took off his bloody tee shirt and replaced it with a dirty flannel that he found within the dank confines of the trunk. Quietly, unnoticed by Rook, he injected a powerful antibiotic into his right arm. "We better get moving; they don't sound too far off." He said.

Rook agreed. They needed to be long gone before anyone official came to investigate the blaze. He climbed back into the passenger's seat. After another minute, Critter was behind the wheel and started the engine. They pulled out of the driveway and headed back east toward where they had come off of The Nightroad. In the rearview mirrors, the lights of approaching emergency vehicles could be faintly seen.

"You sure you're alright to drive?" Rook asked, though it was too late for them to stop.

"Never been better." Critter flashed a bloody grin.

The dark blue sedan sped along through the waning darkness of the evening. After another half hour, the sun would begin to creep over the horizon, trapping Rook and Critter into whatever version of reality The Nightroad had dumped them into. "You remember where the ramp was, right?" Rook said.

Before Critter could answer, a police cruiser sped past them, heading toward the commotion in their wake. It had barely passed them when it spun around, lights and sirens blazing.

"Ah shit, hold on," Critter said. He slammed the gas pedal, and the sedan lurched forward, its engine roaring.

This was the worst possible situation, Rook thought. Critter hadn't even considered stopping and trying to appease the cop. An extended chase would seriously jeopardize their chances of getting back home. Once the sun rose and the ramp to The Nightroad vanished, there was no telling if it would still be there the following evening. Especially considering that the situation in the cultist hideout (which Critter had conveniently cleansed with fire) was likely the anchor holding The Nightroad to this location. Between the fire and the hypersonic mine, it would be miraculous if there was anything alive in that house.

Critter pushed the car through a curve at incredible speed, and Rook felt momentarily ill. The cop in pursuit was not impressed and held fast in their rearview.

"We gotta lose this guy!" Rook shouted.

"You think I don't know that!" Critter shot a glance at Rook, that bristled with madness.

The sedan took another tight turn, and the spent husk of the mine slid across the back seat. It collided with the rear passenger door with a clunk.

"That gives me an idea," Critter said. "Open the glove box and hand me the square box-looking gizmo."

Rook opened the glove box. Inside, amidst the usual mess of manuals and various (fake) forms of identification, sat a small black rectangle that looked in part like a jewelry case and in part like the internal workings of some fantastic computer.

"This?" Rook asked, handing the device to Critter.

"Heh, yeah, that'll do." Critter opened his window and tossed the box out into the path of the oncoming cruiser.

Less than a second later, a great black hole tore itself into existence behind them with a peeling screech. From the abyss within, what looked like several large plant tendrils uncoiled and engulfed the oncoming cop car. It was crushed in an instant and dragged off into the depths from whence the tendrils had come. Then, just as suddenly as it had appeared, the tear seemed to collapse in on itself, leaving only empty space where once it had been.

Critter slowed the car to a stop and pulled over.

"What the hell was that?!" Rook was near to panic.

"Emergency plan," Critter answered apathetically. "We don't have time for your customary rookie explanations. We missed a turn back there before all those curves; we gotta find the on-ramp." Critter was breathing harder than usual. "It's gonna be morning soon."

Critter turned the sedan and headed back in the direction they had come. Not too fast this time, but with an earnestness that seemed to permeate all present.

It was another five minutes before they reached the turn they had missed.

"Should only be a couple of miles. There was a barn at the end of the dirt road we came off of, right?" It was uncommon for Critter to seem unsure of things, and his question unsettled Rook.

"Yeah, man, dirt road with a big barn on the corner. Looked like it hadn't been used in ages. You sure you're alright?" Rook looked at Critter, concern for both their lives now racing through his brain.

"Yeah, I'm fine. I told you that already. Just been a long night." Critter brushed him off.

In silence, the pair drove on. With each minute that passed, the dawn and their doom crept ever closer. Rook began to feel his control over his emotions ebb. Then, just before the crest of an oncoming hill, the barn could be seen. Critter floored it. Moments later, they turned onto the dirt road, dust and gravel spraying like waves in their wake.

A sign on the side of the road whistled past. "Dead end," it had proclaimed, though the local signage mattered little in this case. The sedan raced into the woods, and before them, Rook could see pavement where there should only have been trees. It seemed they had made it, and he sighed heavily.

"Don't get too comfy yet, partner." Critter chuckled. "This is gonna be close!"

Suddenly, some fifty yards before them, a tree appeared out of nowhere. Critter swerved, barely managing to miss the tree and barely keeping the car on the road.

Rook braced himself. On either side of them, strange lights flickered and images seemed to manifest and fade. Trees, bushes, animals, both familiar and strange, and even buildings all appeared around them and then vanished as reality bucked and thrashed. Ever the road was present beneath their wheels.

A loud "POP!" brought the chaos around them to an end, and they were once again driving in silence along the purplish-blue landscape of The Nightroad. Critter slowed the car but didn't stop. "Now that was a fun night, I tell you what."

Rook shook his head. He was sure he'd never be used to this. "So what now?" He asked.

"Well, see, I was kinda lying about being fine and all," Critter said, as his eyes rolled back into his head and he passed out. His head fell hard into the steering wheel.

"Oh Shit!" was all Rook managed to get out.

The Pale House

I.

Deep primal woods are still thriving in the modern world. Often demarked as government land or protected parks, these places are allowed to wallow in their ancient decadence. One such woodland, called simply The Old Woods by locals, reaches down into the northeastern edge of Hueta County and spreads out along its northern border, where it butts up to the farmlands and small residential communities that make up the county proper.

Majestic old-growth forests commonly become attractions or travel destinations, but throughout the townships of Hueta County, the woodlands were only ever spoken of with fear and revulsion. Indeed, several people had gone missing within its bounds but, in truth, no more than in any other similar location. Alone, that could never explain the avid distaste for The Old Woods the local citizenry had acquired.

Perhaps expected then, homes near The Old Woods were often abandoned and became difficult for realtors to offload. So it was that the McMasters family, Edgar and Ruth, with children Eve, Armin, and Allen, found an affordable house for a family of five in the early spring of 1985, just southwest of the terminal end of The Old Woods.

The mid-century colonial was in remarkably good shape. The house was large and painted a pleasant light blue with white trim. The wraparound porch was covered with the same deep brown hardwood floors as the interior and stopped sharply at the back of the house. A small two-car garage with bright white doors sat not far to the right of the house on the eastern side, marking the end of the long white sand driveway, its most distinguishing feature. A row of high bushes bound the east edge of the property, though the remaining northern edge was the literal edge of The Old Woods. The area had something of a hidden quality to it, seeming as though it were carved out of some primal wilderness to which it never belonged. Open on the south and west, the roughly rectangular property was the last bit of civilization before the looming specter of the woods.

The McMasters had moved out to rural Hueta County from the "big city" after Edgar was promoted at his job selling life insurance. To take the promotion, he was forced to work out of the local Hueta County satellite office in Eagle Creek. Some people, Ruth included, would have argued that the promotion was anything but; however, Edgar had been quick to accept the position as the increased status within the company had been something the small-minded Edgar had longed for.

For their part, the children of the McMasters clan had taken to moving out to the countryside. Neither life in the city nor the intervening six months in various Eagle Creek motel rooms had been to their collective liking. The youths, aged 14, 13, and 10, respectively, had all inherited their mother's ruddy brown hair and curious mind. Only Armin had gotten their father's bad eyes and wore glasses as a result. Though Armin's NES had kept them entertained during the long house hunt, they were all, at heart, naturalists, people who deeply loved and needed the outdoors. As such, the trio were eager to set foot on their new territory.

From March to September 1985, the three inseparable siblings explored and mapped as much of their new backyard forest kingdom as possible. The new responsibilities of Edgar's job kept him away or otherwise occupied most of his waking hours. With the strain of leaving the only people and life she had ever known (along with festering underlying alcoholism) weighting down Ruth, it was no real surprise that the children spent as much time as possible away from their home.

In the woods, Eve, Armin, and Allen could be anything they dreamt of, and for a time, they were free to live in relative bliss thanks to the woods. The trees and streams had become their silent fourth companion.

Then, on Thursday, September 19, 1985, the dawn would break on a chain of events unlike any other. At approximately 4:00 p.m., the Mc-

Masters children found themselves, as usual, in The Old Woods. They were returning from a hike that had taken most of the afternoon and plumbed the depths of the great and terrible Old Woods—a place whose foreboding reputation had had no effect on Eve, Armin, or Allen.

Led by the impetuous and headstrong Allen, the three crested a small hill and made their way toward a trail that would lead back to their property. After several hundred yards and nearing 4:30, Allen stopped suddenly. Stunned, he stood motionless and silent as Armin reached his location.

"Holy shit! Sis, you gotta see this!" Armin called back to Eve, who was lagging behind.

A moment later, Eve stood in silence with her brothers. Ahead of them, perhaps fifty yards away, where any of the three would have sworn only trees stood just days before, a large Pale House with an attached and manicured lawn rose up amidst the trees.

The siblings' location, still within The Old Woods, was effectively out the backside of The Pale House's yard. A small gazebo sat in the yard between the children and the back of the house.

All three stood silently for a moment regarding the Gothic monstrosity that now towered above them. The Pale House seemed to ooze out a colorless silence and palpable dread. Its great curtained windows hung far too large upon its sides, and something about its general proportion seemed wrong. Worse, however, was its color or lack thereof. It was not simply white or gray but seemingly of some ancient tone, now gone and faded away. Its color was emptiness, Eve thought, and she shook her head at the strange notion.

Suddenly, there was a loud crash of metal against stone. The commotion roused a flock of chickadees to flight from a nearby bush. The three McMasters children let out a collective yelp almost in perfect unison. The passing shock lifted the children's stupor, and again, they seemed free to act upon their surroundings.

"Where did it come from?" Eve was first to speak as the collective gloom lifted. "It wasn't here just, what, yesterday? It hasn't been more than two days since we've been out this way," she continued.

"We should check it out!" Allen piped in, ever the eager adventurer.

"There isn't time; it's already almost dark," Eve interjected, though, in her gut, she felt some gnawing unnameable desire to flee from this strange encounter.

"Eve's right, Al, we don't even have a flashlight." Armin quickly added, knowing that Allen's impetuous nature needed immediate addressing.

"Okay, fine." Allen relented. "But we are coming back here tomorrow to check this place out. Do you guys think we have new neighbors?"

"Something about this place makes me think we don't want to know the answer to that, Al. C'mon, let's go home," said Eve. She was sure there was something about the strange Pale House that she didn't like, though precisely what it was escaped her.

The children made their way through the last leg of their journey. They emerged from The Old Woods at the very edge of their property, slightly east of a makeshift bridge they had constructed over the creek that ran along the northern border, just within the confines of the trees.

The remainder of their evening was uneventful, but there was much talk about the mystery house in the woods. The idea that such a thing could have been constructed right under their noses was galling, and there were far too many questions unanswered about the strange dwelling.

II.

After school the following day, the McMasters children convinced their mother, Ruth, to drop them off at the local Eagle Creek Municipal Library on her weekly shopping trip into town. It had been Armin's idea that they should look into the public records available at the library to see if someone had indeed moved into that strange spot in the woods. While neither Eve nor Allen were as studious as their brother, they were nonetheless curious and readily agreed to the bit of detective work. That the weather that Friday afternoon had turned rainy and glum only played a mildly significant role.

There was no record of someone purchasing a house near theirs or constructing anything in the area. Though their skills in the matter and the library's resources were somewhat limited, they had managed to pique the interest of the librarian, Mrs. Krum, who, in turn, introduced them to a book of local folklore.

Inside the musty tome, the children discovered something exciting. Amidst a somewhat rambling section on local customs and unsolved mysteries, there was mention of a "ghost house of the woods" that suddenly appeared at various locations throughout the woodlands of the American Northeast. Though its mention was brief, it was lauded as being particularly dangerous. Apparently, if the publication was to be believed, several groups of investigators had gone missing attempting to research this specific "aberration," as the book called it.

"You don't really believe this, do you?" Eve wasn't sure herself yet, but the sinking feeling in her gut hadn't abated. She looked at Armin with questioning eyes.

"I don't know; I mean, it does sort of fit what we found." Armin was busy looking over the book of folklore and missed his sister's earnest gaze. "Do you think this will spook Al?"

"Where did he even get to?" Eve looked around their close proximity for signs of her youngest brother.

"He ran into that Andy kid from school. The one from his class. I think they are in the comics section." Armin waved his hand dismissively in the general direction of the periodicals wrack.

"Oh God, not Andy. That's the last thing we need." Eve cringed. "He'd better not tell him anything about the house." She looked over her shoulder nervously as if expecting someone coming up from behind.

"I don't think he will. It's too big of a mystery for Al to want to share it." Armin smiled. Both he and his brother were known for having a knack for trouble. If Armin was the brains of the operation, Allen was certainly the bravado.

As if on cue, the youngest of the McMasters siblings rounded the nearby bookshelf and rejoined his brother and sister. He seemed more excited than usual.

"You guys are never going to believe what I heard from Andy." He started earnestly. "You know how his great-great-uncle, or whatever, runs that weird farm."

"Not the mushrooms again, Allen." Eve groaned.

"No, no, this isn't about the farm. Just Andy's great uncle." Allen tried his best to press on. Eve and Armin's distaste for his friend Andy was well known. A feeling shared by many of the local juvenile population, who, by and large, found the clever and talkative Andy to be something of a boring know-it-all.

"That guy is creepy," Armin added, the conversation rapidly escaping Allen's grasp. "What does he have to do with anything?"

"That's what I'm trying to tell you." Now, it was Allen's turn to groan. "His uncle, or whatever, the creepy guy. He knows all kinds of stuff, right? Well, it turns out he knows a story about a creepy house in the woods!"

"Wait, does that mean you told Andy about the house?" Eve was beginning to get upset with Allen, though they had made no explicit decision to keep their discovery secret.

"I did, but I made him promise not to tell anyone." Allen put on his most serious expression. "Besides, he knew the story, so we don't even have to go talk to his creepy great-uncle." Allen smiled then, clearly proud of his discovery.

"So anyways, Andy said that the house supposedly moves around in the forests, and people have seen it around here in the past. It hangs out for like a week or something, and then 'poof' it's just gone." Allen paused and looked between his siblings to ensure they were listening. "The kicker is anyone who goes into the house ... is never seen again." Allen's voice rose as if he were narrating a movie trailer.

The depiction was not overly welcome to either Eve or Armin. "Here, Al, take a look at this." Armin held the folklore book out for Allen to read.

"That's basically the same story Andy told me!" Allen said after a moment. "That's gotta make it true, right?"

"That means Andy has read this book, maybe." Armin was ever the skeptic and seemed to take the source of Allen's information as proof of its falsehood.

"But it has to be true; what else could explain it?" Allen caught himself before he got too angry with his brother. This sort of reticence on the part of the middle McMasters child was not uncommon, and Allen was adept at handling the emotions of others despite his tender age.

"You mean that someone built a house out in the woods? It can't be that uncommon, really." Armin persisted, sure in his belief that a rational explanation existed for the current mystery.

Eve was less skeptical. "I don't know, Armi, it is really creepy how similar those stories are. And you saw this book when Mrs. Krum dug it out for us. No one has read this thing in years." Eve's observational skills were, at times, hard to argue with.

"I still say this doesn't change anything. There is only one way we'll ever get to the bottom of this." Armin was confident if mildly nervous about his coming assertion. "We have to go back and check the house out again."

"Yeah, I was already going to do that," Allen added with characteristic charm. "Do you think we have any ghost-catching supplies at home?" He asked only partly jokingly.

By the time they returned home, the rain had passed, and while it was still dreary, it was not overly cold. Buoyed by all the information they had gathered, the three McMasters children could scarcely contain their excitement and thirst for adventure.

After customary promises to their mother to be home in time for dinner, Eve, Armin, and Allen headed out into The Old Woods toward their most recent discovery. The path heading directly toward the house was much shorter than their trip the previous day, and in a matter of less than a half-hour, they were again nearing the hill from atop of which they had first spied The Pale House.

Just as it had been the day before, The Pale House stood looming up amidst the trees. Everything about its proportions was wrong. The windows were both too large and too narrow, and their entire vertical shape seemed almost stretched. The roof hung down near the edges, practically dripping, and the image was repulsive to all three children.

Repulsed though they were, they would not have let this stop them, for the whole of the McMasters clan was known for their bravery had there not been some new ripple to the proceedings. Something seemed different about the house now, something ominous in its strangely angled walls.

"I still say we check it out." Allen was the bravest of the three and always up for the exciting thrill of the unknown. That there now might be ghosts involved seemed only to fuel his desire to explore this new mystery.

"Do you two hear that?" Armin interjected, "I swear it sounds like someone is around to the front of the house."

The three again paused, listening for the sounds of life that had caught Armin's attention. Indeed, there were sounds of commotion and work being done coming from somewhere not overly far from their location. Relieved by the possibility of a rational explanation, the youths relaxed.

"Maybe Al's on to something; let's go check it out," Armin said in his customary dry calmness.

"I don't know, guys, there's something wrong about this place. You can feel it." Eve hesitated, always the most cautious of the three. However, in this case, her reticence seemed far more reasonable than usual.

"It looks strange, that's for sure," Allen added as he hovered between his brother's support and his trust in his sister's instincts. "And there was all that stuff in the library about the ghost house."

"C'mon, there has to be a reasonable explanation here. So what, just because something looks out of place, and we read a vague snippet of similar folklore, suddenly you two become scaredy-cats?" Armin chided. "This is no weirder than that old busted-down pickup we found when we first moved here. The one you two swore must have been from some prison escape or some nonsense. They probably just have one hell of a construction crew or something." Armin's voice had an added insistence as though he needed to have this rational explanation more than he wished to admit.

It seemed for the McMasters children that time stood still as another moment passed between them in silence.

"Oh, what the hell," Allen said as he burst forth into the yard of The Pale House. Armin and Eve were close on his heels.

Just as she was about to emerge from The Old Woods, Eve caught a glimpse of movement from the house. Behind the curtain of the window overlooking the backyard, something moved. Something very large and swift dashed off into the darkness of the house, and Eve shuddered in spite of herself. She quickened her pace to catch up to her brothers, who were now nearly to the gazebo in the yard.

By the time they reached the side of the house, the siblings had caught up to one another. Activity and tents could be seen around the front of the house, and a collection of cars was parked on a makeshift driveway, though there was no road for it to connect to. Several tough-looking, stout men worked at setting up more tents and tables as if for a festival or a great feast.

Though initially cautious, lest they be run off for trespassing, the siblings quickly realized that the workers had no interest in them or their comings and goings. In fact, they barely seemed to notice the children at all as they went about their work. Instead, the men worked in eerie silence, and all three McMasters children seemed reluctant to go any closer to them. Something in the way they moved hinted at dark and terrible things, and the children felt an instinctive pull to shun the presence of the workers.

Staying to the side of the yard and out of the area actively used by the workers, the McMasters children made their way toward the front of The Pale House's yard, back toward where the woods again crowded in.

As they walked through the tidy yard, a realization dawned in Eve's mind. Even allowing for some fantastic construction crew that could have built the house so quickly, Eve wondered how they hadn't noticed the trees being removed, located as their home was, on the only possible road into or out of this part of The Old Woods. Something in her intuition made her doubt that she would like the answer to where the trees had gone.

"My, my! What do we have here?" The sudden advent of a foreign voice visibly startled the children, who all turned toward the sound. Behind where they had been watching the house stood a tall, gaunt man with deep tan skin and hair and a beard of almost shocking white. He was dressed in dark clothing, and a heavy-looking, long, black leather coat hung from his shoulders. A tremendous black top hat adorned his head. With the hat, he was easily seven feet tall and stood towering over the young children. There was, however, an air of calm, of safety, that surrounded the man, and after a moment's recovery, the children again found their ability to speak.

"We were just out for a walk ..." Eve began before Armin interrupted.

"Which we are allowed to do 'cause this forest is public land!" he added, worried they were about to be run off their newest discovery.

"Hi! I'm Allen." The youngest added, determined to be part of the conversation.

The man chuckled warmly. "No need for explanation, kids. This must all seem pretty odd from your side of things." He paused for a moment. "So you just stumbled on us here? I apologize; I've been watching you since you entered the yard. I didn't think it was possible to stumble upon this place."

Allen, again, was the first to reply. "We just live on the other side of the creek back there. We're always finding odd stuff in the forest."

"Never a whole house, though," Armin added.

Eve eyed the tall man. "So, who are you people?" She asked despite a deepening fear that grew in her stomach.

The man again chuckled. "You don't like surprises, do you, miss?"

"Eve. My name's Eve, and this is Armin. You've already met Allen. But you didn't answer my question, who are you?" Eve pressed the tall stranger, though she felt her discomfort growing with each passing moment.

"I suppose that is a fair question, seeing as we are in your backyard and all." The tall man smiled. "My name is Melantonth Qualiaris Vescaro, but you may call me Mel. I am the proprietor of a sort of carnival. You inadvertently stumbled upon an event as we were setting up. You see, the carnival itself isn't open just yet and will only be so for a day, tomorrow, to be specific."

"A carnival? Like the county fair? With games and cotton candy?" Allen's interest was piqued at the prospect of carnival games and cotton candy.

"Yes, in a way," Melantonth continued, "we are more a traveling carnival of oddities—a place where someone comes to see the strange and unique. And, of course, have something to eat. But now I must ask you children a question. Would you be interested in visiting us again tomorrow when the carnival proper is in full swing? As I mentioned before, your finding us here is quite peculiar, even perhaps a heinous breach in our, frankly, incredible amounts of security. As such, I would rather look at this as an incredible opportunity and offer you three an unprecedented invitation to come out tomorrow and see us in all our glory. In a place safe and secure from outside influence," he added almost ominously.

The McMasters children looked amongst themselves. Allen was still taken by the incredible turn of events that day. But Armin, too, had begun to sense something strange around them and was quickly coming to the same ominous fear as his sister Eve.

"So, how'd you build the house so fast?" Armin asked, ignoring the matter of the invitation altogether.

"Right! And who builds a house in the woods for a carnival?" Eve added, emboldened by her brother's implied support.

"Well, that's simple," Melantonth chuckled, "we didn't. I imagine it will spoil some of tomorrow, but this house, known as The Wandering Pale House, is our main attraction. It is notoriously difficult to locate and even harder to determine its movement patterns, but we found it this time, and tomorrow we celebrate." There was something dark and foreboding about the casual way Melantonth spoke of the apparently motile house and the cold assuredness with which he described the impossible.

"All will become clear if you accept my invitation and join us tomorrow. I promise. For now, there is still much I must attend to, and you children should be off. Come back here tomorrow; any time is fine as long as the sun is up, but come by the same path you took today when you found us. Do not bring any guests, and tell no one of the carnival. Should you decide to decline my offer, please respect our privacy and stay out of this part of the woods tomorrow. For your own safety more than anything else." And, with a wave of his hand, Melantonth motioned the children along a side path back into The Old Woods.

Somewhat in a daze, the siblings made their way down the path, unsure how to proceed. As they were about to turn on the trail and put the house out of sight behind them, Melantonth called after them.

"Whatever you do, don't go into the house. The woman that lives there is not as she seems."

The words echoed as the McMasters siblings continued unabated.

"So someone lives there?" Eve asked aloud.

"I guess so," Armin said. "I guess we'll just have to come back tomorrow to get any real answers."

"I just hope there's cotton candy," Allen added, his youthful innocence a stark contrast to the bewildering and ominous day they had all experienced.

"Yeah, I suppose we will," Eve answered. From there, the siblings traveled home in silence. Each was wrapped in thought over the events of the day and the potential of the coming morrow.

III.

The McMasters siblings gathered in Eve's room upstairs that evening after supper. Eve, being the eldest, was given the first choice of bedrooms when the family moved in, and, like any kid would, she chose the largest room.

Nothing further had been said between the children about their strange adventure, but all three had clearly been preoccupied by the possibilities laid bare before them. What mysterious purpose did the house serve, and did it really move? What of the strange carnival with no roads leading to it? What secrets did it hold? There was one course by which they could learn these things, but whether or not they would have the strength to take it remained to be seen.

As usual, Allen was first to speak. "So, we're going to that carnival, right?" He seemed almost pleading.

"Are you nuts! No way!" Eve had been working all evening on convincing arguments to dissuade her inquisitive brothers, but they all failed to materialize in the heat of the moment. "That guy was way too creepy and everything was way too weird." It was all she could muster, and she added it as convincingly as she could.

"But carnivals are awesome, Sis!" Allen continued, "And who knows what will be at this one."

"I've gotta agree with Al on this one; it sure seems like the only way we'll get to the bottom of what we saw today." Armin chimed in for the first time. "There's still a ton of stuff we don't know about that place. How can you want to pass up an opportunity like this?"

"How can you not!" Eve caught her voice rising too late to stop it. She was beginning to get flustered, though she had traditionally been the rock of the group. "Didn't you feel it? There is something really bad happening out there in the woods, something we are better off just ignoring."

Eve was barely able to maintain her composure, and the unabated advance of this uncontrollable sensation chilled her. "If we go there tomorrow, something terrible will happen." Hot tears began to run down Eve's cheeks, and she felt the hold she had struggled to keep on her emotions release.

"It'll be okay, Sis!" Allen was quick to her comfort. "Don't cry; we don't have to do anything you don't want to." His concern for his sister quickly outweighing his desire to see this adventure through.

"Oh, come on! It's not that big of a deal, Eve." Armin was less compelled to acquiesce to such displays. "I mean, I'll go along with whatever we decide, but I'd certainly rather that we check it out. Sure, it was weird and a little scary, but that's no reason to throw in the towel. Think of how big of an adventure this will be!"

"Also, the cotton candy!" Allen added quickly, back into the excitement of the unknown.

"Look, I didn't mean to get so upset," Eve spoke, regaining her composure. "I don't know what came over me. Something about this just really creeps me out. I can't really explain it." She looked at her brothers, and there was more concern on her face than she realized.

"Really, we'll be completely safe. There's no need to give us that look." Armin smiled at his sister. "What's the worst that could happen? We eat too much carnival food and get sore stomachs?" His attempt to underscore the doubt he himself felt was only mildly successful.

"I doubt that's the worst that could happen." Eve started before Allen interrupted, "I dunno, I can eat an awful lot." He smiled broadly. Allen was always the most cheerful of the three, eager to see the others laughing and happy.

Eve laughed despite her concerns. Armin, too, was caught by his brother's sudden injection of humor. In short order, all three were laughing nearly uncontrollably as children do, and their conversation's worry and stress faded.

As they settled down, Eve was the first to speak. "Okay, so say we do go to this thing, this carnival. Do either of you have any plans for what to do there? We don't exactly have any money to spend." Eve's pragmatic issue seemed potentially to derail their plans.

"Shit, that's a good point," Armin said surprised.

"Don't swear in the house, Armin, you know better," Eve added, suddenly more caretaker than sister.

"Sorry. But your point still stands." Armin looked dejected at the continued realization.

"Well, what if we don't need any?" Allen asked, determined not to give up on their pending adventure.

"Don't be stupid, Al; of course, you need money." Armin chided dismissively.

"I'm not stupid, Armi, I'm serious. Mel never mentioned we would need any money." Allen glared at his brother.

Eve looked up quizzically. "Wait a second, Allen is totally right!" She exclaimed. "Melantonth would have told us if we needed to bring anything. I bet we'll be his personal guests." And she shivered momentarily at the thought.

"So you're in then?" Armin was quick to seize on the opportunity. "We would have to be pretty safe being guests of the carnival boss, I'd think." He added the last part to do his best to seal the deal.

"Okay, I guess so ... fine, let's go. But if there are any signs of trouble, we're getting out of there in a hurry, you hear me?" Eve wasn't sure about her decision, but her curiosity was finally getting the better of her. She was, after all, not so very different from her brothers. There was still a nagging fear, but Eve was strong and courageous; she was their leader, after all, and she was quickly becoming determined to see this adventure through to its end regardless of what would come.

The rest of the evening the children spent conversing, imagining the sights they might see the following day.

That night, the siblings went to bed wreathed in an excitement seldom seen in children outside of the holiday season. Something tremendous was bearing down on them, and they could almost taste it in the air. Little more remained than to wait, with bated breath, for the break of dawn.

IV.

A bright, crisp autumn morning was quick to greet the McMasters clan. All three had managed a decent night of sleep despite their collective excitement and anticipation for the coming day. They had agreed, the evening before, to head to the carnival around noon after an early lunch. Armin had insisted that they attend at a time when there were likely to be more people in attendance. He had become somewhat obsessed with figuring out how people would arrive at the carnival.

Eve felt an added comfort in the bright sun and the lack of clouds in the sky. Over and over, in her head, she heard Melantonth warn her to attend the carnival during the day, even though the siblings had come to agree that the extravagantly named Mr. Mel was putting them on more than anything.

By lunchtime, Allen's excitement was palpable. He was barely able to sit still long enough to eat anything. Eve and Armin, too, were becoming nearly overwhelmed with anticipation. It was a wonder their behavior didn't elicit more notice from their mother. By then, Ruth was barely a husk of her former self, and she noticed little outside of the presence of her libations.

The McMasters siblings carefully followed their previous path as they left their home, not knowing what they would find in The Old Woods that day. As they neared their destination, they were met with the faint din of commotion. They followed the path toward the front of The Pale House that Mel had shown them.

The Pale House stood silently amidst the trees as it had the day before. At a point approximately halfway between the forest's edge and The Pale House's front porch, a veritable city of tents had risen up. The tents, alternating in color between a deep maroon and a bright purple, created a sort of tiny village arranged in a loose circle that stretched into the woods. A group of tents was arrayed in the center of the loose circle, and a throng of bodies moved along the path they created. The attendees were dressed in wildly divergent and incredible clothing, so much so that the siblings agreed that Mel should have told them it was a costume party.

Upon mention of the peculiar carnival man, the siblings began to scan the crowd for his whereabouts. Finding nothing at a distance and noticing that there was no ticket booth or other checkpoint for entry, the McMasters children decided to try their luck within the carnival itself.

As they crossed the threshold and entered the carnival proper, the world around them changed. Wholly new smells and sounds assaulted them, and all three of the McMasters siblings struggled for a moment to maintain their wits. How could something like this even be possible? As they came back to their senses, more and more oddities began to occur to them.

The most obvious was the circle of tents, originally more of a semi-circle interrupted by the woods; now, the circle was complete, and a great stone arch stood where before there had been only woods. The underside of the arch shimmered with a strange light that reached down to the ground. From within the light, people emerged, all extravagantly and bizarrely dressed, and went about into the carnival. Others walked back into the light only to vanish moments later.

"Well, at least we know how people are getting here, eh Armi," Allen said, still mildly in a daze.

"Yeah, I see it too, Al, but I don't think it really answers anything," Armin added with nervousness in his voice.

"We need to try and find Mel." Eve was trying her best to take charge in the maddening face of what was occurring around them. "This might have been a bad idea, but I don't even know what else we're going to do here, so get it together, and c'mon!" There was an added anger in her voice that she hadn't intended. The boys were to blame for dragging her into this, she thought momentarily before coming to her senses. What was happening to them?

"Ah! There you are!" The booming call came from behind them. With relief, the siblings turned to see the towering Melantonth approaching quickly. He was dressed as he had been the day before, although his entire attire seemed somehow a deeper, darker black than should have been possible on fabric.

"I had hoped to catch you before you entered the gates." The gracious, if strange, man began. "This place, once it's all going, you see, it can be a lot to take in for the unsuspecting mind." He led the children to a nearby tent and motioned for them to sit in the chairs arranged therein. Then, with something of an exaggerated flourish, he produced three bags of brightly colored cotton candy, seemingly from nowhere, and handed them to the siblings.

"Cotton candy!!" Allen nearly fell out of his chair.

"I had a machine brought in yesterday after our conversation," Mel explained, quite happy at the youngster's reaction. "It's been far too long since we served any of this wonderful fluff. Plus, the food should help you adjust to everything."

"What's going on here!" Eve blurted out, still entirely on edge and not nearly as mollified by the sudden appearance of a sugary treat. She felt the hot rush of blood to her cheeks and lamented that she was having such a hard time with everything. Over and over, her mind rolled in tumult, torn between the mystery and drive of her curiosity and an unspeakable horror that grew in the back of her mind.

"My sister does kind of have a point, Mr. Mel," Armin pressed, seemingly the calmest of the three, "There is a lot of stuff going on here that doesn't really add up; this place isn't like any carnival I've seen."

"Heh, Mr. Mel. I kinda like it." Melantonth chuckled, "But of course, you have every right to have questions and should have every expectation of having those questions answered. At least, I shall do my honest best. Why I've even brought literature!" And he produced several pamphlets from somewhere in the recesses of his enormous coat. "As for what I can guess, first and foremost, you are safe here. As long as you remain on the carnival grounds, I can personally guarantee it."

"Secondly, you are correct; this carnival is unlike any other that you, or likely anyone you know, has ever seen. Though we have had many names and are known differently in different places, most commonly, our endeavor is known as The Carnival Macabre. We travel the length and breadth of causal reality in search of the bizarre and unique so that our patrons may experience truly one-of-a-kind events. See truly rare things!"

"Everything about this place is so strange." Eve still seemed reluctant to relax. "Like, what's the deal with that arch? How come we couldn't see it before?"

"Yes, about that. Would it surprise you if I told you there were roads all over the place, great moonlight passages through the night, connecting everything that is to everything else? Roads that can be accessed if one simply knows where to look. Perhaps I am giving too much credence to the imagination of children."

"We aren't children. Armin and I are in our teens." Eve interrupted.

"Well, perhaps that's it then," Melantonth continued. "Regardless, that arch, as you call it, is something like a door that connects to a road like what I described. It is how our guests arrive and depart from our wildly varied locations. I can assure you, however strange it may seem, it is completely benign. Why, come here tomorrow, and you'll never know it was even there."

"Okay, well, what's up with the house then?" Allen asked, finally managing to pull himself away from his treat.

"Ah, yes, our main attraction." Melantonth smiled. "That is why I brought the pamphlets; they give a brief history of the house. You should read them while you rest here."

Suddenly, a young, disheveled-looking man with thick glasses burst into the tent. "Mr. Vescaro! Thank god I found you!" The man exclaimed.

"I left specific instructions that I was not to be bothered while I was with my very important guests," Mel responded coldly without even so much as a glance at the young man.

"I know, sir, it's just … the Marquis, sir, he seems to have consumed one too many Rundle Pies, and he's gotten forward with Madame Bellis of Taryll. No one noticed before it was too late, sir."

"Oh my! That's far worse than I was expecting." Melantonth suddenly looked up from the children and turned to face his attendant. "This is no good at all; something will need to be done." And a look that none of the children had yet seen on the animated carnival barker's face passed across Melantonth's visage.

He stood then and walked to the edge of the tent. "I must leave you to recoup at your own pace, children. Give the literature a read, and then feel free to explore the carnival." Melantonth then produced a small red cloth pouch. "This should have enough tokens in it to purchase anything you desire. There are games, gifts, and food in abundance. The main tents nearest the house will be the most crowded, but don't let that stop you from having a look at our mysterious guest of honor." And with that, the eccentric carnival man ducked out of the tent and vanished into the crowd with the nervous and entirely worn-out-looking attendant close behind.

"Wait!" Eve called out only moments too late. "Oh, hell! That wasn't all of my questions!" She sighed and tried to make sense of everything they had seen. "So now what?" She asked her brothers.

"Well, I suppose we should have a look around." Allen began, already watching the crowds of strangely dressed people passing outside the tent.

"Hold on a sec, Al. We should at least read that thing Mr. Mel gave us." Armin was not yet sure if he shared his brother's excitement or his sister's hesitation.

"Ugh! You know I hate reading Armi; just read it aloud. Or, better yet, let's just go." For a moment, it seemed as though Allen would disappear into the crowd just as Melantonth had moments before.

"Okay, okay, hold on!" Armin sounded increasingly nervous. "There isn't much here, mostly pictures of the house, here we go:"

The Wandering Pale House is one of the rarest sights known to patrons of the Carnival Macabre. First encountered in 763 of the common era, no means of predicting the House's movements has ever been discerned. What is known is that exactly 72 hours after a human first views the House, it relocates. Again, the mechanism by which it accomplishes this is unknown. There seem to be two occupants of the building: a tall female human who is always seen dressed in yellow and gold and a statue of a large human male seated in a massive stone chair in the front room. Notably, the human female is the only witnessed part or occupant of the House to possess any true color, seemingly unaffected by the pale that spreads around the House."

"Does anyone else dislike how often this pamphlet says 'human'? It's unsettling." Eve was trying her best to contain her fears.

"Just let me finish, there's only one more part:

Research into the House's origins point to it potentially being some sort of time or dimensionally lost entity, unbound from causality. Original records indicate that contact was attempted in the early encounters, but all attempts were met with hostile opposition from the female occupant, resulting in total loss of all parties involved. Henceforth, the female occupant has been listed as an extreme threat, and all attempts at contact have ceased. Safe viewing from within Carnival Macabre grounds is recommended."

"Wait, so the house just came here? How's that work?" Allen seemed to pause at this strange new information.

"It says nobody knows. Weren't you listening?" Eve chided, her nervousness coming out as unsolicited aggression.

A cool autumn breeze brought the smells of the Old Woods into the tent and, with them, a sense of familiarity and calm to the McMasters siblings. Though they were all affected still by the strangeness of the day, this draught of the comfortable brought back much of their adventurous spirits.

"Al's right, let's go exploring. What's the worst that could happen?"

"Don't say that, Armin, it's bad luck." Eve shivered at the thought of their situation worsening in terrible, unimaginable ways. "But I get what you mean; we did come here to check everything out. No point in chickening out now, I guess."

And with that, the courageous siblings set out together into the growing multitude of visitors to the carnival. There were few games to be found among the sea of bright maroon and purple tents, and those that were there were peculiar and nothing like anything the children had seen before. Most of the stalls sold various odd bric-a-brac and strange clothing or offered services that were akin to fortune telling. The other visitors were all friendly, however, and the children soon began to feel comfortable in spite of the strange things all around them.

For several hours, the McMasters siblings explored the carnival at large. They sampled the food, both strange and delicious, and bought several small keepsakes (a pair of dice, a stone rose, and a colorful necklace) with the tokens provided by Melantonth. Eventually, they found themselves in one of the main viewing tents across from the front door of the Pale House. Allen and Armin sat at a table, finishing off the apple tarts they had just purchased while nearby. Eve listened to a group of travelers who claimed to be from New York City but were dressed as though they lived in feudal Japan.

"I still don't get the deal with the house," Allen said to Armin as the youngest of the McMasters siblings finished off his fifth treat of the afternoon. "I mean, if, like, it vanishes or something, that'll be weird, but other than that, it's just a house."

"Okay, well, what about the color of the thing?" Armin was always one for a good bit of devilish advocacy.

"What do you mean?" Allen cocked his head to the side and regarded the house more closely.

"It's color is all wrong," Armin continued. "It isn't white or gray or anything really, like the color has drained out of it. And look at the grass over by the front porch; it's losing its color too, like it's spreading."

"Whoa, I guess I didn't notice." Allen swallowed hard as a peculiar look passed over his face. "Is Eve still talking to those samurai folks?"

"Yeah, she's just over there."

"Okay, let's go get a closer look." Allen's smile was equal parts mischievous and daring.

"I probably could have guessed you'd say that." Armin calmly replied, "You know she's going to be furious if she comes over here and finds us missing."

"Then we gotta be quick!" Allen said as he rose from his seat. He took Armin's lack of outright rejection as tacit acceptance. "C'mon, if we scoot around the side, I bet we can get close enough to look inside without anyone seeing us."

No more conversation was needed, and quickly, Armin followed as Allen cut a surreptitious route along the side of the woods and the house, doing his best to keep them out of sight. In moments, they were behind the Pale House and cautiously approaching the window on the backside. As they neared, the anticipation was almost too much for either of them to bear. Then, something extraordinary and completely unexpected became readily apparent. The window they were carefully and quietly approaching was open.

The boys froze, now only an arm's length from the window. Strange, foreign smells wafted from the opening, but no sound could be heard originating from within.

"Wadda ya say, Armi? Gimme a boost?" The look in Allen's eyes was dead serious.

"You can't be serious," Armin protested. "Coming to have a look is one thing, but going inside was never part of our plan. Nobody knows what's inside this place." His voice was beginning to tremble. "And remember what that pamphlet said about the lady living inside. This is a bad idea, Al."

Allen looked back and forth between the window and his brother for a moment when their quiet was abruptly broken.

"Ow!" Winced Armin as his hand reached up and smacked the back of his neck.

Allen practically jumped onto the roof. "What is it? What's wrong?" he shouted as quietly as he could.

"Son of a bitch!" Armin grimaced. "Felt like a bee sting. Is there a mark?" He turned and exposed his neck to his brother.

There was indeed a red welt in the middle of Armin's neck. "Yeah, looks like it," Allen sighed. "You scared the hell out of me, though."

"Sorry," Armin said flatly as he looked at his brother with strange eyes. "So are we doing this or what?" He asked.

Allen was still recovering from their brief scare and looked puzzled at his older brother. "Hell, yes, we are!" He puffed his chest and did his best to ward off any rising fears and apprehension.

With practiced cooperation, the brothers deftly went about their infiltration. In moments, Allen was inside and leaning back out the window, arm outstretched to the waiting Armin. With a quick tug, both of the boys were inside the mysterious Pale House.

Some twenty feet away, around the back of the house, a small pipe lay splayed open next to a large rock. From out of the pipe oozed a viscous polychromatic liquid that seemed strangely animate. No immediate purpose for such a pipe would have been apparent had anyone noticed it or its obvious damage. A small, oddly shaped pool of polychromatic liquid was beginning to collect at the base of the pipe.

Back at the carnival, Eve continued to listen in on the fascinating tales of the travelers gathered therein. She had not noticed that her brothers had moved from their seats and was blissfully unaware of their current escapade. So much of what was going on seemed unreal that it was hard for her to focus. Were they really going to believe that some portal was bringing people here? And houses don't get up and move; it's not possible. It seemed to Eve that this was a lot of trouble to go to just to throw some strange party in the woods. After all, that was all it really could be, right? Eve was uncomfortable with her doubts about the answer to that question.

Suddenly, Eve noticed a tall blonde-haired woman looking out the right front window of the Pale House. Eve tilted her head but stifled any outward appearance of shock. There was something peaceful about the woman's appearance, yet something strange as well that Eve could not place. She felt strangely compelled to wave to the woman and made a slight waving gesture before she could stop herself. The tall, blonde-haired woman nodded her head and turned to walk deeper into the house.

Eve's heart raced. Had the woman seen her and responded? Eve could barely think straight as she caught sight of something truly shocking. Allen and Armin were passing by the window of the front left room of the Pale House. Their clothes and general possession of color standing out brightly against the sickly colorless surroundings.

A quick turn of her head confirmed her brothers were no longer sitting at the nearby table. Eve cursed their impetuousness and wished she could believe herself mistaken, though she knew she was not. Her instincts to protect and safeguard her siblings rose as quickly as her growing terror. She remembered the warnings in the pamphlet about the dangerous woman in the house that she had herself just waved to. Eve knew it would only be a matter of time before her brothers ran into the blonde-haired woman as well.

Eve raced directly toward the Pale House, disregarding any danger or breach of protocol. As she reached the porch, she hesitated and looked back to the carnival. No one seemed to notice her or what was happening. Steeling her nerves, Eve walked to the front door and found it to be open. She crossed the threshold into the Pale House and hoped desperately that she was in time to intercept her brothers.

In a viewing tent to the left-hand side of the carnival, Melantonth watched as the front door of the Pale House closed behind Eve. A short elderly man in a blue robe stood at his side. "So they are all inside then?" The old man asked.

"Yes, it would seem so." Melantonth furrowed his brow. "I wonder if I shouldn't have done more to stop them. They are so young, after all."

"You said yourself that you suspected the house lured those children out here. There was nothing you could have done to stop this. It's going to be an incredible carnival, that much is certain." The old man concluded as he turned and left the viewing tent.

The ancient Melantonth stood in silence watching the Pale House, and he felt deeply the weight of his many years. Experience told him that something terrible was coming, but, in the end, that was what everyone had come to see.

V.

The air inside the house was cool and thin. No lights shown and all but a few of the curtains were drawn. Here, the telling paleness of the outside was replaced by a deep, wet darkness, not unlike the interior of a cave.

In the center of the large room the boys had entered was an immense stone throne carved from a bright white rock. Upon the throne sat an enormous imposing statue of a man seemingly cut from the same stone. The statue's countenance was stern and powerful and looked to be sculpted in the style of the ancient Greeks. Something about it spoke to an age far more remarkable, though neither boy could say precisely why. The statue wore a toga that looked to be of soft linen, though surely it was carved of stone as well, the boys reasoned. Great laced sandals were sculpted upon its legs.

The brothers regarded the statue with awe and wonder. Though they had both been to art museums and seen various works of sculpture on numerous school trips, nothing in their experience could compare with what now sat before them.

"This is weird, Armi. What's wrong with this thing?" Allen sputtered in a nervous whisper.

"I don't know," Armin replied. "The guy looks like a jerk to me." There was an uncharacteristic venom to Armin's voice. "Let's keep looking around; there's got to be something better in here than this."

"Seriously?" Allen exclaimed. "First you don't want to do this, then you do, and now we find something bonkers, and you're like 'meh'?! What gives?" Concern laced Allen's voice in a way he had not coped with before hearing it aloud, and he swallowed hard.

"What's bonkers? Some weird statue? C'mon, let's just see what else is in here." Armin pressed his brother to act as he had so many times before.

"Fine, whatever. This place is extraordinary." Allen relented, not wanting to escalate things given their current circumstances. There was something extraordinary going on and Allen was sure that it was more than just the house.

Following Armin around to the right side of the statue, Allen turned and passed in front of a window open onto the carnival. He reasoned that the door to his right was then the front door, and for a moment, he considered just opening it and walking back outside.

Meanwhile, Armin had turned again at a hallway along the stairs to the upper level, directly across from the front door. This path led deeper into the house and the unknown, but Armin forged ahead nonetheless.

Allen caught up with his brother about halfway down the hall. Together, they made their way to the end of the hall, which terminated at a small table about fifty feet further along their path. Openings on either side led off into other rooms of the house, both dim and seemingly unlit within.

The door on the left was Armin's destination and where he led their erstwhile exploration.

Inside the dark room, the boys could make out large shelves along the walls and, as luck would have it, a candelabra with a book of matches sitting on a small table just to the left of where they were standing. Quickly, almost as though it were a practiced behavior, Armin made for the matches and lit the candelabra.

In the growing light, it became apparent to the brothers that they had stumbled into a study or library of some sort. The shelves they had initially perceived were, in fact, bookshelves, each filled to capacity with books of all types and sizes. It was but a matter of moments before they were busy looking through the collection of strange books and magazines, the madness and fear of their exploration momentarily assuaged by the joys of discovery.

VI.

On the porch, a nervous but determined Eve tried the front door and found it open. She paused once inside and made a conscious effort to remember to close the door behind her. She took a deep breath of the strange air of the house and wondered how best to proceed. Assuming her brothers were on a collision course with the tall blonde woman, Eve moved to her right into the room where she last saw the woman.

The small, dimly lit room appeared to be a sort of parlor with neat, delicate couches arranged along the walls. Eve considered resting on one for a moment but brushed off the impulse. In the back of the room, a half door connected to what looked to be a large kitchen. Finding herself still alone in the house, Eve decided to follow the presumed path the tall blonde woman took and crept into the kitchen.

In the kitchen, the environment dramatically changed. A flood of sunlight through several large bay windows painted everything in a bright golden hue. Gone were the paleness of the exterior and the gloom of the hallway and parlor. Here, finally, Eve felt as though she was actually able to see through her own eyes rather than through some filter. So significant was the change and the relief that it brought that it took several moments for Eve to realize that she was not alone in the kitchen. The tall blonde woman was standing directly in front of her. The woman's gaze was alien but gentle, and she seemed unfazed by Eve's sudden appearance.

"I believe you may be lost, young lady." A quiet, melodically beautiful voice fell from the mouth of the tall blonde woman. A mouth that was far too wide to be human.

"Sorry, yeah ... um ... you see my brothers," Eve stammered, suddenly caught off guard by the turn of events.

"Are in the study, I believe." The woman continued. "They are neither as stealthy nor as quiet as they believe themselves to be, but they are unharmed." There was an air of calm around the woman, and Eve wondered how she should proceed.

"You're nothing like I expected." Eve smiled shyly. She wasn't sure what was causing it, but the longer she was around the tall woman, the more she felt compelled to trust her, to tell her things, and to care for her.

Eve shook her head and tried her best to collect her thoughts. "Okay, well, I'll just go collect them, and we'll be on our way. Sorry again to bother you." And she moved to head back toward the hallway.

Suddenly, there was a loud 'thud' as if something of great mass had fallen in another room. The tall woman moved with impossible speed and, in a blink, was past Eve and into the parlor. Another moment passed, and she was again standing next to Eve.

"You need to come with me now; time is short." Gentle but firm hands gripped Eve's shoulders and moved her along toward the back of the kitchen, which wrapped around the back side of the house. The tall woman rushed Eve along toward a strange door in the corner across from the last bay window.

"Head along this hallway until you come to the stairwell. Take the stairs down, but do not stop on any floor save for the last. And do not go up." There was a terrible power emanating from the woman's eyes.

"My brothers!" Eve protested as the tall woman pushed her along.

"They are already lost, my sweet. I am sorry. You must do as I say now, or you will be too," the woman implored.

"What!?" Eve shouted as the door slammed shut in her face. Tears rolled down her cheeks and she collapsed, overcome for the moment. Were her brothers really gone? How could that woman know for sure? There was a sick feeling deep within her stomach.

After a time, Eve collected herself and rose from the floor. She was determined to press on as the woman had instructed, but moreover, she was now driven by the need to discover the true fate of her brothers. Perhaps, she reasoned, if she could make it outside somehow, she could go back to the front door and attempt what was now a rescue mission.

The new hallway Eve found herself in was again wholly different from any of the environments the house had previously shown itself to possess. Color and normalcy reigned here, and it looked, for all intents and purposes, to be a completely normal hallway, though one that looked to belong to an office rather than a house. The truth seemed far from that to Eve, but the illusion of normalcy was calming all the same.

There was clearly no going back the way she had come, especially given how insistent the woman had been. Pressing on was really Eve's only choice, even though she had already decided to do so.

Proceeding down the hall, Eve noticed several things. The first and most apparent was the clutter. Everywhere along the walls of the hallway, there were boxes, cleaning implements, or random pieces of furniture. There was an appearance of someone in the process of moving or remodeling and needing a place to store objects of a specific size.

The second thing she noticed pertained to the appearance of normality in the hallway. Light shone through small half windows high up on the wall to Eve's right. The light was full of color, and the world of monochromes she had just left melted away. Further, she could clearly see trees and bits of The Old Woods through the windows. No matter how far it felt she may have gone, she was still really just in her backyard. Her mind wondered about everything that was going on around her. Where could such a long hallway have hidden within the Gothic-style house Eve knew herself to be in?

Eve slowed her walking as she came upon a door to her left. The door was plain, essentially an unadorned piece of wood with a large handle on it, not unlike what might be found in a school or a doctor's office. Eve approached the door and tried the handle absentmindedly. The door was unlocked, but Eve paused before swinging it open. She recalled the tall blonde woman's warning not to go off onto any other floor. She had said nothing about the different rooms along the hallway. For that matter, who was to say this wouldn't lead to the stairwell Eve sought? It certainly wasn't the end of the strangely long hallway, but Eve wasn't searching for an ironclad excuse at the moment either.

Eve pushed the door open onto another seemingly out-of-place sight. Row after row of desks and chairs were set up in the large room. Broad windows sat at the top of tall walls, reaching twelve to fifteen feet up to the ceiling. The Old Woods could again be seen. Strangely, there was no sight of the house or the carnival, just the trees. Toward the back of the room, the desks gave way to shelving units stacked high with boxes of various sizes.

From among the shelves and boxes, Eve perceived an odd yellow glow. She worked her way to the back of the room past the rows of desks. Once there, she began to search for the source of the strange light. Halfway up a shelf on the middle row sat a likely suspect, a small but wide rectangular box with a lid. The yellow glow seemed to be seeping out from under the lid.

Eve slowly opened the box. As she raised the lid, the yellow glow dissipated like steam. Remaining in the box was a large knife, complete with a scabbard and belt. As Eve, almost instinctively, drew the blade from its sheath, she noticed small intricate writing along its length. The letters, though unrecognizable, were carved of the same glowing yellow as the light that had drawn her near. With only a moment's thought, Eve decided to fasten the belt about her waist and bring the knife with her. Though she was not particularly violent nor overly fond of weapons, something had drawn her to this knife, and she felt powerful and safe with it hanging from her hip.

Having claimed the strange knife, Eve returned to the hallway. She had a sick feeling in her stomach that all of her actions were not entirely her own. The thought made her shiver, and she wished that she had never agreed to come with her brothers that day. And if they had gone without her, then they'd be gone for sure, she thought and took a deep breath. Not today. Not if she had anything to say about it.

Eve began again down the long hallway, her right hand resting on the hilt of the blade. She was met with more clutter and the light of a waning afternoon. Considerable time passed in remarkable sameness, and as the light of day began to fade, Eve reached the end of the hallway.

Here, at the end of the hall, Eve was greeted with the gaping maw of an open entrance onto the stairs. As she cautiously explored the aperture and stairs, she noticed small electrical lights along the walls of the stairwell. It was the first artificial light source she had yet seen in the house. Clearly, it seemed the stairs went both up and down several stories, though that blatantly made no sense to Eve.

Hoping that she was right to trust the tall blonde woman, Eve prepared to head down to the bottom of the stairwell. Then, a sudden commotion occurred—several floors up, by the sound of it. Whatever had made the ruckus was headed down, directly towards where Eve now stood. Eve swallowed hard and braced herself, her hand tightening its grip upon the blade she had unconsciously drawn.

VII.

"Okay, fine, I admit it does look a lot like your flower." Armin practically growled. He and Allen were both huddled over a large book bound in leather and with gilded pages.

"It doesn't look *like* it, it *is* it. The little stone flower I bought at the carnival is right there in this super old book, next to a picture of that statue in the other room!" Allen was about to lose his temper in the face of his brother's stubbornness.

"So what if it is? What would that even mean?" Armin, too, was becoming upset, though he was known to be the most difficult of the three.

"I don't really know, to be honest," Allen admitted, "but I am going back to that statue to see if I can figure it out. Are you coming or not?" The question hung in the air.

"Yeah, of course, I'm coming; I just don't think it's a good idea." Armin glowered at his brother.

"You know, if I didn't know better, I'd say you were afraid of that statue." Allen was becoming tired of dealing with the stress of their endeavor.

"Whatever, man, you know I don't get scared by shit like this." Armin protested, though he was not entirely convincing to either of them.

The boys headed back past the stairs along the path they had traveled to reach the study. Along the way, Allen swore he noticed movement in the other room across from where they had turned at the stairs, but he pressed on, determined to address the mystery at hand.

Again, in the living room containing the statue, the boys regarded the carving with renewed scrutiny. There were indeed many peculiarities to it aside from the absurdity of its proportion. The throne itself possessed numerous faint carvings and depressions along its surface. More unnerving, the man on the throne seemed unerringly to be staring at you no matter where you looked at it from. Lastly was the peculiar air in the house, the coolest and thinnest near to the statue, enough that breathing was difficult in close enough proximity.

The boys pored over the statue, though Allen noticed a certain reluctance from his brother. Armin's head was constantly cocked downwards, deliberately refusing to meet the ever-present gaze of the statue.

After some time, they began to lose heart that a solution would be found to their mystery. Armin moved back toward the window through which they had entered The Pale House. "Maybe it was just a coincidental similarity between your flower and the picture. Like how I was saying before."

"I can't explain why," Allen gripped the stone flower tightly in his hand, "but I know they are the same. I just can't figure out what that means." In his frustration, he placed the flower down on the edge of the throne. A slight vibration rose in response. "Whoa! Did you feel that?" Allen jumped down from the side of the statue.

As if in response, the vibration rose again, more substantial this time. There seemed almost to be a peel of sound that accompanied the tactile sensation.

Then, with a mighty crash, the sides of the throne fell to the ground. Allen leaped back, barely missing being crushed by the huge stone slab. Armin lifted his head to call out to his brother, and Allen saw the look of abject terror on his face.

The great stone figure on what remained of the throne stirred and began to move.

"Run!" Armin shouted, moving as fast as he could back towards the stairs. Allen was first to reach the stairs, and he hurried up them toward the second floor, with Armin close behind. The stone man crashed through the intervening wall and roared in defiance.

The boys rushed up the stairs. Allen gained the second floor and turned right down the hallway.

The great stone man tore through the stairs, and the floor between Allen and Armin began to come apart beneath their feet. As the world collapsed around him, Allen caught a last glimpse of his brother, a great stone hand crashing down upon him.

Everything was black for a time, and Allen's mind was grateful for it. When he woke, Allen was in the collapsed hallway of the second floor of

The Pale House. He tried desperately to purge the image of his brother's terrible demise from his mind and, with great effort, stifled a complete breakdown.

Allen scraped to his feet and tried to assess his situation. The way behind him was now blocked, but it seemed at least that the stone man had ceased its assault.

As he was now trapped in the hallway, Allen had but one choice before him: a strange green door at the end of the hall. He proceeded onward rather than crumpling at the immensity of everything that had occurred. It was a trait he shared with his sister. Once he reached the door, Allen proceeded inside, desperately hoping to find some escape.

Instead, he found a thin set of stairs, weak-looking and no wider than a few feet across, that wound and twisted precariously upward in what was, for all appearances, a bell tower. Allen couldn't recall seeing such a tower on The Pale House, and he shuddered at the passing implications.

With no other real option, Allen pressed on and made his way slowly up the stairs. He had, by then, amended his previous opinion that the stairs he was now on were part of some archaic bell tower. Instead, he reasoned, he must be headed toward the attic of the Pale House, though certainly by circuitous and complex means. After climbing the equivalent of several floors, he had to admit that this, too, seemed unlikely. Eventually, after far too long of a climb, Allen reached the top of the stairs and was greeted by another door, this one painted red but clearly faded with time.

Allen hesitated on the cramped and narrow stairs. For a moment, thoughts of poor Armin almost overwhelmed him. Allen breathed deeply but shook with fear and mania in spite of himself. How was he supposed to go on?

One thought occurred to him over and over. Rimmed with panic, he wanted only to get out of that cursed house and again feel the light of day. This need to survive, this need to flee, was driving Allen's hand as he gripped the handle of the red door and prepared to move on.

Inside, the blackness was complete. The little light that existed came from the square windows placed sporadically along the narrow stairwell, and the night was rapidly approaching. Allen hesitated again, but as he sat in the doorway, his eyes began to adjust. Deep in the gloom of the upper room, Allen was sure he could make out a faint glow.

There was nowhere else to go and nothing for the fear but to face it, Allen thought to himself. Always headstrong, he dove into the darkness in search of the faint glow of light.

For a moment or two, Allen's pitch-black adventure was uneventful. Then, with a loud whack and a louder yelp, Allen collided with what seemed to be a small table. As his hands felt along the top of the table, he again yelped, but this time in delighted surprise. Indeed, fate, luck, or something else entirely was in his favor as his hands moved unmistakably along the recognizable form of a flashlight. Someone must have left it here for some mundane purpose, Allen mused, and the thought of commonplace occurrences happening in this strange place seemed to quell some of his fear.

Allen pressed the power switch on the flashlight, entirely expecting it not to work. To his continued surprise and momentary relief, he was mistaken, and a bright beam of light cut through the inky blackness. Then, just as the light had brought comfort, it also illuminated horror.

Resting in the spot where the light landed hung a bat-like creature roughly the same size as Allen. Its skin was a sickeningly human paleness and seemed devoid of hair. Its head was bulbous and far too large, with mammoth closed orbs for eyes. Allen panned the light upwards towards the peak of the roof, clearly now in the attic. The once-saving glow illuminated another five of the awful bat things sleeping in the rafters above him.

Allen's heart raced, and he needed nothing more than the sight of the things sleeping to realize he was in mortal danger. He panned the light around the attic room and had the uncomfortable consideration that it was perhaps a roost more than a proper attic.

Allen turned the light back to the original monstrosity he had encountered. He hadn't expected its eyes to be so deep blue. It took his addled mind a moment to catch up. Its eyes were open, wide open.

Allen froze, locked into a terrible staring contest with a horrifying creature far beyond his comprehension. Its face now turned toward him, showcased a vile sucker-like mouth lined with horrible thin needles for teeth.

Survival instinct would come to Allen's rescue. Throwing caution to the wind, he darted toward the far wall of the attic roost. He had briefly glimpsed a door there as he had scanned the room, and that door seemed to harbor the light he had initially sought. He ran towards the door with all the speed he could muster. The vile bat-thing appeared to sense the coming climax as well and dropped from its perch with a terrible wail. The others in the rafters roused, and they, too, dropped down, screeching towards a terrified Allen.

Allen reached the door on the far wall just barely ahead of the bat-things. One of his pursuers crashed into the wall to his right in a bid to catch him that only narrowly missed. The room inside that Allen had reached was another, more traditional stairwell. Tiny electric lights along the wall lit the area reasonably well, but Allen had no time to ponder what that may have meant. He leaped down the first flight of stairs and turned the corner, running for his life.

VIII.

Outside, the carnival was in full swing. The crowd of revelers had swollen to near capacity and the noise was becoming deafening. Strange music played in many of the tents, and guests danced amidst the thoroughfare. Food and drink were abundant, and the smells, while somewhat foreign in many respects, were nonetheless enticing. Cheer and merriment reigned.

Beneath the great arch, the shimmering sheet of light no longer glowed, and the forest beyond could be seen through its alien architecture. No new guests would be arriving that day. The energy to run the arch was precious and needed conservation. Melantonth stood near the base of the arch, attended by his thick-spectacled assistant.

"Are you sure it's safe to shut it off, sir? There are quite a few guests here at the moment." The nervous, small-framed man was beginning to pace.

"We've been over this, Helms. I say, 'jump,' and you say, 'how high?' I say we shut off the Arkway for now, and you shut it off. I've been doing this a lot longer than you have." Melantonth said.

"Of course, sir. I didn't mean to question you. It's just, well, the last few events we've hosted ..."

"What about 'em?" Melantonth said as he moved from the base of the Arkway and headed back toward the crowd.

"... have all needed to be evacuated, sir. We've already had one incident today that nearly started a galactic war. And from all of our records, everything we're seeing with the House this time is entirely unique. There is no telling what we are in store for here." Helms might have been the new man around the carnival, but he was, nonetheless, good at his job.

"That's part of the excitement. The evacuation, everything going wild. It's the illusion of danger that allows us to charge such exorbitant prices for entry, my good man. No one is in any real danger; the Arkway can be relit in a matter of minutes. Unless, of course, you were attempting to insult me." Melantonth stopped just outside the crowd.

"How do you mean, sir?" Helms raised an inquisitive eyebrow.

"By claiming that I cannot protect the guests at my carnival. Do you think my strength has waned so much that we should be frightened by a simple time-lost building?"

The sounds of commotion prevented Helms from answering. Something was happening back at the House.

"This way," Melantonth called to Helms as he moved along the right side of the great crowd that was beginning to gather. Darting between patrons and skirting through tents, the pair made their way to Melantonth's modest and reserved personal tent. Sitting to the right of the central viewing area, the tent was deserted save for an elderly man in a deep blue robe.

Melantonth and Helms stood, watching the house. "What happened?" Melantonth asked the elderly man.

"There was a great 'thud,' like something heavy fell over. Then, more crashing and commotion, like someone was tearing the place up inside. You could see something through the windows, but it was hard to make out specifically." The old man answered.

Suddenly, more noise erupted from the house. Banging and what sounded like fighting could be heard by all in attendance. As the sound began to climb to a crescendo, there was a terrible crack, followed by a low, rumbling cry. The cry grew louder and began to take on a sinister and vile quality. The people gathered closest to the front of the crowd became sick or lost consciousness entirely.

"Sir?" Helms said expectantly.

"Let's just see where this goes. Has anyone seen the kids?" Melantonth never took his eyes off the house.

"Your preoccupation with those children is dangerous, old friend." The elderly man in the blue robe spoke up. "You must accept that they are lost and see to your duties. Nothing else can be done."

"You don't get to tell me how to run things, Adgric. Not here anyways. We are waiting to see if those kids are alright before I pull up a single solitary stake." Melantonth seemed, ever so slightly, to be growing taller.

The awful cry swelled, and the tall blonde woman appeared on the porch. She scanned the crowd briefly, then, with a speed that made her movement seem instantaneous, appeared standing before Melantonth's tent. In the bright light of day, her features no longer seemed human. Her head and hands were too large, and her mouth seemed to stretch from ear to ear—a fact confirmed when she began to speak.

"You, Carnival Barker; you are known to us," the woman's long finger pointed directly at Melantonth. "The prison has failed. He seeks to remove the last of his bonds and be free of this place. I have no choice but to deploy the weapon. Collateral damage will be great unless you do something. I will not be able to warn you again. Do not let this loss of life be upon your hands, for they are stained enough." And just as suddenly as she appeared, the tall blonde woman vanished from sight.

"Sir?" Helms asked again.

Melantonth stood motionless for a moment. "Try not to cause a panic. Head back and fire up the Arkway. Order a full evacuation as quietly as possible. No show. No drama. Get these people out of here." Melantonth looked worried for the first time in a millennia.

IX.

The clamorous rumble was coming closer. Eve knew she needed to act. Bracing her back leg against the far wall, she tightened her grip on the blade. The letters along its length began to glow with the now familiar yellow light.

As Allen came tearing around the corner, Eve nearly took his head off. Mad with fear, she had swung blindly at the first thing she saw attached to the approaching cacophony. Fortunately for them both, Allen managed to duck and slide past Eve just below the blade's treacherous arc.

The closely pursuing bat-thing was not so lucky and caught the force of the blow mostly with its face. Blood sprayed in a crimson gout, and the monster roared in pain. The unexpected violence from their intended prey sent the remaining bat-things fleeing back to their roost. The injured horror raced after its fellows, and after just a moment, the siblings were alone in the gore-covered stairwell.

"Sis?" The words came out of Allen's mouth as barely a whisper.

"It's me, Al. Are you okay? God, I almost hit you with this thing." The letters on the blade seemed to glow brighter now that it was slick with blood. Eve slid the blade back into the scabbard at her hip. "I'm so happy you're okay. Where's your brother?"

Tears welled immediately in Allen's eyes. "The statue in the living room." He sniffed. "It came after us, and it caught Armi as I was tossed clear. Sis, I don't think ..." But Allen couldn't finish the thought.

"Okay, okay, just try to calm down. We'll find Armin and figure this out." Eve did everything she could to seem strong and sure for Allen's sake. In her heart, a sinking feeling betrayed her hopes. "Look, someone already told me you were done for, but here we are, right? Just try to pull yourself together and we can get through this."

Allen gave one last snort and steeled himself. The McMasters children had found reservoirs of courage during this harrowing day that they had never imagined dwelled within them. "Okay, so what's the plan?" Allen looked up to his sister expectantly.

"My plan was to go down. I met the woman inside the house, and she sent me this way. She said that there was an exit at the bottom of the stairs. I figured that outside, I could get back around to the carnival and get help." Eve was cautious not to explain everything she had thought or experienced to Allen. The youngest of the McMasters clan was beginning to show signs of extreme stress.

After a short reprise, the siblings began to go down the stairs. At each successive floor, there would always be a doorway opening onto the floor beyond. "Shouldn't we see what's down these hallways?" Allen asked as they passed the third such doorway.

"The exit's at the bottom," Eve replied quickly. "I don't have much hope we'd find anything useful there. There's nothing in this place but evil. We just need to get out of here." Eve was insistent and she could feel her heart race more the longer they lingered in the doorway.

Faintly, a stirring could be heard from down the unlit hallway.

"C'mon! We gotta go!" Eve pulled at Allen's arm and managed to yank him along the next few steps.

"Okay! Okay!" Allen shouted as he wrenched his wrist free. He had never seen his sister this agitated before, and the reality of it was unsettling to his nerves.

The two continued in silence, descending the dimly lit stairwell. They no longer stopped on each successive floor and instead rushed past the now daunting apertures. After another six floors, they seemed to finally reach the bottom, but by Eve's reckoning, they were now deep underground. This time, the doorway, still with no actual door, opened on the opposite side of the stairwell, and light could be seen from a moderate distance within. Both Eve and Allen were taken aback by the sudden appearance of the exit, but it was unmistakable; the light within was clearly sunlight.

X.

The door to the supposed basement sat perilously atop a steep hill, which seemed to be comprised mainly of old belongings and discarded furniture, strangely matching the clutter Eve had encountered in the hallway. This mountain of ruins was much more dilapidated and decrepit than anything found within the house proper; certainly, it was much older. At the base of this artificial mountain, off some fifty feet or so into the distance, was an opening that led back out the saving light of day.

"If we're just careful, it won't be hard to climb down." Allen began as he made the descent. "Is that really sunlight? I thought you said we were underground?"

"It sure looks like it." Eve was quick to follow Allen's lead and head down the pile of discarded human furnishings. "Look, nothing in this place makes sense. We won't really know anything until we get down there." She was eager to put some distance between them and the dimly lit stairwell where she was sure she still heard some distant commotion.

In a matter of minutes, the siblings descended to the ground floor, as it were. On this side of the doorway, the composed and common walls of the house had given way to sheer stone, not unlike the interior of a cave. The hard earth below their feet was damp but firm. Allen and Eve wasted little time examining their new surroundings and headed directly for what was now clearly the mouth of a cave.

Outside, they were greeted by the bright light of day as it showed through the bows of the Old Woods. At that moment, a great sense of relief passed through both Allen and Eve. Briefly, the weight of all they had endured abated.

Allen began to sob. "What are we going to do about Armin? We have to try to save him!" He looked at his sister with desperation and terror bright in his eyes.

"It's okay, Al. Just try to breathe." Eve did her best to comfort her brother, who, at that moment, seemed so much younger than her. "Of course, we're going after Armin. He's tougher than he looks; I'm sure he's okay."

With their relief rapidly passing, Eve took a moment to survey the area of the Old Woods they found themselves in. To her amazement, she recognized the general location they were now in, and by her best estimation, they were actually not terribly far from the house and the carnival. There was a sharp ridge some 200 yards past where the carnival had set up shop. It seemed to Eve that they were, in fact, at the bottom of the said ridge in some previously unheralded cave.

Eve explained her reasoning to Allen, and the two turned back toward the cave entrance and the cliff face before them. Not once did they discuss going back the way they had come, and a tangible fear surrounded the prospect of returning to The Pale House.

The climb out of the small ravine was slow going, and nearly an hour had passed when, finally, they were both atop the ridge. Wet with sweat and breathing somewhat heavily, Allen paused atop the ridge and peered into The Old Woods before them. "It's too quiet." He said almost suddenly. "I know we're still a little ways off, but we should be able to hear something. It's completely silent."

Eve shuddered as she came to accept her brother's assessment. There was no sound of commotion or the goings on of the carnival, something they could clearly make out from a similar distance on their original approach that now seemed so long ago. Moreover, there were no sounds of the forest coming from before their course, and an eerie stillness hung upon the scene.

"I don't want to go back," Eve said flatly. "I know we have to, for Armin, but I really am having a hard time with this." Her eyes darted frantically between her brother and the path before them. "Nothing here makes sense. None of this should be possible. And that house ... it's just wrong and bad and awful, and I don't want anything to do with it anymore." Eve's hands were shaking.

"I know, Sis," Allen smiled, his courage far outpacing his years. "But we gotta. It's not too far, and you've got that blade; we'll be okay. We just have to get Armin out of there. Then we can put this place behind us." He smiled again and took Eve's hand. "C'mon, the sooner we start, the sooner it's over." And with that, the two headed into the Old Woods again. They would face that terrible house and learn their brother's fate, one way or another.

XI.

The walk back to The Pale House was not long, but Eve felt an eternity pass nonetheless. Thoughts of an uncountable magnitude assailed her mind, and each step she took was an expression of her will and determination. So much could be waiting for them once they completed their journey that it was difficult for Eve to focus. She desperately wished for some sort of answer that could explain everything they had seen and experienced. None was forthcoming.

Armin was likely already dead. The thought should have been more revolting, but Eve was numb. Perhaps if he were, it would be a mercy, she thought, the coldness of her emotions causing her to swallow hard. She was about to call out to Allen, who had gotten slightly ahead of her, when, instead, Allen called back to her.

"It's all gone!" The shock in Allen's voice painted a clear picture of his emotional state. "The carnival, everything is just gone." A note of defeat ringing in his voice.

"What? That can't ..." but Eve stopped mid-sentence when she caught up with Allen. Indeed, it was clear that the carnival was no more. Not so much as a scrap of paper or a discarded ticket had been left in the wake of the once large and quite involved carnival. All that remained now, in its placid manicured lawn, was The Pale House. Its loathed visage looming before the siblings.

"What do we do now?" Eve asked, deeply afraid of the answer.

"Same as before, right?" Allen steeled himself for their coming endeavor. "With any luck, Armin is in the front room where we got attacked by the statue."

"Yeah, but what about that statue?" Eve was not entirely convinced of Allen's planned frontal assault.

"I don't know." Allen was beginning to crack under the ever-increasing stress.

Eve motioned to her brother. "Okay, I get it. We go in, get Armin, and get out as fast as possible, right?"

"Yeah, let's hope so," Allen said, regaining his composure. "Keep that knife handy; there's no telling what's going to be in there."

"Right." Eve reached for the handle of the strange blade that hung from her hip.

Together, the McMasters siblings stepped forward toward the Pale House. The eerie silence seemed to grow stronger as they neared the porch. Now, even their footfalls no longer made any sound.

The large front door was slightly ajar. Stopped on the porch, the two exchanged grim glances and took a moment to speak softly.

"Ready, sis?" Allen looked as frightened as Eve felt in spite of himself.

"No, but that's never stopped me before." Eve nodded her head in determination. The time was finally upon them.

Following Allen's lead, the two entered the Pale House again. The sight that greeted them was something neither had anticipated.

The stairs across from the entrance were destroyed, as Allen had described, but at the bottom of the resultant rubble lay the statue. Its body was crushed into several large pieces that were strewn about the area. Eve let a brief scream escape when they found its head, a terrible expression of horror etched onto its stone face.

"How did this happen?" Eve felt her sanity beginning to ebb. "Why does it look like that?! What could even cause this?!" The fever pitch of madness rising.

"Don't look at it. Aw, hell, this is bad." Allen turned back towards the front door. For a moment, he had to resist his body's natural inclination to flee from this terrible place.

"Let's go this way toward the kitchen," Eve said as she moved past her brother.

Calmness again seemed to reign in the small parlor before the kitchen where the siblings now found themselves. Here again, they paused, both noticeably more at ease out of sight of the statue's mangled body.

Faintly, a sound became audible to both Eve and Allen. It was soft and terribly sad. A sort of whimper or cry but unlike anything either had heard before.

"Do you hear that?" Eve started, mildly convinced that she was imagining the sound. "It sounds like it's coming from the kitchen."

"Yeah, I hear it, but what is it? This doesn't feel good; something is incredibly wrong here." Allen looked past his sister to the now ominous half-door to the kitchen. A sickly pallor seemed to seep out of the cracks around the door and over its top. Allen noticeably shivered, considering the prospect of crossing the seemingly cursed threshold.

"There's nothing for it," Eve said grimly. "Let's just go slowly; maybe we can remain hidden for a bit."

Now, it was Allen's turn to quell the fear and doubt that rose within him. Sweat began to build on his brow, but he shook off the encroaching enfeeblement. Any chance his brother had rested squarely on the siblings' shoulders, Allen dug down to find renewed strength within himself.

The two crossed the room and slowly made their way into the kitchen. The warmth and bright sunlight Eve had experienced before were now replaced by a sickly gloom. Beyond the gloom stood a sight neither could have anticipated.

In the middle of the kitchen stood Armin. He was messy and dirty and stood with his back turned toward Allen and Eve. Armin's hands were clenched into fists, and blood and gore dropped freely from them. At his feet laid the tall blonde woman, broken and beaten near to death. It was from her that the pitiful whimpering was emanating.

Armin was speaking as his siblings entered the room unnoticed. "... As I did to your beloved guard dog. Would you like to see it? His cursed stone form managed to capture the exact moment I tore out his soul. It is quite exquisite!" He laughed then—a terrible, truncated sound that seemed to emanate from all around the room. It culminated with a swift kick to the tall blonde woman's midsection that caused a gout of blood to erupt from her mouth.

"Armin! Stop!" The shout erupted from Allen's mouth before Eve had a chance to steady him. Armin spun around with incredible speed. A terrible polychromatic light leaked out from his mouth and from behind his eyes. Almost imperceptibly, a thread of silvery light rose up from behind his head and disappeared into the gloom.

"Well, well, if it isn't my erstwhile siblings. Come to see the show?" Armin spoke with a voice not his own.

"We came to save you ... to make sure you were ..." Allen stumbled through his words on the verge of hysterics.

In an instant, Armin was before Allen, staring directly into his eyes, mere inches from his face. "To make sure I was really dead, dear brother!" As Armin's voice rose with anger, so too did it seem to originate from somewhere other than Armin's throat.

The suddenness of events had spurred Eve into motion. With Armin distracted, she rushed to the tall blonde woman's broken form. Though she felt helpless, she tried desperately to staunch the flow of blood coming from a deep wound in the tall blonde woman's chest.

"It's no use," Eve said out loud.

The tall blonde woman smiled weakly at Eve. "Indeed it is not." Her voice was barely a whisper. "You must be swift, child. Take the blade and cut your brother free from his infernal grasp. You found it, didn't you? It was gone when I went to retrieve it." Spent from this final exertion, the tall blonde woman slipped from the bonds of the world.

Eve reached toward the blade hanging at her belt. The handle was warm, and the blade seemed to be humming. She turned her attention again to her brothers. Armin was still ranting and menacing the younger Allen, who had gone white with fear.

Eve had seen the thread that hung from above Armin. She felt a pull from the blade. A hunger. A yearning. As she pulled it from its scabbard, a bright golden light poured off its blade and into the room.

Armin froze. Turning slowly now onto his sister, a terrible visage was drawn on his once familiar face. Armin spoke in a dreadful low growl. "How! How could you have that?!" The voice again bounced around the room. "I'll kill you!" He raged and made for Eve's throat.

Or, at least, he would have had Allen not reached out then. Allen's instincts to protect his sister overrode his fear; he swung outward and got his arms tangled up in Armin's legs.

Armin lurched forward, falling towards the floor, and Eve saw her chance. With all her might, she swung the glowing blade above where her brother's head was falling. She caught the thread but stuck on it, impossibly hanging in the air. Eve screamed and pushed forward with everything she had. The thread tore, pouring the sickly polychromatic light into the air. A terrible voice, everywhere at once, shrieked with pain and horror. Armin fell to the ground unconscious.

Around the siblings, the house began to shake as if some great earthquake had risen suddenly.

Eve sheathed the blade and moved to collect Armin. "C'mon! We gotta get out of here!" She shouted to Allen, who was still lying on the floor.

The two picked up Armin's limp form and rushed back through the parlor. As they passed the awful remains of the statue, Eve wondered at the sight. How could they have missed all that blood?

Shaking off the gloom of the house, they rushed down the porch and back into the waiting safety of the Old Woods. They passed where the carnival had been and were some hundred yards down the trail back home before they stopped.

A groaning sound rose from Armin, and Eve and Allen froze, not knowing exactly what to expect.

"What? What happened? Why aren't we at the house?" Armin's voice was weak, but it was his own again.

XII.

There was a calmness under the leaves of The Old Woods. At a distance behind them, sounds of crashing and rumbling could be heard. The McMasters siblings struggled with everything they had endured.

"So you don't remember anything?" Allen was happy his brother was safe but had trouble grasping what was going on around him. "None of this makes sense, " he concluded.

"I remember the carnival; I remember us trying to sneak into the house. Then I woke up out here with you guys." Armin was surprisingly hale, considering the circumstances.

"Maybe that's for the best, Al. I wish I didn't remember that awful place." Eve was shaken the most of the three and absentmindedly fidgeted with the blade at her hip. "Let's just get home, you two. I don't like this part of the woods anymore."

"Yeah, agreed," said Allen. Armin was quick to follow his siblings' lead. Together, the three made a steady pace back towards their home.

As they crossed the makeshift bridge that marked the far edge of their property, Eve paused and looked back on the path they had tread. Some part of her had expected something to have been following them, but only emptiness greeted her gaze. She waited for a moment longer, then decided to cross the bridge and catch up to her brothers.

In their backyard, the children were greeted by an unexpected sight. Their family picnic table was set for a meal, and their father stood at the grill, as fathers are known to do.

"Ah, there you are," he called to the siblings. "I told your mother you'd be back by dinner." He smiled warmly, and all three of the McMasters children were nearly overcome with relief. Somehow, in spite of everything that had happened, only a morning and subsequent afternoon had passed since the start of their fateful adventure.

Allen sat down hard on the picnic bench. "Boy, am I glad to be home," He said absently as he began to feel the weight of all they had endured.

Eve sat next to her brother. "It's funny. I kinda didn't know if we'd really get home." Her voice trembled, but she was still hardened by the day's events.

"Armin, go see if your mother needs help in the kitchen," Edgar said as he went back to tending the grill.

In silence, time again began to pass. None who were there particularly noticed, and for an undetermined amount of time, all of the family simply existed there in the gathering darkness.

Eve noticed first that the sun had begun to set. "Wait, what?" She said aloud and looked at her brother.

Allen met his sister's gaze and felt a new fear rising in his stomach.

"What could be taking them so long?" Edgar said suddenly and headed toward the door at the back of the house.

Eve and Allen looked up in time to witness their father crossing the threshold of their home. From inside the house, a vile, sickening, polychromatic glow emanated.

"No!" Eve shouted as she leaped from the table. Two steps toward the house, and the blade was out, glowing in the growing darkness. Four more strides, and she was at the door, crashing into the house.

Allen was slower onto his feet, owing in part to being thrown off balance by his sister's sudden explosion of movement. He raced behind but lost sight of her as she plowed into the house. In another second or so, Allen would follow her in.

The explosion tossed Allen clear across the yard. Plumes of strange, thick smoke and flame rose into the sky. Allen could feel fires burning all around him.

As he rose to his feet, still dazed from the blast, Allen was overcome by the deep-seated instinct in all things to survive. Allen ran for the front yard. He passed the white sand driveway and barreled through the bushes on the far side.

Terrible sounds rose behind him—screams and explosions. Still, he ran, heedless into the darkness. He charged headlong into the dark figure before him.

"Easy, kid," Melantonth said. The carnival proprietor held the frightened Allen and attempted to calm him. "I'm amazed I found you," he said.

"We have to go back!" Allen interrupted. He pulled himself away from his newly arrived associate, but the strain finally caught up with him. Allen, who was but a child of ten, succumbed to the terrible weight of all he had seen and fainted.

Melantonth caught Allen before he hit the ground. "Rest now, kid. Nothing I can do for the others, but I can get you out of here." And with that, Melantonth carried Allen to his waiting car and safety.

In the local newspapers, it was proclaimed that the light blue colonial on the edge of The Old Woods had been consumed in a fire. Tragically, its occupants, the McMasters family, were all lost in the blaze that was eventually blamed on a faulty propane tank. No mention was ever made of any other houses within The Old Woods, nor any carnivals that might have occurred therein.

A large town car of peculiar make, with a unique deep purple color, was witnessed by several parties on the fateful night of the fire. All reports agreed the strange vehicle was headed toward the city of Eagle Creek.

Mountain Song

I.

The tale of Marcellus Emil Ott began many years before his actual birth, with his great-great-grandfather, Sir Heinrich M. Ott, in their ancestral homeland of Germany. It is a tale of the consequences of careless actions and the hubris of man, born on through time by persons who were not even so much as a twinkle in their parent's eyes when a profound insidious evil was allowed to slither into the fabric of their very being. Heinrich, as legend had it, was so incompetent and generally unpleasant that it almost cost his family their titles and holdings in the Rhineland Mountains. It is no wonder then, that locals amongst the little towns of the Rhineland still speak with awe at the incredible success Heinrich achieved after emigrating to the United States at the turn of the twentieth century.

In truth, Heinrich and his immediate family had been sent west by express order of several more prominent uncles among the greater Ott clan in hopes of distancing their good names from Heinrich's disastrous endeavors. The belief was that Heinrich's eventual failure in America would be easily explained and, with luck, would prove fatal.

While he was generally unpleasant and fond of strong drink, Heinrich was not so out of touch as to be unaware of his situation and the implications of his pending departure. He spent the months before the trip sojourning in the Rhineland Mountains. There, amongst the ancestral peaks, something in his character changed. By all accounts, he was reserved and thoughtful as he had never been before, and he left for America with a cautious optimism.

Heinrich's first move arriving in the States was to use the remainder of his fortune to purchase an abandoned mine in the northeast. This was widely seen as the prophesied death toll, but no one had dared to hope it would come so soon. Two months into excavating his new purchase, Heinrich struck gold. After hiring miners and a larger crew, it was clear that the seam was deep and ancient, and would produce obscene riches for all those involved in its excavation.

Two years later, some of the proceeds from the mine went to purchase land in the American South, where oil was promptly struck. In a matter of a decade, Heinrich had become an American magnate with considerable interest in the oil and precious metal markets.

Heinrich's image transformed from that of a bumbling idiot into a champion of American industry. And so it was that his family viewed him over the preceding generations up through the birth of his great-great-grandson Marcellus.

Marcellus, which he insisted on being called, without abbreviation, from age six onward, was the fourth son of Heinrich "Henry" Ott IV, a titan of a man both in form and function. Marcellus was, by all accounts, an odd child who lagged behind his three older brothers (Henry Jr., Hugo, and Harvey) in terms of both development and character. Even as a small child, he was prone to wandering off and getting lost, once causing a state-wide manhunt after wandering in pursuit of an errant butterfly that had caught his eye and led him nearly to the state border. He was regularly picked on by his older brothers, which did little to improve his condition. His father was a hard man, however, and felt that Marcellus's rough treatment at the hands of his brothers would serve to toughen his frail body and mind. Predictably, it had the opposite effect.

When Marcellus was eight, tragedy struck. His mother, Annabelle, died suddenly, afflicted by an ailment that had plagued the entire family but to her proved fatal. The cold, or infection that claimed her life, was never identified, and indeed, all members of the family had suffered symptoms of a terrible head cold for the entire month since the return of Marcellus's father from a trip back to Germany to reunite with members of his estranged European relations. Doctors could offer no explanation outside of the family having come in contact with some particularly nasty local pathogen that was resistant to treatment by modern medicine. Prior to Annabelle's passing, the cold had simply been a nuisance for all of its mysterious reputation.

It is likely that here, Marcellus's tale might have turned out differently if not for the intervention of his remarkably ancient great-grandmother and her vast personal fortune. Marcellus had never taken to his studies and was far too physically frail even to attempt most athletics. Painting was the only talent the boy had ever taken any interest in. He was spurred on by the encouragement of his great-grandmother, and, indeed, at her insistence to her grandson Heinrich IV, who would have otherwise not heard a word of such endeavors.

As a teen, he continued to drift apart from his immediate family. His skill with brush and paint, honed at the finest private art schools, had grown in accompaniment with his love for painting. By his nineteenth birthday, he had secured admission to NYU under circumstances that were never exactly clear. His centenarian great-grandmother was his biggest supporter and had endowed him with a trust fund that was easily enough to support a life with no need for work regardless of his successes, but he still strove to make his own future.

At first, college was the panacea Marcellus needed. Forward-thinking professors and a campus with a diversity he had never even conceived of excited and inspired him. Consequently, the first semester passed in a blur. By the spring, however, it was beginning to become clear that the youngest Ott boy had at least inherited his father's legendary arrogance. Marcellus never fit in at the university, though he never tried to. He was convinced he knew more of the spirit of the artist, more of his own personal greatness than those stuffy old men in smocks gave him credit for. At first, it was manageable, but by the start of his sophomore year, he had grown tired of arguing with professors and stopped attending class. It wasn't long before he dropped out and, with no intention of returning to his family, decided to remain in New York City and make his way as an artist.

In New York City, Marcellus finally felt he had found himself. Free of the disappointment of his overbearing father and older brothers and the cold, formulaic nature of the university, Marcellus dove headlong into a new phase of personal expression and growth as an artist.

Then again, the Grim Reaper struck close to home as Marcellus's great-grandmother, along with the entire company of her flight, went missing when their plane mysteriously vanished. After several months of investigation, the flight was declared lost, with all aboard presumed decreased. Marcellus was heartbroken at the loss of the last member of his family that he genuinely felt any connection to. To further complicate matters, with the official demise of his connected and influential great-grandmother, his father took over control of the administration of her estate. Using the opportunity to finally mold his youngest son into the hard man he had become, Heinrich IV promptly cut Marcellus off from his fortune.

Undaunted (and still with some funding set aside in case anything like this ever happened), Marcellus pressed on. For months, he continued to attempt to make his way in New York City, selling his paintings on the streets. Marcellus had, however, overestimated the value of living so purely by his convictions when weighed against that of an actual starving stomach. The neighborhoods where he was able to make his way were far from the places he had known in his youth, and his general standoffishness, coupled with his lack of social graces, made finding the other comforts of life difficult. He was alone, tired, and heartbroken, but Marcellus poured that pain and anguish into his art. He scraped for every penny, for each new piece of canvas, each fresh pot of paint. He worked all week long, bussing tables at a local greasy spoon, and spent each weekend on the street attempting to sell his wares.

Finally, his big break came. A passerby took notice of his work, and through pure chance, Marcellus had managed to impress one Cornelius Ebbsworth, owner of the famed Aleppo Art Gallery. Cornelius was quick to arrange a show for the aspiring Marcellus, and in the course of a few days, Marcellus went from barely scraping by to headlining his own one-man show. He had managed, in a few months, what took some artists lifetimes to accomplish. Marcellus was vindicated and still conceded enough to be unbearably entitled. To his studio apartment, Marcellus retreated to frantically prepare for his big coming out.

A week before the show, Marcellus met up with some friends, primarily coworkers from the diner, though a few of his former classmates from NYU had come out as well to celebrate his sudden change of fortune. Walking home that night, mildly inebriated, Marcellus stumbled and fell into an exposed section of the sewers along an area of construction that was haphazardly roped off. The street had been full of onlookers who, along with getting a laugh at his expense, were quick to help Marcellus out of the pit. Still, the entire ordeal took some time and was wildly disorienting for Marcellus. Refusing to seek medical care, he made his way home that night in a daze.

The sudden brush with potential danger so coincidental with what Marcellus perceived as his huge turn of fortune, coupled with the recent loss of his great-grandmother, had shaken his thinking. Marcellus decided that evening to paint an entirely new series of pictures for his upcoming show. It was of little matter to him that this new course was neither practical nor what had been agreed upon (and handsomely paid for) by the gallery. Marcellus was the artist, and Marcellus knew best, so Marcellus painted. He stopped sleeping at one point, wholly consumed by his new work, and in spite of the time constraints, he managed to complete what he considered his masterwork in under a week.

The day of the show arrived with all the pomp and circumstance befitting the arrival of New York's next big thing. What they got instead was a horror show. What was depicted in the three paintings offered on that fateful day by Marcellus Emil Ott is not entirely clear. Reports from the surviving eyewitnesses vary wildly, but what is known is that Cornelius Ebbsworth shut down the show after only ten minutes and ordered all three paintings to be immediately destroyed. Of the fifty attendees, thirty-six needed immediate medical attention, suffering from conditions ranging from nausea and vomiting to spontaneous advent of vertigo and loss of consciousness. More severe were the ten initial viewers, all of whom attempted suicide (eight successfully) with various implements available throughout the gallery. One unfortunate individual even managed to smash his skull partway through the concrete wall of the gallery.

The show's result was telling on Marcellus, though the paintings seemed to spare their creator from their more vile effects. He was arrested that afternoon, though charges were never formally brought, and Marcellus was released later that day, in large part because the artwork in question and the only reasonable evidence from the scene had been destroyed.

His reputation was now entirely and irreparably destroyed; the few remaining Ott family members who still spoke to Marcellus were quick to excommunicate him. Destitute and running out of what remained of his fortune, Marcellus resolved to leave New York City and head into the vast anonymous stretches of America where he could simply disappear.

II.

There was no more welcome left for Marcellus in New York City. Sure-ly, none was to be found where Marcellus had come from. Where exactly he had planned to go, even Marcellus was not entirely sure. But he knew he needed to leave, so he used some of his remaining funds to purchase a beat-up sedan and headed out on the road.

The passage of time began to ebb as Marcellus got further and fur-ther away from New York City. Eventually, it seemed as though he were simply driving endlessly, unmoored in the currents of time. He was sure that he could recall the passage of day into night and back again, but never did he seem to stop driving.

Marcellus noticed that he had made his way into the mountains when the weather began to turn unseasonably colder and the air awash with the cleanliness of altitude. The shock of that thought was the first clear thing he recalled of the trip. He had intended to head south from NYC, of which he had no doubt, even imagining possible careers as a fisherman or beach bum once he reached the forgiving warmth of the Caribbean. Marcellus had never intended to go north, and that he did, that he must, at that moment, have been somewhere in the Adirondack mountains, shook him from whatever stupor had clouded his mind during the earlier portion of the trip. He pulled over at the nearest rest stop, some fifteen miles further down the road, and tried to regain his composure.

After a moment, Marcellus decided to chalk up the mishap to the stress he had been under. The hard work and then abhorrent failure of the past few weeks must have mixed up his perceptions, and he reasoned that he mindlessly drove off in an unintended direction. There seemed to be more going on, more to what had happened that he couldn't entirely pin down. But Marcellus was extremely tired, and he resolved to rest for the evening in a local motel just a mile or so further from the rest stop. For the remainder of the day, all he could do was try to piece together what had happened and try to shake off the ominous feeling that he was somehow unaware of something terribly important.

The following day, Marcellus was in surprisingly good spirits, better than he had been in some time, and he spent longer at the motel than he had intended. Something had clicked with his accidental new surroundings. Although he felt himself slightly mad, he began to consider just stopping somewhere nearby and trying to make it there by whatever means he could. It seemed as good of a place as any, and there had been no plan for his intended southern wanderings outside of intoxication and decadence with the hopes of forgetting the recent past. Some depths of miscreant behavior would undoubtedly be more challenging to come by out in the wilds of the mountainous north, but perhaps it was what he needed to get a fresh start.

By dinner, Marcellus had decided both to stay in those strange mountainous lands and not specifically stay in the tiny motel/gas station/McDonald's complex that made up his current lodgings. He knew some of the more famous cities of the area but was becoming quickly enamored with the idea of "getting back to nature" and wanted to find somewhere out of the way, somewhere almost secret, to escape into this new identity he was constructing for himself.

Local maps and some digging the next day had pointed him slightly northeast, away from the big interstate roads to a small grouping of towns some thirty miles away. "All nice little places, friendly folks," Marcellus heard over and over from the small cadre of locals that huddled near the interstate. No one was ever overly keen to answer when he asked why they lived there instead, or quick to name an actual resident of these "pleasant towns," but he hadn't expected much different and so paid it little mind. He planned to head for the largest of the three towns, Artemia, as its size would hopefully make it the easiest to find work. He set off first thing on the third morning after arriving at the seedy little motel by the interstate. Marcellus was strangely excited, but still, he felt that something was amiss. Something small and unimportant, he reasoned, an artifact of the stress he was trying to shed, and nothing more.

The drive to Artemia proved more difficult than he had hoped. Away from the large, straight interstate roads, the narrower local roads were winding and prone to sudden drops and turns. It was easy to miss intended turns and harder still to find safe places to reverse course and correct such errors. Mercifully, the roads were pretty quiet and nearly bereft of traffic, but still, their geography alone was enough to tense the knuckles and bate the breath. Marcellus drove through strangely dense wooded areas that loomed over the road and seemed to threaten to devour the sky, only to turn onto a field of wildflowers and low bushes awash in sunlight. The smell of the woods was constant, however, and welcoming in a manner he had not anticipated. He came over a hill, having just thought to himself that he had again been driving for a peculiarly long amount of time, and saw a small village not far ahead at the base of where the road and the mountain met. Marcellus had finally arrived and breathed an audible sigh of relief.

As Marcellus approached the town, he saw to his right an old and terribly worn town sign indicating that he was in Cobbled Hills, not Artemia as he had intended. He brushed aside the wave of frustration that threatened to overwhelm him and tried to resist the sudden urge to turn around and head back to New York City. It seemed that the entire trip had been accidental to this point, and Marcellus thought that perhaps he should just go along with this new turn of events. He stopped at what looked to be the local diner and resolved to do a little digging as to his change of course and then decide on his next move over some much-needed sustenance.

Marcellus quickly entered the diner and sought for a place to sit down. He was still mildly in the grip of delirium when a young waitress arrived at his table. The waitress was about his height, with long blonde hair and an athletic build. Her nametag proudly proclaimed her moniker "Leann," and she said she was happy to answer Marcellus's questions after some brief small talk. It was clear that passing travelers were something of an oddity there, and Leann was excited to hear that Marcellus had actually come from NYC.

"No one ever manages to make it out here from the big city." Her voice was soft but confident and commanded an air of authority one would not expect.

"No, they always get pulled to the tourist traps, Lake Placid, and the like. Rich people sure love skiing. So how is it you ended up in little old Cobbled Hills?"

Marcellus was mildly taken aback as the question seemed to drip with accusation. He had thought himself the questioner, and feeling that he had somehow come to some place he shouldn't have, he rapidly began to lose his cool.

"Well, I, I was hoping to make my way to Artemia, and I must have gotten turned around or missed my intended route or something," Marcellus stammered, clearly feeling the gaze of several other patrons of the restaurant turn toward his direction.

Her sudden burst of laughter brought his reeling mind to sharp attention. "Calm down, sugar," she said as she lightly placed her hand on Marcellus's arm. "I don't mean to be all prying into your business; I'm sure whatever brings you here is of no matter." And then she smiled broadly and continued. "Or is it just talking to pretty girls that makes you seem so jittery?" She finished with a wink. For once, Marcellus's propensity for being easily embarrassed and the rush of warmth to his rapidly blushing cheeks filled him with comfort and eased the sudden panic he had been feeling.

She took his order and, after returning with a modest sandwich and fries, they managed some more friendly and surprisingly informative conversation. It turned out that Marcellus had missed an eastward turn about ten miles back the way he had come and that he had instead headed more north and missed not only Artemia but its two neighboring towns as well. In truth, he had missed Artemia by more than a little bit, Leann confessed, and they both puzzled as to how he had managed to be so far west of the most common routes one would take from New York City to Artemia. Marcellus knew his reputation with directions had never been good, but this seemed beyond the realm of ordinary occurrences. Cobbled Hills was at least as far to the northwest of Artemia as the pair figured Marcellus to have been to the southwest when he left the motel and rest stop. This explained why Marcellus had not recognized the name Cobbled Hills when he came upon the town. The mounting evidence of something occurring to him beyond his understanding was beginning to take a toll on his general state.

It must have been fairly obvious, for Leann was quick to recommend that he get a room at the inn in town, much nicer than any seedy motel, she assured him, and try to get some rest before moving on. She promised to come by to see him that evening after her shift and to bring him some dinner. She seemed confident that everything would sort itself out by then. Marcellus was certainly not in control of the entirety of his faculties at that point, and her kindness had been the highlight of his strange trip so far. Seeing the wisdom of her advice, Marcellus acquiesced and made his way to the inn.

The Black Pines Inn was more polished and luxurious than Marcellus had any right to hope for. Deep, dark wooden fixtures and walls all seemed to be carved by hand, and an air of antiquity hung about the place, similar to that in a museum. The caretaker, a stout man by the name of Billings, had been amenable once he was located and helped to settle Marcellus into one of the nicer rooms on the ground floor. There was apparently some remodeling occurring on the floors above and the clutter was deemed unacceptable for guests. Still, the room was spacious, with a large bed and several pieces of furniture. There was a small kitchenette and what looked to be an exceptionally inviting shower. There was no television, and Mr. Billings had admitted upfront that there was no internet service, or Wi-Fi, or "whatever else technological nonsense" people were used to in New York City. Marcellus was content, however, even with what was lacking, and after a hot shower, it was only a short time before he managed to drift off for some much-needed sleep.

He awoke later to the sound of knocking at his door. It was Leann, who had just arrived with the previously mentioned meal and was apologizing profusely for the unintended delay. It was only then that Marcellus realized that it was evening outside and far later than one would customarily take dinner. He accepted her apology and admitted that he had just woken up himself to the sound of the knocking. It was after midnight, and though she had brought the meal she had promised, it was cold, and the package was damp with grease. She was different, too, on edge, and as Marcellus's mind began to come awake fully, it became clear to him that she had been crying. Marcellus fumbled with the assorted prepackaged accommodations of the room, attempting to make them coffee, and they both moved to sit on the sofa. After taking a moment to devour the sandwich she brought him, Marcellus tried to gently ask what was wrong.

"You're sweet to ask, but it's nothing." This time, it was Leann's turn to blush at his apparently unexpected sympathy. "I have this friend in town, and no, it's nothing like you're probably thinking; he's just a friend. But he gets into trouble a lot, and he drinks a lot, and then he gets into more trouble, and I'm really the only person he has to turn to." She paused and looked over to the doorway. "Not that he wanted any help from me tonight; just told me to fuck off and leave him alone." She stopped for a moment as if saying it again had been like experiencing it anew. "And that's why I'm so late getting over here with your cold dinner and so damn upset."

"The sandwich was fine, really; I don't even think I tasted it," Marcellus said with a smile, hoping to lighten the mood. "I'm sorry you still had to come by and check in on me after the night you seem to have had. I am feeling much better than this afternoon. I guess I really needed that sleep." Again, he chuckled, but oddly, he wasn't really lying either. He was feeling much more relaxed, and again, the sense of wild chance and coincidence put him somehow perfectly at ease. "If you need to get going, I understand, and I truly appreciate the sandwich."

Leann looked him over strangely then, like there was something she was expecting to see but never did. After a moment, she seemed to agree, and they parted company with Marcellus's promise that he would come by the diner in the morning for breakfast and that he wouldn't leave without saying goodbye. Marcellus had agreed as coyly as he could, for in the back of his mind, he had already decided he was going to be staying in Cobbled Hills for more than just the night.

The following morning, Marcellus was greeted by an idyllic mountain town freshly covered in a blanket of snow. The snow must have come deep in the night and was entirely unexpected to Marcellus, given that it was still early November. Everything seemed particularly magical to him, and he began to imagine his journey at its end.

On foot, he explored the tiny hamlet. There was precisely one road that cut through the town proper -the same one he had arrived on the day prior. There were also two dead-end streets, Ellis Avenue, which pointed back to the southwest, and Henry Boulevard, which pointed toward the mountains and ended some hundred yards before the forest edge at the base of the towering local scenery.

All told, Marcellus counted fifteen residential homes (though a couple had looked abandoned), the inn, the diner, a school, and a general store. On the far northeastern edge of town, he spotted what looked to be a dreary dive bar, though he wondered to himself how such an establishment could ever be profitable in a place like Cobbled Hills.

The eponymous hills of the town hid a small creek, now little more than a tiny stream located along the western border of the town. Marcellus was making his way back toward the diner and the center of town when he noticed a further building that had somehow managed to evade his previous reconnaissance work. Staring at the massive neo-Gothic cathedral, Marcellus felt himself practically struck dumb by how such a thing could have remained hidden from his view. For a moment, he again felt the disorientation that had accompanied his trip the days before, but he managed to shake it off before it collapsed around him.

The cathedral was made of dark, heavy stone and looked to be a relic of another time. An elderly priest tended the walkway and waved to Marcellus as he passed. Something about the man gave Marcellus the creeps, and he hurried his pace.

Arriving at the diner for his planned breakfast, Marcellus again made his way to the booth he had occupied the day before. The strange, disorienting feeling was again crawling up his spine, and he struggled to control it. How could he have missed that evil black monstrosity of a building when he first scouted the town? How was it that he was so confident it was evil? Hadn't he seen it before?

Marcellus jumped slightly when Leann asked what he wanted to drink.

"Yeah ... sorry, I'll have a coffee, black." Marcellus tried his best to smile and not look the least bit like he felt at that moment. Leann returned his smile, and he began to feel his nerves settle. The diner was empty, save for one couple seated on the opposite side of the dining room.

Marcellus ordered a modest breakfast and chatted with Leann. As his emotional state finally settled, he decided that now was as good of a time as any to tell Leann he was thinking of sticking around in Cobbled Hills. Leann smiled in response to this new information but didn't seem overly shocked at Marcellus's change in course. Instead, she reverted into something of a de facto welcoming committee and spent the remainder of the time telling Marcellus everything she knew about the small mountain town of Cobbled Hills.

By the end of his meal, Marcellus had arranged to meet up with Leann later that evening, toward the end of her shift at O'Malley's, the bar Marcellus had spied earlier. Leaving the diner, he now became convinced that he should make Cobbled Hills the permanent end of his journey.

Marcellus spent the remainder of the day making inquiries about possibly renting one of the houses he had seen in town. As luck would have it, one of the homes Marcellus had assumed abandoned, the one on the corner of Ellis Avenue, was not only available to rent but also owned by the kindly Mr. Billings, who ran the inn. The home was already furnished, and it was a simple matter in the end for Marcellus to make arrangements to stay in Cobbled Hills.

In the late afternoon, Marcellus rested in his room at the inn for the last time. He was still not entirely comfortable with everything that had transpired over the past few days. If he thought about it for too long, especially the drive that brought him to Cobbled Hills or the mammoth cathedral in the center of town, a great dread began to rise in his gut. Still, he brushed everything off as a consequence of the magnitude of his recent life changes. He was eagerly awaiting his evening rendezvous, and, in the end, the companionship and calmness he had felt in the mountains seemed more than enough justification to start this new life despite his reservations.

When evening finally fell on the sleepy mountain town of Cobbled Hills, Marcellus made his way, again on foot, to O'Malley's Pub on the northeastern edge of town. As he neared the bar, an unexpected sight greeted him. Though it was still very early in the evening, two squat, stocky-looking individuals had taken it upon themselves to work over a third, much more normally proportioned, man. Marcellus acted before his mind had time to reckon with what exactly was off about the two assailants. "Hey! Get off him!" He shouted.

Much to his surprise, the relatively large aggressors quickly turned tail and fled. They were out of sight before Marcellus had made it to the wounded victim, followed moments later by the sounds of a vehicle leaving the area.

Marcellus rushed to the man who was crumpled just outside the bar. He was bleeding profusely and unresponsive to Marcellus's attempts to rouse him. In another moment, Leann had burst from the front door of the bar with an apparent coworker in tow.

"Oh fuck! Hank!" Leann shouted as she rushed to Marcellus's side.

"I just came up on these guys ..." Marcellus was trying desperately to piece together what was happening.

Leann looked briefly at Marcellus's panicked expression. "It's okay. Hank has a real way with people." She smiled weakly. "I've gotta get him to the hospital. Terry ..."

"Go, go." Terry, the coworker, said calmly.

Marcellus helped Leann get the barely conscious Hank into the backseat of her car. "So much for our first date." Leann laughed, but a deep sadness permeated her voice.

Before Marcellus even knew it, she was gone with the terribly wounded man, and he was alone in the cold outside of a strange dive bar.

"C'mon in, drinks on the house," Terry said as he turned and headed back inside.

III.

Over the next few weeks, Marcellus adjusted to his new life in the tiny town of Cobbled Hills. The house he rented on the corner of Ellis and Main was nicely furnished and surprisingly modern. In spite of his initial reservations, the local general store always managed to carry everything he could think to need. All told, Marcellus's transition to small-town life was going as smoothly as one could hope.

It had taken a week and a half for Leann to return to town. Marcellus ran into her at the diner shortly after her return, unexpectedly as it were, for the restaurant had become his customary morning eatery. "You're back!" He blurted out with singular grace.

"Yeah, I got back into town last night." Leann looked tired but resolute.

"How's your friend?" Marcellus asked, attempting to recover from his earlier shock. He was sure there was something different about Leann, but he couldn't exactly put his finger on what.

"He'll survive. Hank's tougher than he looks." Leann moved around the diner with practiced efficiency. "It'll still be a bit before they let him out, though." She added.

"They can keep him!" Someone from the diner called out. Leann shot a withering glare across the dining area. "Don't listen to them." She continued more softly to Marcellus. "Hank's a good guy. He just likes to get drunk a lot. He lost his parents when he was little; it kind of messed him up." Leann paused as though perhaps she had said more than she intended.

"Sure, I'm glad to hear he'll be alright. He looked pretty rough that night." Marcellus did his best not to think too hard about how badly Hank had been beaten up. The memory chilled him, and Marcellus thought uncomfortably about the day at the Aleppo Art Gallery.

Leann smiled at Marcellus's obvious discomfort. The two quickly fell back into step and Marcellus was excited to learn that he and Leann were now neighbors. Leann's house, on the other side of Ellis and one house in from Main, was the other house Marcellus had assumed was abandoned when he first took the measure of the town.

"No, it's just a dump." Leann laughed, and the pair shared a moment of unexpected levity. "Maybe you'll get to come on the tour if you're lucky." She smiled at Marcellus, and his heart skipped a beat. The idea of falling in love and starting a new life in the mountains was becoming more than Marcellus's romantic artist's heart could handle.

He left the diner that day invigorated by his decision to start a new life in Cobbled Hills. Though his remaining fortune was rapidly being depleted, Marcellus had discovered a peculiarity about the quiet little town. One that, he rationed, he could turn into a manageable living. Aside from himself, Leann, Hank, Terry the bartender, and Mr. Billings, who ran the inn, the entire population of Cobbled Hills was elderly. It wasn't overly complex for Marcellus to imagine that there would be plenty of handiwork needs in the little town, and he was right. In the order of a week, Marcellus had set himself up as the local handyman, owing in part to the years of tutelage in various crafting and repair techniques from his father (an attempt by the latter to instill what he viewed as a useful set of skills in his artist son).

Over the next month, Marcellus continued to endear himself to his new neighbors with his handiwork. Regardless of his skills at the start, he at least had some cursory knowledge about a great many of the things that need fixing in a typical household. He soon seemed to be making himself indispensable to the town.

His relationship with Leann continued to develop, though it had hit something of a snag. One night at the bar, Marcellus met Hank. The two couldn't have been more different, but somehow hit it off famously. They shared a bleak sense of humor and, in the course of that first night, became fast friends. So it was that Marcellus found himself in possession of everything he had ever really wanted: a good friend, a cute girl, and a promising little life.

By the start of the new year, Hank had begun working for Marcellus. The two had become quite inseparable, and, along with knowing everyone in town, Hank was incredibly talented working with his hands and excelled under the guidance of Marcellus's know-how. The effect on Hank was widely viewed as a change for the better, and the added assistance allowed Marcellus to entertain thoughts of the one thing that he was still without: his painting.

Ever since the incident at the art gallery, Marcellus had refused even to pick up a brush. Though he could not explain the effect his work had had on the collected attendees, he was sure that he did not have any control over it. That it had simply erupted from what he took to be expressions of his angst and sorrow chilled him that it could happen again. Still, painting was all that had ever mattered to him, and he missed working on new pieces the way someone would miss a lost lover.

Amidst his new life, however, practically drunk on the mountain air, he could no longer resist. As it always did, the general store in town carried a wide variety of art supplies, and Marcellus was able to amass a suitable collection of paints, canvases, and brushes with a single trip. He would paint the landscape only in as lifelike a manner as he could, reasoning that the beautiful scenery he was now effused in could never have a negative effect on another living thing.

Still, Marcellus was cautious lest something like the disaster at the art gallery happen again. He painted only in the very early mornings or late at night in a side room of the basement that he had quickly converted into a tiny studio. For a time, Marcellus kept up the charade, but, as was inevitable, he was eventually spotted painting one morning. The Sanders were on their morning walk through town when Mrs. Sanders spotted Marcellus in the backyard of his house, peering out over the mountains as the sun crested them for the first time that day, painting away frantically before he lost the light.

In a day, it had gotten out that the town's new golden boy was also a talented painter. By the end of that week, Marcellus had already turned down three separate offers for commissioned work from the citizenry. He was torn, though, given his love of painting. Additionally, he feared that people would learn of the disaster at the Aleppo Art Gallery and come to shun him as people in New York City had. Everything he had so far accomplished hinged, he imagined, on keeping his dark secret.

As February rolled in, a change came over Marcellus. He spent more and more time painting each day and started a new piece in secret in the basement studio. He always kept this painting covered with a heavy sheet when he was not working on it, and he told no one of its existence. He completely changed course with regard to creating artwork for the people of Cobbled Hills. Now, he would endeavor to run a small art studio from out of his rented house, as well as manage Hank in the daily handy work jobs. The move seemed to slight Hank, who did not especially take to the added responsibility of working on his own. Still, the friends managed, and the return to the work Marcellus so truly loved seemed to be the last ingredient in completing his perfect new life.

Business boomed. By the end of the month, Marcellus was a veritable celebrity within the tiny mountain town of Cobbled Hills. He learned something else about the town then, namely that its elderly occupants were all considerably wealthy. They seemed to love nothing more than to compete with each other over who could best curry the new artist's favor, and Marcellus was not one to stop them fawning over him. It had been four months now, living his new life in Cobbled Hills, but something of Marcellus's former life still lingered in his presence. He kept his painting in the basement a secret and purchased and installed a shiny new lock on the door to the basement studio.

IV.

Everything began to go south on a chilly morning in March. Spurred on by his successes of late, Marcellus had taken a commission from the mayor to paint a rather large portrait of the town's massive cathedral, "The Church of The Solemn Vow." Marcellus had never liked the ominous building, and alone, he and Leann were the only members of the town who were not within its soundless walls every Sunday. Even Hank and his elderly Granny never missed a week.

Inexplicably, around the same time, Hank's drinking began to become a problem. Jobs were completed poorly by a hungover Hank, if not missed entirely. On two occasions, Hank got into shouting matches with the clients, once almost coming to blows with poor Mr. Roosevelt. Marcellus's preoccupation with the cathedral painting, coupled with Hank's slide back into alcoholism, conspired to sink the handyman business.

Marcellus seemed barely to notice and now rarely slept. Each day was spent laboring over the cathedral painting and its sinister visage, while each night, he devoted more and more time to his secret work in the basement. These behaviors persisted for a few weeks until things finally came to a head. With Marcellus on-site at the cathedral, Hank broke into the basement art studio. It was impossible for Marcellus to hide that something secret was kept in the basement, especially from Hank, who was at Marcellus's home almost daily in connection to their handyman business. Fueled by alcohol, Hank broke down the door to the studio, determined to see what was hidden there in the dark.

Marcellus came home that afternoon to an empty house. The door leading to the basement from the kitchen was open, but Hank was nowhere to be seen. Marcellus rushed into the cellar practically in a panic. His fears only rose as he saw the old basement door leading to the studio, broken off of its ancient hinges.

Strangely, inside the small room Marcellus used in secret for his mysterious work, the painting was undisturbed. It was covered as it had been the night before in its heavy grey sheet. It would have seemed as though nothing had happened in the murky basement save for the presence of the fallen and shattered door.

Marcellus was at a loss as to how to proceed. He attempted to contact Hank, but his calls went unanswered. Still, it was a small town, and after regaining his composure for a minute or two, Marcellus headed out on the short walk to Hank's house.

Hank lived with his grandmother, whom everyone in town simply called Granny, at the last house on the end of Henry Avenue before the mountains. The towering manse must have been a sight in its day but, at present, wore a coat of wear and age that made it seem ancient. Hank was not home, but Granny had seen her troubled grandson earlier in the day. "He had that look on his face again. I don't imagine we'll be seeing him for a few days. Or when I get a call from the county sheriffs to come pick him up from the drunk tank. Try not to worry too much about him; he always comes home eventually." The elderly woman smiled in a kind and easy manner. Even for residents of Cobbled Hills, Granny was ancient and looked the part. Marcellus wondered that she would be alright without Hank around but passed the thought off, reasoning he had bigger problems at the moment.

A quick check to O'Malley's dashed any hopes Marcellus had of ending his search quickly. Indeed, Terry, the bartender, had not seen hide nor hair of Hank. However, he was able to provide Marcellus with the name and location of several other "local" bars around the area that might have been harboring the erstwhile Hank.

Into the early evening, Marcellus searched through several of the establishments he had learned about from Terry. All were dead ends. As the night threatened with a coming storm, he decided to return home.

On the coming dawn, Marcellus had recovered from the shock and intensity of the night before. He reasoned there was nothing he could do, having no earthly idea where Hank went and feeling strongly the pull to continue working on his paintings.

Four days passed and still, no one had seen or heard anything of Hank. Marcellus continued to work diligently on the painting of the cathedral. He resisted the urge to work on the painting in the basement, going so far as to not even enter its murky confines. Instead, he purchased a second lock and installed it on the door leading to the basement from the kitchen.

Leann had been asking questions, too, and she seemed to suspect that Marcellus was keeping something from her. On the afternoon of the fourth day since Hank's disappearance, she surprised Marcellus at home. Marcellus resisted the urge to let Leann in on everything. He knew, at least on some level, that the painting in the basement was dangerous and wished to spare Leann of any ill consequence of knowing of its existence despite his worries for his other friend.

"Well, he wouldn't just up and leave without telling me. We have an arrangement. That's what I'm saying; something else is going on here." Leann's look was stern, and a strange light seemed to glow in her eyes.

"He didn't say anything to me either, and there are jobs that need to be finished in town. I need to know where he went." Marcellus hoped changing the emphasis to work would help to hide his true intentions.

"Bullshit, you haven't cared about the handyman stuff for weeks. It's just been the painting. What aren't you telling me?" Leann seemed to be getting upset with Marcellus and was utterly immune to his deceptions.

"I can't ... It's not safe." Marcellus couldn't help but glance toward the basement door.

"You're not even making this challenging sugar. So what's in the basement?" There was no fear or aggression in Leann's voice, and she was in complete command of the situation.

Marcellus began to panic. "Look, it's nothing. He didn't see it; I'm pretty sure of that, at least."

"Didn't see what? It's time to come clean, hun; just tell me what's going on. I can help." Leann moved closer to Marcellus and placed a hand on his arm. She was comforting but also forceful; she wasn't asking him again.

"Look, I have a studio in the basement. It's just a little thing I set up when I started painting again. I've been working on something. But it's covered, and I put a lock on the door. If I don't show it to anyone, then no one can get hurt." Marcellus felt compelled to tell Leann everything but still resisted out of fear.

"How would a painting hurt someone? This doesn't make a ton of sense." Leann continued, direct and calm, her every word carefully chosen. "Now talk."

It was then that Marcellus lost the battle in his mind over his dark secret. Cold and detached, he rattled off the details of the Aleppo Art Gallery tragedy as though it had happened to someone else. There it all was, plain as day. Marcellus's paintings caused people to hurt themselves, and he worried that his friend was now under their spell.

"Wait, why did he cover the picture back up then? That doesn't seem like something you would do if you were compelled to hurt yourself uncontrollably." Leann was far more observant and quick-witted than Marcellus had ever given her credit for.

"That's why I don't think he's seen it. I haven't moved the sheet on it since the incident. I haven't even gone back in there." Marcellus felt strangely back in the present moment. Was this the same disorienting effect he had experienced several times since leaving NYC?

"So what's it a painting of? Can I see it?" Leann seemed to be commanding rather than asking.

"What?! Are you serious? After everything I've told you about this? Now you want to see the damn thing?" Marcellus had never raised his voice to Leann before.

"Yes. Right now, please." Leann continued with a countenance of stone. "I'm not losing Hank to whatever this is. And I'd rather not lose you too. So right now, you are going to show me what all the fuss is about, and then I'm going to figure out how to get the two of you out of this mess." Marcellus had never seen Leann like this, and it both excited and terrified him.

"The paintings don't seem to affect me any, but it's the strangest thing. I couldn't tell you what I'm working on even if I tried. When I try to think about it, my head just hurts. All I know is that I want to keep working on it all the time. I really don't think it's safe for you to look at." Marcellus shuddered, thinking about painting. It sounded strange to admit how little he actually was in control of regarding the now sinister work in the basement.

"I know, it's okay. I'm a big girl; I can take care of myself. Let's just go take a look." Leann smiled reassuringly to Marcellus, who seemed about to collapse under the stress. The pair made their way downstairs, Marcellus turning on each and every light he could along the path. They passed the remains of the shattered door, still cluttering the hard basement floor. Reluctantly, Marcellus led Leann into the side room that served as his studio. He withdrew the cloth covering the painting and pulled back, anticipating the need to prevent any harm from coming to Leann.

The shock and horror, the danger Marcellus had imagined, never manifested on Leann. Instead, she simply remarked that the painting was indeed awful and cause for concern. She shrugged and looked Marcellus squarely in the eyes. "I've never really liked your paintings, I'm sorry. They just aren't my kind of thing."

Marcellus looked on dumbfounded for a moment.

Leann continued, unfazed. "Look, there's more going on here than you realize. Let's go back upstairs to talk. I needed to see it for myself, and now that I have, I'd just as soon put some space between it and us." She moved back toward the stairs with Marcellus in tow.

Leann led them into the living room and took a seat on the couch. "I don't know how exactly to start this, so here goes. Would you be surprised if I told you that I'd seen the awful things in your painting before? Well, I have. There are other images in the cathedral, statues too." She paused to make sure Marcellus was still following. "I got in there once. It's a labyrinth inside, all hallways and bad angles. I think those 'things,' whatever they are, are real. And I think this town is some weird pagan cult that worships them. Hank and his Granny are tied up in it, too."

"But how would you know about all of this?" Marcellus interrupted.

"You'd better not be about to follow that with 'you're just a waitress,' or you're going to be nursing a sore jaw in addition to everything else." The look on Leann's face was dead serious.

"That wasn't what I meant." Marcellus backpedaled as fast as he could.

"Whatever. You aren't entirely wrong, either. It's complicated." Leann smiled, a disarming tactic that worked almost every time on Marcellus. "I work for a group of people who have an interest in things that fall outside what you think of as 'normal.' Have you noticed how old everyone in town is? How are there so few people who aren't elderly? My bosses think maybe people here are too old. You follow? So they sent me in two years ago to check things out and keep an eye on the place. And, aside from some bizarre artwork in the monster cathedral and confirmation that Hank is somehow involved in this, I really didn't have much to show for it until you showed up." Leann looked concerned again, as she had that night when Hank got attacked.

"Look, we need to find Hank. If half of what you've told me about your paintings is true, he is going to be in rough shape. I think it's also safe to assume that he saw the painting." Leann looked sternly at Marcellus. "I think this might be getting out of hand. I usually have a good sense for this sort of thing." She grabbed Marcellus's hand to cement his attention on her. "I'm going to go get help. I need you to stay here in case Hank shows up. If he does, just keep him here, and don't let him back into the basement. And don't go in there yourself! I don't really understand why, but I think you're right, that painting is dangerous. Can you remember if you covered it back up before we left?"

"I don't recall." Marcellus felt the look of horror as it crossed his face.

"Yeah, same here. Still, don't go back down there. In fact, how about you go over to Hank's house and keep an eye on Granny? If he comes back anywhere, it'll be there. Make sure to lock up as we leave."

"Okay." Marcellus agreed, starting to feel himself in a bit of a daze. Outside of the house, the two exchanged a brief goodbye, and, as quickly as could be imagined, Leann was gone. Alone, Marcellus stood in his driveway. He decided to take his car over to Hank's house this time to ensure he would not need to come back home.

V.

Marcellus never managed to make it over to Hank's house. Sitting in his car, idling in the driveway, he had stopped to think through what he was going to tell Granny. Then, with a peal of sound that split the white noise of the old motor, Marcellus's phone rang. He had left his contact information at several of the bars he had visited initially in the hopes that Hank might show up in the future. The gambit had born fruit, and now, the bartender of a sleazy little hole-in-the-wall two towns over, a congenial woman named Betty, was calling to inform Marcellus that Hank had just left. There had apparently been a commotion involving other patrons at the bar just moments before and Betty was worried that someone might hurt the impressively inebriated Hank.

Marcellus was on his way out of town before even having a plan in place. The outlying town he was headed to was approximately a ten-minute drive to the west, but he worried that he would still be too late to help Hank. With as much abandon as he could muster, Marcellus raced to his friend's aid.

Arriving in the equally backwater town of Bywater, Marcellus saw the scene from a distance. There was a commotion going on in the parking lot surrounding the bar, and Marcellus could make Hank out clearly in the middle of a group of four other individuals. Though he looked drunk as he staggered about, he seemed to be holding his ground all the same. Marcellus thought perhaps he recognized the assailants. They were similar in build to the two men who had assaulted Hank that first night at the bar. They moved with a strange gaping motion, as though their arms and legs were too long for their considerably limited height. But there was something else as well. It would seem, at least from a distance as Marcellus approached, that all four of the mysterious figures held their heads down towards their chests. It had an unsettling appearance, as though perhaps they had no heads at all. But that would be madness.

As the light from Marcellus's sedan illuminated the collected group, Hank looked up and smiled. Almost in response, the assailants fled from the light toward a van not far away in the lot. They piled in with remarkable speed. The black van lurched into the thoroughfare, disappearing around a corner some two hundred yards down the road.

Everything had become quiet, save for Marcellus's running car, as he exited and went to his friend. Hank spat blood onto the tarmac and chuckled. "It took ya long enough," and he let out a loud burp, "I had the fuckers right where I wanted 'em. See anybody ya knew?"

The question struck Marcellus as exceedingly odd. He moved closer toward Hank, but the latter backed away.

"What the hell is wrong with you? Are you so drunk you don't recognize your friend and business partner? Let me get a look at you; that cut on your head looks pretty bad." Marcellus pressed on regardless, worried for his friend's well-being more than anything else.

"Stay fucking back! Or this is going to go the same way as it did with your goon squad!" Hank raised his fists and spat again, the look in his eyes gleaming with madness.

"What goon squad? It's me, Marcellus. I just want to get you back home so we can sort everything out there. Leann went for help; we just had to wait a little while. Hell, maybe she's already back. Just get in the car and we can talk about it on the way." Marcellus was pleading and dreaded the thought of coming to blows with his friend. He remembered the beatings he had suffered at the hands of his older brothers and winced reflexively.

"How do I know I can trust you? I saw the painting; I know you're working for them." Hank had a look on his face of utter loss and defeat.

"I don't know what to tell you. I can't remember what the painting is of. I know I work on it all night, and this makes no sense whatsoever, but I couldn't describe it to you. I don't know anything about this 'them' you're referring to. But I know we need to get out of here before those guys come back to finish the job." Marcellus's voice quivered as fear of some coming physical altercation began to overwhelm him.

Something in the admission seemed to jar Hank from his combative stance. "What? How could you not know what you're painting? Man, I must really be drunk." Hank looked around, seeming to come back to reality. "Okay, maybe you're right. Let's get out of here; my head is killing me." And with that, the imposing visage of Hank swooned and collapsed toward the ground, overcome by both his injuries and his inebriation.

Marcellus lunged forward and caught Hank just inches before he struck the pavement. Hank was considerably larger than the thin and frail Marcellus—built with the physique of a linebacker, Granny always said. The collision was detrimental to Marcellus, but he seemed to survive it, minus some bruises and pain. Hank was passed out in his lap and injured, though it was nothing like that first night.

Marcellus roused himself with all his might, lifted by his fear over Hank's assailants' imagined return. With great effort, he managed to drag Hank to his nearby car and load him into the passenger's seat. Then, after settling himself behind the wheel, he headed back to Cobbled Hills.

In town again, after some fifteen minutes, Marcellus headed directly for Hank's house. His passenger was beginning to come to as he pulled up the drive to the large house at the end of Henry Avenue. Stepping out into the early evening air, Marcellus felt something wrong. There was a darkness to the night that seemed unnatural. Hank groaned as he got to his feet and began to head into the house. Shaking off the sensation, Marcellus followed his friend inside.

Inside the old manor house, Hank made for the drawing room in search of his grandmother. Granny was seated in a high-backed, upholstered chair that made her ancient frame seem impossibly tiny. She sighed loudly as she saw the extent of the injuries to Hank. "You never will learn, will you? One of these days, I ain't gonna be here to stitch you up, ya big lummox."

"Cut the act, Granny, we've got trouble. I'm gonna need some of the medicine, and I think we're going to need to tell Marcellus a couple things about Cobbled Hills." The matter-of-fact manner with which Hank now spoke was leagues away from the drunken mess he had been just a bit earlier.

Granny lowered her brow and looked at Hank with an odd glint in her eye. "So that's what all this is about then. I knew once your friend here showed up the other day but I didn't want to admit it. I've not been looking forward to this."

"I could use something of an explanation. What the hell is going on here?" Marcellus felt out of place and completely lost amidst the proceedings. He had hoped that Leann would have been back by then, but it seemed otherwise.

"Heh, I suppose you could." The old woman chuckled before taking a sip from a glass of tea at her side table. Hank had disappeared through a door in the back of the drawing room, and at present, only she and Marcellus were in the room. "Well, if Hank says it's time, then so be it." She said. "You should probably take a seat; some of what I'm about to tell you is shocking, but not more so than what is coming next."

Marcellus felt his pulse quicken but complied with Granny's request. The other chair in the room was of similar style to Granny's but without the high back. It gave the strange appearance as though Marcellus was sitting with royalty, he thought to himself.

"This town isn't what it seems. There's an evil here, old as time itself. We made a deal with it years and years ago now." Granny paused again to drink from her tea. "How old would you say that I am? Don't be shy, sweetie, just give it your best shot." She shot Marcellus a wry grin.

"Well, I suppose you remind me most of my great-grandmother before she passed, and she was in her hundreds. So that would be my best guess, somewhere near a hundred. Though you don't look a day over eighty." He added at the end, worried that he might offend.

"You're sweet to say such a thing. It's nonsense, too, by the way. I was born on October 14, 1785, right here in Cobbled Hills. What is that, 225 years ago now? Spry for a shade over two centuries, wouldn't ya say?" Granny chuckled. "You must have noticed how old everyone in town is by now; you're a smart boy. Well, they're older than they look, too. Every family in town 'cept for you and Leann, and that boy Terry that works the bar was one of the original families that settled here in the late 1700s. Back then, we were just settlers, fresh off our nation's newly won independence; my parents were among a group of people looking for somewhere to set up a town. They chose to build near the creek for access to the fresh water, and maybe that was the first mistake. There's something in the water; it comes up from below the root of the mountain. Must get diluted once it moves far enough away from the source, but here it's strong, and has an effect on everything that drinks from it. Makes you live far longer than you should and ages you slower. It was hard even to notice at first, at least before the majority of us were in our 60s. No one lived that long and looked and felt as young as we were. But that's when the trouble started, too, really. Some people came from Europe with plans for the mountain. They had money and means, and we were still coming to grips with how different our lives might be in this place; no one ever thought to question it, you understand." The recollection seemed difficult for Granny, but she continued. "Well, those men from Europe were the ones who built the cathedral—and the inn, too, now that I think of it. Their real goal was to get at the gold and silver that was under the mountain. They carved a mine into the depths below the mountain and we all got rich from the precious metals and stones that came to the surface. But they just kept digging, deeper and deeper, until they hit something else. Something they had been looking for all along. There is a race of creatures that live deep below the surface. The Europeans had known of them from others of their kind that they had encountered in the mountains of the Alps and Himalayas. More than a simple rescue mission, however, the Europeans venerated the things below the stone and wished to bring their glory to the surface."

Marcellus sat stunned as Granny continued with the tale. "That was when people finally started to question things, but those crafty foreign devils had an ace up their sleeves. They told us that the reason we all lived longer, the reason the water carried such power, was because of The One Below The Stone. Once freed, they promised to bring riches and longevity to all who helped them. We didn't know about the price then, but I'm sure some suspected. It didn't matter, really; none of us was eager to get old or give up the lavish lifestyles we had gotten accustomed to here in our little hidden paradise. So we agreed, and the Europeans kept digging. It was true too, you know, for a while. We had riches and youth beyond anything we had ever imagined. We met the Voul then as well. The stocky individuals that you chased off of Hank that first night after you came to town."

"Oh god," Marcellus felt suddenly sick as the pieces started to fall into place in his mind, "They were there tonight, just a little while ago in town. Those things aren't human? What the hell is a Voul?" The creeping feeling rose along Marcellus's spine.

"Take a deep breath. I know this isn't easy to hear or easy to believe, but it's the honest truth. The Voul are servants of The One Below The Stone; they see its will fulfilled here on the surface. They are roughly human in shape but with larger arms and legs. Normally, they aren't out on the surface, and if they are, they are disguised. They are horrible, evil things, and we should have known then that we had made a grave mistake. Not that there was anything that could be done by then. The Europeans hightailed it out of town shortly after the Voul were freed, I imagine, to dig more mines somewhere else."

Hank returned to the drawing room then, remarkably healed from his earlier state. "That's what's in your picture if you wanted to know. The Voul and their foul rituals. That's why I thought you were in cahoots with them; well, that and the drunkenness." Hank was fully recovered from earlier. His head bandaged, there was little else to his appearance to suggest that he had recently been on the receiving end of a beating. Additionally, he seemed no longer to be drunk, which, in and of itself, was hard to believe.

Marcellus tried his best to gather his thoughts. So, these mystery monsters were in his painting? Were they in the other paintings from the art gallery, too, he wondered. That at least explained why there hadn't been a more negative effect on Hank, Marcellus reasoned, and there was now some comfort to the reality of his faulty memory regarding the picture.

"There's more to this. I don't really want to think about it, but you're gonna need to know if we're gonna have any chance at getting out of this. Tell him the rest, Granny. No point in holding anything back." Hank was pacing along the back wall of the small room.

Granny sat up in her seat. "So you really mean to go through with it then? There's no going back from this."

"There's no going forward as it is. We won't ever get a better chance." Hank seemed resolute about some coming altercation that Marcellus knew nothing of.

"Very well, you still sitting, city boy, 'cause this is where it gets bad." There was a strange manner to Granny that Marcellus had never before encountered, and it made him feel oddly afraid of the old woman. "It took nearly a hundred years. All the Voul, and whatever else is down there, ever asked of us was to keep their existence secret and to attend their strange masses every Sunday. In return, we had virtual immortality and riches beyond imagining. We had already been keeping our longevity a secret, you understand; it wasn't that much more to ask that we keep this secret now in exchange for these gifts. Bah! It was all just a setup.

"About a hundred years in, the Voul came to us and demanded a new tithe for their unspeakable god below the ground. It was required that we give the young from one family, once every 20 years, to be taken by the Voul and used in their rituals. Any who resisted or refused would be cut off from the source of our immortality.

"This, at first, almost seemed the lesser evil to many of us, having lived as long as we already had. But there was more to it. Cut off from the power of the waters and addicted to their strange properties as we now were, our bodies would be doomed to transform into the wretched sub-human slaves the Voul used for menial labor and sustenance. Still, some resisted, but the doom upon them was swift. It was more than sufficient to horrify the rest of us into compliance. We drew a lottery every two decades and what was required of us was done.

"To my shame, I played along with it for an age, only ever coming to my senses when the price they asked for was my sweet Hank. He was supposed to have been taken when he was a child, but we arranged a 'payment' in his stead so that he might be spared. We've been working desperately on a plan to get him out ever since." Tears were welling in the old woman's eyes, and Marcellus wanted to tell her that everything would be okay, though such a thought was almost laughable at this point.

"You've gotta excuse her; the old age makes her emotional. These things are evil; we have a responsibility to rid the world of them. Regardless of whether or not I make it out of this." Hank was calm and had an air of power about him. "I've always needed someone else to pull this off, and now I think I've found him. See, I figure, if these things are haunting you and compelling you to paint their awful pictures, then you probably have a vested interest in seeing them gone." He looked at Marcellus with a commitment and deep concern that was uncommon for his character.

Marcellus wavered. He had not expected to be presented with an explanation for his painting suddenly; instead, he had simply been concerned for his friend's well-being. Now, with this new information, he paused and tried his hardest to think through everything. Could there really be a way for all of the danger from his paintings to be averted? The thought was exciting to him on a primal level. There was also the implied danger of Hank's still unexplained plan. Was he sure he could trust his friend with something of this magnitude? He began to feel the eyes of the others in the room on him as he still hesitated to say anything.

"Yeah. That's a lot to take in. So, the things in my painting, like the paintings in the church, are real? A menace, which I can't deny. You say there is a way to stop this; how can that be with just the two of us? I don't know; this is not what I had expected when I raced out to save you from a bar brawl." Marcellus stopped, unable to continue on his line of thinking.

"Look, it's simple. We have something, an amulet. It has some weird name,"

"The Stone of Hy'anakc." Granny chimed in.

"Yeah, that." Hank shot a look at Granny. "It's basically a cloaking device, like on a stealth jet or something; it makes you completely invisible to The One Below The Stone and its various minions. It took a lot of effort to get it, and originally, I was just going to wear the amulet and leave town one day. That wouldn't have sat right with me, though, leaving Granny and everyone in town to the mercy of those things. So, we did some more digging. It turns out there is a ritual you can perform to release the power within the gem in the amulet. The kicker was that you need two people, near the same age and of the same sex, to pull it off.

This put Leann right out, not that I would trust her as far as I could throw her, and Terry is a ton older than he looks. According to some old books we uncovered, the release of the energy of the stone should be enough to level the mountain. Keep those wicked fucks buried for all time." Hank smiled, though there was a look of desperation on his face. "So I've been waiting for someone who might fit the bill, and then you showed up."

"And you've been hatching this plan ever since?" Marcellus was not sure exactly what to believe. Were it not for Granny's corroboration of Hank's story, Marcellus would have thought it a delusion caused by his painting. Was it not too much of a coincidence that everything going on in this town was somehow related to the curse on his paintings? "I can't say I like this idea. Why don't we just wait for Leann to get back? Maybe there is another way out of this."

"No chance, dude, the people she works for are bad news. At least as bad as the things we're trying to be rid of. No point getting in bed with a demon just to avoid a devil." Hank seemed to know more than he was saying. "But, I get you; this isn't easy to grasp, really, unless you can see what we're really up against." Hank looked over to Granny.

"So that's you're plan. I should have guessed. There won't be enough for more than the two doses. We'll need to get more supplies afterward if you intend to do this again." Granny looked with concern to her grandson.

"Wait, what's his plan? I really don't appreciate being left in the dark on so much that's going on." The stress was starting to show on Marcellus.

"It's something we came across during the years of research. It's called Dreamwalking Tea. You drink some, and then it's essentially a really accurate lucid dream. You can move around freely and check out anything you want, completely invisible, but you can't affect anything either. It's like you're a ghost."

"Okay," Marcellus raised an eyebrow, "and what are we going to check out?"

"Best to hear this sort of thing right from the horse's mouth, ya know." Hank was calm and resolved. "We're going down below the mountain."

VI.

The air was cold as Marcellus took a bracing draught of the night air. Standing on the front porch of Hank's home, he could see the edge of the forest to his left, at the foot of the now-dreaded mountain. He shuddered, thinking about everything, not entirely able to come to terms with what he had heard. It wasn't so much that he doubted Hank and Granny, nor that he could otherwise explain the effect his paintings had on people, but there was something in his soul that caused Marcellus to pause and seek desperately, in his mind, for some other solution.

Hank came out onto the porch and looked cautiously at his companion. Over the short time that they had known each other, Hank had come to expect a degree of resistance from Marcellus. The latter was undoubtedly accustomed to things being a certain way, and Hank, much like Leann, had come up with several ways of dealing with it. "Look, man, I won't go through with this if you think it's a bad idea. I respect your judgment, but I also know that if you could just see what I've seen, then you would be 100% in on this plan. We will be completely safe going to take a look with the tea; I've done it before."

"I appreciate that, and I get where you're coming from. There is a lot I would give to make my paintings safe again. But the things you're suggesting showing me, I'd be crazy to say I believed them."

"Which is why you need to see it for yourself," Hank added.

"And what happens if I see these things and then I go nuts too? I honestly don't hate that I have no recollection of my work. The things you and Granny described sound awful," Marcellus said shaking his head.

"That isn't going to happen. Whether or not you remember it, you've seen them before. If you were gonna lose it as a result, it would have happened by now." Hank was confident and still possessed a strange air of power and command.

"Okay, fine, I suppose that makes sense. I still think we should wait for Leann, regardless of what you think of her. But that also means waiting for the moment. I suppose, in the meantime, we can try this tea idea of yours. Did you say it only lasts a few hours? Take me through it again." Marcellus was amazed at the things his mind was beginning to believe.

Hank smiled. "Okay, so Granny is brewing the tea as we speak. It comes from this fungus-slash-mushroom sort of thing; it's bright red and kinda looks like skin or meat. Anyways, she brews tea from it, and we drink it. Shit tastes awful. Then you just lay down. You're usually asleep in a minute or two, and then it's go time. You wake up right next to your sleeping corpse. From there, you have about two hours to explore in your 'ghost' state while your body sleeps safely here at the house. I'm gonna drink some, too, so I'll be right there with you. It's hard to describe, but moving is easier when we're on the 'Walk; it should only take about ten minutes for us to get to the mine entrance at the foot of the mountain. From there, it's a bit of a slog. It's about an hour and a half to get to the bottom, where all the trouble starts. That should give us about twenty minutes to have a look around, and then, 'poof,' you wake up back at the house." Hank had settled into the large chair on the porch. "Look, you're completely invisible, undetectable, and safe. Most of the time is going to be spent walking down a mine shaft. Even if we encounter a Voul in transit, they won't be able to notice us any more than someone in town could."

"Speaking of town, wouldn't it be easier to just show me something from the cathedral? Why not just Dreamwalk there or something." The thought of the mountain terrified Marcellus.

"Yeah, I thought about that too, but it's a no-go. There are weird properties about the inside of the cathedral; moving from room to room, it doesn't make sense. Even going in there every week, there's only one path any of us knows to get to one specific room. Going off in any other direction results in a person becoming lost. Like, never-see-the-light-of-day-again-lost, you get me? It's too much of a risk. Plus, like I said, I've been down the mine before; I know the way, and I know we'll see what we need to. Simple as that."

"I knew that place was evil the moment I saw it; I just couldn't ex-plain why. Okay, so let's say I'm starting to come around on your plan. What makes you think we'll be safe here at the house? Won't those things, the Voul, come back for you? I assume they know where you live." Marcellus said. All things considered, they were closer to the source of the trouble than he would have liked.

"We've got a back room in the house. It's super hard to find if you don't know where to look. That, plus we're gonna use the amulet. You remember how I said it was like the stealth fighters and shit; it's really more of a bubble. Everything inside the bubble is totally undetectable to all manner of evil nonsense, not just what we're dealing with here. I figure we hang it on the back of the door to the back room, and we should be all set. Invisible bodies, ghost forms to go exploring in, you've gotta admit you're at least a little curious just to see if I'm full of it or not, right?"

Marcellus caught himself, indeed curious, in spite of everything that had happened. Could any of what Hank was telling him really be true? It was hard to believe even a fraction of what he had been told, but it was still more challenging to shake the feeling that his friend was telling the truth.

"Okay, fine. Fuck it, what's the worst that could happen, right. We'll just be sleeping in your house after all." Marcellus added the last part for himself as he felt his courage wavering even then.

"All right! That's what I'm talking about. Just wait, this is all going to work out." Hank rose and quickly made his way back through the front door. With Marcellus following close behind, the pair made their way into the kitchen at the rear of the house. Granny had been busy working on the tea, and Marcellus could see some of the remains of the strange fungus on the cutting board by the sink. It was so brightly red that, for a moment, Marcellus thought it was glowing.

"Everything's ready. Got the tea poured and everything." Granny motioned toward the two steaming tea cups sitting on a pewter tray on the counter. The tiny ceramic cups seemed in stark contrast to their supposed contents, and Marcellus started to wonder at the wild possibilities that now emerged before him.

"Alright, buddy, drink up." Hank handed a cup to Marcellus and then quickly downed the other one with a grimace. "God damn, that's awful; drink it quick. Trust me." Hank poured a glass of water from the nearby decanter.

Marcellus paused and examined the odd-smelling reddish liquid. It was a wholly unique smell, though he did not think it as terrible as Hank was making out. He took a sip and realized his friend was being modest, proclaiming the drink as simply awful. He paused again. "You really want me to drink this? It's worse than I expected." He looked at Hank, but the latter simply nodded and reiterated that Marcellus should hurry.

There was nothing else for it. Marcellus closed his eyes and swallowed the foul drink in one painful gulp. Hank handed him a glass of water and motioned for Marcellus to follow as he let out a loud yawn. They went through what looked to initially be a closet in the back of the kitchen but turned out to be something of a foyer in a back area of the house that would have been otherwise hidden. Hank went into a room on the right side of the small hallway they entered into. Inside were two small cots, several folding chairs, and an end table. Hank lay down on the cot nearest to the door. "Better get comfy; I can already feel it; I'm about to pass out. See ya on the other side."

Marcellus watched as his companion fell fast asleep. He settled quickly onto the other cot and prepared his mind as best he could for the expected journey. Laying on the tiny cot, Marcellus imagined what they might encounter on this strange quest. Could there really be monsters under the mountain? Certainly, that wouldn't be possible. It was just people that were assaulting Hank earlier that evening.

"Nah, man, totally monsters," Hank answered. He was sitting in one of the folding chairs in the small back room. Wait, was Marcellus dreaming? What about the Dreamwalk? They were supposed to be doing something important!

"Whoa, calm down, buddy, everything's going according to plan. Shit, I forgot how disorienting this can be for a first-timer. Just hang in there a minute, and things will start to clear up." Hank was standing now just to Marcellus's left.

"What? Did I say that out loud? Feels like I'm drunk, but just the shitty spins part." Marcellus thought he must be wobbling or swooning but seemed motionless all the same.

Slowly, the world around him began to come into better focus. The color of everything was off, as though he were looking at a film negative. Aside from that, though, everything seemed to be the same. He looked below himself and saw his body sleeping on the cot before him. Then everything threatened to go bad for him. How could he be sleeping there and standing here? Hank steadied his friend, calm and relaxed in the face of this unbelievable circumstance.

"Just try to breathe; this is just like I told you; it's like you're a ghost, and I'm right here with you." Hank looked different outside of the color; Marcellus was not used to seeing his friend as the purveyor of knowledge that he seemed to be on the subject of things unimaginable.

"Okay, I'll try. I'll be honest, I didn't think this was going to work. I figured, what was the harm in a weird mushroom buzz for a couple of hours while we waited for Leann? This is way more than that. How is this possible?" Marcellus said.

Hank smiled at his friend. "It's just like I was saying, bro, Dream-walking. I don't understand the specifics, and you don't want to know the hassle it was to find someone who knew how to grow the stuff. But fuckin' works like a charm. It's how I've been able to stay free this long. And why I don't trust Leann. I ain't gonna lie to you; I spied on her like this. Not in some pervy way, just to see if she was on the level. She's a good person, I'm sure, but the people she works for? No, thank you. Anyway, I'm getting off-topic; we have to be careful not to lose track of stuff. Dreamwalking is sort of like being stoned; it's easy to get distracted."

"Yeah, I'm getting that," Marcellus said, shaking his head. The world around him had indeed settled from the film negative nightmare it had started as. There was a strange sort of light, as if a full moon shone, though they were still indoors.

"Okay, let's get moving," Hank said as he headed for the door.

"Wait, I thought you said we couldn't effect anything like this." Marcellus stopped.

"Yup, that's the case, wassup?" Hank raised an eyebrow.

"The door," Marcellus pointed, moving his hand consciously for the first time, "is still shut. How are we getting out of the room?"

"Yeah, you aren't gonna like this part. We are really ghost-like while Dreamwalking. It's not super pleasant to do, but we are gonna just walk through the door." Hank smiled at Marcellus, though he was sure the latter would not appreciate this additional ripple.

"What? This gets odder and odder the longer it lasts. Whatever, let's just get this over with." Marcellus was getting used to moving now; it was more about thinking about where he wanted to go and less about the actual moving of his body.

Hank agreed and, with a solemn look, stepped through the door and was gone. Marcellus moved up to the door and envisioned himself plunging through it. There was an unpleasant grating sound, and suddenly, he was in the hallway with Hank.

Together, the two made their way back through the little closet-foyer and into the kitchen. From there, Hank changed direction and headed toward the back door, which was located just a few steps away from the kitchen. It was conveniently open, and Marcellus marveled at the preparedness Hank and Granny showed. He would never have imagined such things possible from the pair.

Outside, Hank made directly for the forest. "Try to stay close." He called back to Marcellus.

Marcellus was still getting used to moving in this strange state and lagged slightly behind his friend. The darkness of the night was banished under the spell of this strange light and he used Hank's slight lead on him to direct his thinking. The forest seemed foreboding, but he kept up as Hank dove past its bounds.

They did move with exceptional speed, and the world around them seemed far away, though it could still be clearly seen. In short order, they were at the entrance of an old mine carved right into the rising height of the mountain. Hank paused at the opening and waited for his friend to catch up.

"Okay, this is it. It won't be dark in there, or at least we'll be able to see, just like we can now. Just try not to freak out if we see a Voul. They are horrible to look at; I can't even really describe it. But they can't see us, so if it's too much, just put a hand on my shoulder and shut your eyes. I'll make sure we stay out of direct contact with anything, and when it's clear again, I can let you know, and we can move on." There was a look of concern on Hank's face. "There's something else too, a song coming from the depths. At least, I think it's supposed to be some sort of song. If you listen to it, you'll become spellbound and just stand there drooling. It will be faint at first; you might feel it before you hear it. Look, you really have to focus on not listening to the song. It's the reason we're gonna put a stop to this, but I won't say anything more of it. You'll see soon enough." Were those tears welling in Hank's eyes?

Marcellus did his best to steady himself. "Alright, stay close and don't listen to the song under the mountain. I think I can handle this. Let's get moving," he said, and the pair departed into the mine. For over an hour, they descended a standard mine shaft. While it hadn't been used for a considerable amount of time, the path was clear and clean, leading ever downward below the mountain.

Then, there came a sound in the artificially alleviated darkness. Not the dreaded song Hank had warned about, but a heavy plodding sound, and it moved ever closer to where the pair had frozen. "Okay, this is probably a Voul. Just stay calm and move over to this side of the path; it sounds like it's coming up from the depths." Hank never took his attention off the direction from which the sound rumbled ever closer.

Marcellus had been dreading this, though he had expected it eventually. As the thing moved into sight, before them and to the left, he had to stifle a gasp. How could he have ever imagined this thing to be human? Thick, almost bulbous, arms and legs hung from a roughly human-sized torso that was anything but. Where a man would have had a chest, instead, the Voul possessed a great beak-like mouth. Above this hideous mouth sat a wicked single eye that bulged upward and gave the appearance of a hung head.

Undaunted, the horror continued to amble past the two hidden trespassers. Marcellus was glad when it passed, though he had managed to keep his eyes on the beast for the entirety of its time before him. And there were more where that came from, he thought, and Marcellus swore he could feel his blood chill. Hank continued as soon as the thing had gone back into the darkness. "You did good; keep it up, and we'll get through this." Hank gave Marcellus a thumbs up, and Marcellus couldn't help but feel pity for his friend. Hank didn't deserve to be tormented by these monsters, and he just kept fighting. There was something admirable in that.

It was another hundred yards before Marcellus first heard it. Hank was right; the song, if the droning broken rhythm could even be called such, was easier to feel resonating through the stone than to hear it at first. It seemed almost as if it rippled the stone, as a sound wave might when passing through water, and it pulled at the conscious mind as it droned on and on. Marcellus struggled to regain his focus. The harder he tried to ignore this strange evil sound, the more it stuck in his thoughts and drew his attention toward it.

Hank put a hand on Marcellus's shoulder. "Pull it together, buddy; we're in the mine; we've only got a short distance further to go; listen to my voice, not the song." He looked directly into Marcellus's eyes.

"What? Where? Okay, okay, I'm here. Keep talking. It helps."

"I thought it might. I have a trick: try to hum a song in your mind or something else to listen to. Probably should have mentioned that part before. If you don't focus on it, the effects will go away." Hank was calm, but there was a sense of urgency to his actions.

Marcellus nodded and dug into his memory for a favorite tune to hum. Within moments of the competing information in his mind, the strange pull of the mountain song passed, and Marcellus was again himself.

"We're going to have to get moving. This is taking longer than I planned. C'mon, just a little farther." Hank headed further down the path. Marcellus picked up his pace and followed close behind his friend. It was easy enough to keep humming something or other in his head as they went. The song grew ever louder and more precise with each step.

As they reached a larger junction area, Hank stopped. "Hold up. This is it. There is a cave entrance in the room connected to this. It's the entrance to their lair. We've been doing pretty good so far, but there are gonna be a lot more of them down there. Plus, the ground gets weird, uneven, and strange-looking. We have to be careful not to pass through any Voul accidentally. It was one thing going through the door; it's something else when it's living stuff. You don't want to find out what it's like. Anyways, we'll just go a little way. I'm sure you'll see enough by then. Feels like we're getting close to the two hours."

Marcellus agreed, and they moved into the adjoining room. Roughly carved into the side wall was the entrance that Hank had described. "This is where we'll perform the ritual. If you decide to go along with my plan, this is as far as we'll need to go." He seemed resolute. Hank moved toward the opening and motioned for Marcellus to follow.

Inside the entrance, the ground indeed became uneven and rough looking. There was a strange smoke that seemed to drift about the long hallway they were in. The walls seemed no longer to be stone but instead resembled the rough surface of the ground below them.

The song, too, had become louder and clearer within these strange halls. As they approached an aperture to the right that looked something like a doorway, Hank again paused. "Shit, I can feel it fading. Marcellus, you have to hurry!" Suddenly, Hank's image appeared to fade. "Look through the doorway! You only have another minute or so. Look and see why this has to end!" Hank's image disappeared completely.

Panic grabbed Marcellus's heart. Had they taken too long coming down the mine shaft? He had never imagined being in this awful place alone. Marcellus pushed forward with great effort. Could he smell Granny cooking something in the kitchen? He had to focus. With tremendous strain on his mind, Marcellus willed himself to turn his head, to look, and there, on large, oddly carved daises, he saw it—the horror that Hank could never bring himself to describe in any detail. Before he could even react, Marcellus woke on the cot in the back room.

VII.

He vomited the moment he came to. Marcellus was shaken and weary. Nothing could have prepared him for what he had just seen, and that he saw it briefly was likely the only thing holding his sanity together.

"Hang on, buddy, I'll grab ya a towel." Hank rose from his seat across from Marcellus's cot. "I take it that means you saw it?" How could he be so nonchalant about the dripping, abject horror Marcellus had just laid eyes upon? Again, the urge to vomit rose in Marcellus's gut and he struggled to control it.

"How? How could anything like that be possible? Are we in hell or something?" Marcellus swooned on the edge of consciousness.

Hank had returned to the room with a towel. "Just take it easy. It's best to try not to think about it. You understand now why this has to stop." Hank was equal parts somber and convicted. "Smells like Granny is cooking us up something to eat. The food will help you settle down. Then we can see if Leann is back and decide on our next move." His settled, calm demeanor was soothing to Marcellus's ravaged psyche.

For several minutes, the friends sat in the small back room, gray and silent like a tomb. Every casual thought threatened to turn down terrible and hopeless avenues. It was all Marcellus could do to keep his focus on anything else. No, he could focus for sure on one thing: making that silent dark trip under the mountain to end those monstrosities, those aberrations against all that was good and decent in the world. There was no way his sanity would accept anything else.

Hank rose first and stretched. "Alright, let's get some food. C'mon." And he moved out of the room into the small hallway. Marcellus was quick to follow, convinced he should not be alone anywhere in that ancient manor built during the heyday of those fiends.

They moved back along the path they had tread, returning to the kitchen moments later. The disarray was immediately apparent. Several kitchen chairs were turned over and an untended pot boiled away at the stove. The room was otherwise empty, and the fear on Hank's face was reflected in his voice. "Granny? Where ya at, ya old bat?" He was out of the kitchen, headed toward the drawing room with haste, Marcellus close behind.

In the drawing-room, more chaos and disarray greeted them. Shelves were turned over, and books littered the floor. More alarmingly, Granny's customary high-backed chair was smashed to bits. "Fuck! This looks bad. Where is she?" Hank was no longer the picture of calmness he had been up to that point.

"What happened here? Was it the Voul?" Marcellus was trying to keep up.

"Sure looks like it. Somebody trashed the place. We gotta find Granny. She's a tough old bird; they wouldn't get her without a fight." Hank was pacing again around the cluttered room.

"Okay, let's just think about this for a bit. Is there anywhere else she could have gone? Other secret rooms in this place, that sort of thing." Marcellus tried his best to hide his worry from his friend. How were they supposed to fight those things?

"Yeah, right, gotta calm down and think. Those fucks better not have hurt her."

"There's no blood or anything. I don't even want to think about those things taking prisoners. That said, it's probably likely they would just capture her. They're after you, after all, right?" Was there really any reason to hold out hope? Marcellus shivered.

"No, that's right too. I'm the one they want; they don't need Granny; she's too old." Hank seemed to be settling.

"That's the part I don't get. Why you? What are they after from you?" Marcellus hadn't wanted to ask, but things seemed to be spiraling out of control rapidly.

"You really don't get it? I was one of the kids promised to those things. What do you think they made those ... instruments ... out of? That's what happens to you when they take you below the mountain. My parents, what's left of them, that's what you saw beyond the door. That's why I knew we would see what we needed to. That was supposed to be some payment, them for me, but they changed the deal and came calling for me when I turned twenty-one. Now they've got Granny. They've taken everything from me; they won't get her too." Hank was shaking with rage and fear, tears streaming down his face.

"It's okay. We'll figure this out. How are we going to get Granny back? Do you know where they would take her? We need to check and see if Leann is back. She was right; this is getting out of hand fast," Marcellus said, unable to fully think about the horror beneath the mountain.

"Probably the cathedral. That place is basically a fortress. There's no getting in if they don't want to let you in. Even the Dreamwalk, not that that's an option anymore." Hank was resolute. "Let's keep looking around the house, just in case. Then we can see about Leann. Maybe we do need some help."

The pair moved on from the drawing room back into the hallway. Hank headed to the central living room, near the stairs to the second floor, when he yelped with surprise. "Aw, sick! That a girl, Granny! Serves you right, you nasty fuck."

As Marcellus caught up to Hank, he saw what had caused the commotion. There, on the floor of the living room, lay the deformed remains of a Voul. It appeared that the thing had suffered some explosion in its torso/skull that had partially blown it apart. The sight was appalling, and the smell was worse. "Well, at least we know you can kill the things. How did she ..."

"Don't ask; Granny has more than a few tricks up her sleeves. And now we know for sure who came for her, or for us, or whatever. Let me grab a couple things from upstairs. You head back to the back room and grab the amulet. I left it on the door." Hank paused. "Don't look at me like that; it's not like they could find it, remember."

"Are you sure we should split up? What if there are some still here?" Marcellus was not at all comfortable with the thought of being alone in the house.

"Nah, they never stick around long. Plus, just put the amulet on when you grab it if you're feeling worried about it." Hank made a face that looked somewhere between amusement and madness. Then he darted upstairs, two steps at a time.

Marcellus did as Hank asked and went back to the kitchen, through the closet/foyer, and back to the tiny hallway that led to the back room. Just as Hank had said, the amulet was still hanging from its hook on the back of the door. Marcellus pulled the oddly heavy charm off the wall and looked at it closely for a moment. He had only seen it briefly when Hank set up the room for the Dreamwalk. Now, under close inspection, he marveled at the craftwork of gold and silver that twisted strangely around a gem of deep black-red. There seemed to be intricate writing all over the metal, but it was far too small to make out properly.

Marcellus slid the chain over his head. The cool metal came to rest comfortably on his neck. The weight of the amulet seemed to fade the moment it was worn. He felt immediately more at ease, this magic amulet being the least unbelievable thing he had so far encountered that day.

Marcellus made his way back to the central living room just in time to see Hank descending the stairs. In his hands, Hank held an impressive-looking sidearm. All black and shockingly larger than Marcellus would have expected, the weapon looked like something out of an action movie. Hank sported a bandolier across one shoulder, strapped full of additional clips for his gun. The idea of fighting the Voul was more than Marcellus could entertain, but at least his partner was ready for action.

The two made their way back onto the front porch. Hank was off towards Leann's house in a flash before Marcellus had a chance to suggest they take his car. Marcellus sighed and followed after Hank. Though it was late in the evening, the pervasive darkness that had colored the night earlier had indeed abated, just as it had during the Dreamwalk. Maybe that was a good sign, thought Marcellus.

After a few minutes, they reached Leann's place. All signs indicated that she was still not back from her trip to secure help. Not the least of which being that her car was not parked in the tiny driveway on the west side of the house.

"Looks like she's still not home. I don't know what I was expecting, given how this night is going, but this is disheartening." Marcellus stood on the porch in front of Leann's door. The loud crash made him jump.

Hank was busy cleaning up the window he had just shattered. "C'mon, let's have a look around. Careful not to cut yourself." He was through the window before Marcellus had raised a protest. Begrudgingly, Marcellus climbed through the broken window and found himself in Leann's living room.

"We shouldn't be in here. What do you think she's hiding? Granny sure isn't here." Marcellus was getting weary as the night dragged on.

"I know that. But Leann got into the cathedral. She must have a map or something of the inside. That's gotta be where they took Granny. It's not like I can just ask Leann to borrow a map at the moment, ya know. I'm sure she'll get over it; she's forgiven me for worse than this." Hank was busy looking about the room and was only partly concerned with Marcellus's objections.

"I still don't like it." Marcellus protested. Unabated, Hank continued about his search. Marcellus sat down on the couch, feeling exhausted. What was it that he heard just in the distance? Was it the dreaded song from below the mountain? How could it have come up to the surface? No, it was something else, more of a commotion than the discordant rhythm of the mind-altering song.

It was far too late when Marcellus finally placed the strange sound. Were those people outside of the house? "Hank!" He called out. "I think we have company!"

Hank emerged from the nearby bedroom with a piece of paper in his hands. Stepping out onto the porch, the pair noticed the crowd of people coming up the street. Most of the town's population was making their way as a group toward Leann's house. Led by Mr. Billings, the crowd was clearly agitated and moved with surprising speed to surround Marcellus and Hank.

"That's enough meddling from you for tonight," Billings said, though he was clearly addressing Hank. "Haven't you caused enough trouble for us yet, boy? First, your parents, now Granny, how many more need to pay the price you were born for?" Billings was angry and seemed to be the de facto leader of the mob.

"Fuck off, Billings. Where's Granny?" Hank was not the least bit intimidated.

"You need to come with us now, up to the cathedral. We're going to wait until morning, and then we're going to hand you over to the Voul when they come up next. This ends now." Billings, too, was unmoved by his counterpart's obstinacy.

"Like hell we are! You have lost your mind if you think this is going to end well for you." Hank waved his impressive firearm about.

"Put your toy away, boy, before someone gets hurt. You don't have the nerve to try to kill one of us. Have you even fired that thing before?" Billings moved closer to Hank. "Your precious Granny screamed when they took her below the mountain. Wailed like a newborn babe. That's what happens when you go against The One Below The Stone. There is no escape for you."

The look on Hank's face was defeat. Tears welled in his eyes and he dropped his shoulders.

"What? Did you actually think you could save her? You're more of a fool than she was. This can all end. Just come with us and play the part you were born for. There is no other choice, boy. Everything goes below the stone eventually."

Marcellus's eyes darted back and forth between Hank and Billings. Was this the end? He tensed his muscles and prepared to make a mad dash back to his car. There was no way he was willingly going into that cathedral or anywhere with this mob. With these people he had assumed were simple elderly townies, now the vessels of unmitigated horror.

"Never." Marcellus heard Hank's voice a moment before the gunshot. The large caliber bullet burst Billings' skull like a ripe melon. Someone in the crowd screamed. Hank fired again, this time into the crowd. The assembled townsfolk fled. "C'mon!" Hank shouted as he sprinted back toward his house and the looming shadow of the terrible mountain.

Marcellus followed his friend. Hank had just killed his landlord. Something about the mundane nature with which Billings had met his demise, in contrast to the terrible, unreal things they were allayed against, made Marcellus feel weak. He had only ever seen someone die on that awful afternoon in the art gallery. The memories were unwel-come.

Hank raced down Henry Avenue. Marcellus struggled to keep up. As they reached the end of the street and Hank's house, Hank blew past and tore through the lawn, headed for the edge of the woods. Marcellus's chest heaved; he knew he couldn't keep this pace up for much longer. Hank stopped at the line of trees that demarked the end of the lawn and the beginning of the forest.

"Hurry up! It doesn't look like anyone's following us." Hank shouted to Marcellus as the latter slowed his pace from exhaustion.

"I gotta stop for a second!" Marcellus said, bedraggled and panting.

Hank walked over to his friend. "Okay, so new plan. They can't be that far ahead of us. If we hurry, we can catch them, then with Granny safe ..."

"You fucking shot him!" Marcellus blurted out. "God, I was right there; I saw everything. How the fuck could you just shoot him!"

"Billings had it coming; he's always been the ringleader. Besides, it got us out of there, didn't it?" Hank was calmer than he had any right being, Marcellus thought. "They're all in on it. If they stand in the way, I'm gonna knock 'em down. Simple as that. Now we need to focus, time's wasting." Hank looked back to the forest with determination and mania in his eyes.

"Fuck, I can't do this." Marcellus was bent over, holding his knees, trying to catch his breath.

"Nah, like hell you can't. It's too late now for that shit. You come willing, or I carry your ass. I told you before I need two people for the ritual. Billings was right about one thing: this ends tonight." There was a look in Hank's eyes that Marcellus had never seen before, and he shiv-ered. There was no getting around it then.

"Okay. Okay, whatever, fine, I get it. Just, you gotta gimme a minute here. I'm not made for this type of endeavor." Marcellus felt weak and the world seemed to spin around him.

"Look, it's alright. You're still wearing the amulet, remember? I don't even think anybody in the crowd knew you were there. It's gonna be the same down below. We're gonna hustle, but I'll try to take it easy on ya as best as I can. When we catch up to them, I'm gonna cause a ruckus. They'll be on me pretty quick, but we've danced before, so I can handle it. You're gonna sneak up and grab Granny and get her somewhere out of sight. Then, just head for the mine; I'll meet you there when I finish off the Voul. We're gonna head down and blow the lid off the fuckers, just like we planned, ya hear. Then you can run away, or go fuck Leann, or whatever. It'll be over." Hank was pacing again.

"Alright, I'm with you. I forgot about the amulet. That's not a terrible plan, I suppose. It doesn't matter; you're right in the end. I've seen it. How could I live with myself, knowing I didn't try to blot it from existence?" Marcellus sighed, regaining some of his composure.

With renewed conviction, the two friends headed into the forest. Hank was moving at a good pace but, indeed, was no longer at the all-out sprint of before. They were in the woods for five minutes with no sight of their quarry. Then, ten minutes. Then fifteen. With every second that passed, their outlook became grimmer and grimmer. There was nothing they could do to save Granny. The entrance to the mine came into view some twenty minutes after the pair had entered the forest.

Stopping at the opening to the mine, Hank's visage wore a gloom it had not possessed before. "We're just gonna have to head down then." He said matter-of-factly. Digging into the pocket of the oversized denim jacket, which was his customary attire, Hank produced two headlamps on elastic straps. He handed one to Marcellus.

"You really have thought about this a lot, haven't you?" Marcellus said. He was still in amazement at Hank's preparedness, a trait he seemed utterly to lack from their working relationship.

"Hell yeah!" Hank smiled. There was indeed something tragic about Hank, a victim of horrible circumstances.

The pair donned the headlamps and prepared to descend the mine. Marcellus was surprised at how little he was nervous now, expecting, as he was, to have run for the hills far before then.

"Well, let's do this. Granny can't afford for us to wait." Hank's face was stern. "Don't forget about the song. It's worse when it's your real ears. And it'll be the end of us if we aren't careful. You fall into a stupor down there, and I don't want to think about Granny's chances."

Marcellus nodded his head. He wasn't ready to do any of this, he thought, but he was determined to try nonetheless. Hank led the way, and with urgency, they began the dreaded trip. Already, faintly, Marcellus swore he could hear the song creeping up from the depths.

VIII.

As the white shafts of light pierced through the darkness, Marcellus caught himself thinking of how much the current scene resembled a horror movie. After the first five hundred yards or so, down the ever-descending path through the mine, they picked up the blood trail. It wasn't much, but it was the first real confirmation of Granny's dwindling condition.

Hank hurried his pace, still in the lead of the pair. It was harder going, now cemented into the real world as they were. Marcellus's legs ached, and his head throbbed. This was madness, all of it. How could he ever come to terms with everything that had transpired in the past day?

Distracted, he collided with Hank, who had stopped abruptly.

"Dammit, pay attention! There's something ahead of us; you can hear it." Hank barely shifted from the impact.

"What? Did we catch them?" Marcellus could feel his muscles quaking.

"Calm down. It doesn't sound like it. It's something else." Hank was looking off into the darkness as though he expected to see something but never did.

Marcellus's mind raced. Something else? What else could possibly be down here in the darkness with them? He strained his ears but picked it up faintly. It was neither the song nor the plodding heavy sound of an approaching Voul but instead a sort of moaning, labored sound.

"Fuck." Hank said plainly. "Okay, look, I think I know what it is. I was hoping not to run into any of them. You remember, in Granny's story, she mentioned the subhuman slaves the Voul keep. They are horrible, deformed things, made through some wicked sorcery, out of living, breathing human beings. Though they only resemble us in a way that'll make you sick to your stomach now. Sometimes, they wander into the mine and get lost, I guess. The Voul don't take much care of them; they eat them without provocation. It's hideous. I don't want you to see it. I'm gonna head off and put it out of its misery. Then I'll be right back, and we can get on with this. Just trust me, okay." Hank's look was grim.

"You can't leave me here!" Marcellus said, louder than he intended.

"I'm not leaving. Sounds like it's just up the path a little bit. I'm gonna clear the way; think about it like that, alright." Hank's command of the situation was all that was holding Marcellus together.

"Okay, fine. Just be quick." He fiddled with the amulet hanging from his neck. Would they get the chance to use it to end this once and for all? Marcellus dreaded the thought of parting with it. Placebo or not, it made him feel safe, and safety was something he desperately needed.

Hank crept off into the darkness. Marcellus kept his light trained on the ground and stained his ears to listen to the proceedings as well as he could. There was the noise of a scuffle or possibly something being dragged along the floor. Then silence, and for a moment Marcellus worried for his friend's well-being. The crack of the sidearm going off almost stopped his heart.

After another minute, Hank was back in sight, a strange, dark purple spatter covering parts of his legs.

"You could have told me you were going to shoot the thing. You scared the shit out of me!" Marcellus was still attempting to regain control of his wildly beating heart.

"Did you think I was gonna give it a hug? Get it together. We don't have time for you to get bent out of shape at every turn. Look, I took care of that thing, but, well, it's not entirely out of the way. I could only get it over to one side; they're heavier than they look. We're gonna have to pass fairly close to it; just don't look, okay? It's too much for you, and like I said, we don't have time for you to deal with this. We've gotta save Granny." Hank looked concerned.

"Okay, okay. I just didn't expect it. Whatever. So, what do we have to do?" Marcellus wasn't entirely comfortable being ordered around like this by Hank. How could he be sure that his companion was on the level? Could there be any hope of saving Granny?

"Stay close to me and keep your eyes to the right," said Hank. "It's in a heap on the left side of the tunnel. Just don't look at it, okay?"

What could be worse than what Marcellus had already seen? The Voul? Those vile instruments in the depths that pounded out that debilitating song, somehow made from those unfortunate ones sent down below. In the place where they voluntarily headed now with reckless abandon. What could possibly be worse?

He couldn't even help it. They had gone about a hundred yards when Hank moved over to the far-right side of the tunnel. Marcellus had been keeping his light trained on Hank's back and over his right shoulder, but he hesitated. What could possibly be worse? The question hung in his mind. His head turned, only for a moment, to the ruined mass to the left. Then he screamed. The sound tore through the darkness, and Hank spun around.

He couldn't stop. How could that be something that was just alive a moment ago? Its hideous face twisted up in agony far beyond that suffered from the bullet that ended its existence, its face he recognized somehow. Wasn't he one of the security guards that his great-grandmother had employed for years? One of the people lost when her plane went missing? His mind tried to reel and snapped like a dry twig.

The slap brought his screaming fit to an abrupt end and nearly knocked him unconscious. Hank was holding him by the shoulder and looking directly into his eyes. "C'mon, Marcellus, don't lose it on me now. There's nothing we can do for them, and there's no way back from that. How could there be? We go through with this and end 'em all; that's the best we can do for any of them now. But we can still save Granny, so get it the fuck together. I told you not to look." Hank was not messing around.

His head was spinning. Marcellus tried his best to fight off the rising tide of anger and fear that the physical interaction with the much larger Hank brought up. "Okay, fuck, don't hit me again. I think I recognize him. Or who he was before. Oh God." Marcellus swooned.

"What? How could you ever recognize what that thing came from? That's not possible, man. Look, you're just freaking out. Let's keep going, don't think about it." Hank had moved behind Marcellus and hurried him along the tunnel back into the black depths.

Marcellus relented, not wanting to stay near the deformed remains. Step by step, he forced his legs to comply and moved them further and further down into the abyss. After another hundred yards or so, Hank again took the lead.

They moved with as much speed as Hank could muster, outside of breaking into an all-out run. Invariably, they followed the slight traces of blood that littered the floor, but there was no other way down to the lair. No matter how far they continued to descend, silence always rose up to greet them.

It had been about an hour, as far as Marcellus figured, when he needed to stop. The pace was wearing on him, and his aching muscles required a moment's reprise to recover. Hank had agreed more readily than Marcellus expected and looked dogged and tired himself.

"How much further do you think we've got to go?" Marcellus asked. The question echoed in the gathered darkness, seeming to twist and distort with each repetition.

"Can't be much farther now. You can hear it faintly if you try. Don't try. Remember the trick from before: hum a tune in your head." Hank was recovering faster than Marcellus and looked as though he was about to head out again into the gloom.

"Okay. Shit. I'm still not ready for this." Marcellus paced in a small circle. "Just give me a moment." He tried to steady his breathing. Just find the old woman and get her back out to the entrance. Simple. Then, set the bomb and get the hell out of Dodge. This was it. The time was now.

"Let's get it over with," Marcellus said as he placed a hand on Hank's shoulder. Hank nodded and headed off again.

After fifty paces or so, he could hear it. It was far worse in reality than it had been on the Dreamwalk, the droning blasphemous song of the depths. Marcellus was repulsed and had to take a moment to steady himself. He started humming one of the numerous catholic hymns he remembered from his childhood in his head. The implied divine mollification comforted his ravaged mind.

He hurried his pace lest Hank move out of sight of his headlamp. As far as he could reason, it was another twenty minutes before Hank let up his pace. Marcellus recognized where they were—in the junction room adjacent to the entrance to the lair of the Voul. He swallowed hard and braced himself.

"This is it then; I guess we'll have to head into the lair to get Granny. Just keep to the plan. I'll take as many of them out as I can, then loop back to the entrance to meet you two." Hank's attention was focused on the exit from the junction room that they needed to take.

"Okay. We'll wait for you, then we end this. Good luck." The sentiment seemed foolish to Marcellus. Still, there was something noble about going out fighting against something as vile as the Voul. He was surprised that he so readily accepted this coming doom. Surely, there was no way they would survive.

In silence, they left the junction room. Reaching the rough carved doorway to the lair of the Voul, Marcellus paused. The ground seemed wrong inside the entrance. Although Hank had plowed in indiscriminately, he too seemed to slow his pace at the strange surface. It was, indeed, the same surface that now covered the walls and the low ceiling above them. It all seemed strangely continuous. Strangely organic.

They reached the odd doorway that Marcellus knew held behind it unimaginable horrors. Those vile human instruments that pounded and groaned out the hideous melody were now so close at hand. Marcellus worried he might have a heart attack before everything actually got started.

Hank stood at the doorway, sidearm in hand. "It's been a real pleasure, Marcellus. See you on the other side." And he stepped through into the lands of the Voul.

Marcellus rushed up to the doorway and, without thinking about it, followed right behind Hank. Inside, it was lit with a sick yellow light that fell from the now much higher ceiling. Everything was a reddish-brown color, the floor, walls, and roof all slick with an oily liquid.

Before him stood Hank, stunned for a moment into silence. Before Hank, stooped what remained of Granny, twisted and bloated into one of the subhuman creatures the Voul kept, her same clothes still clinging to her now deformed frame. Behind what Granny had become stood a group of Voul, all oddly chortling or squawking.

With surprising speed, one of the Voul leaped forward toward Granny. With one awful, crashing bite, it tore off the front half of Granny on a gory display. The other Voul hooted in triumph as Hank screamed, the cacophony nearly maddening to Marcellus.

He turned from the scene and staggered off. The world spun. In the back of his mind, he could hear more screaming and the thunderous crack of Hank's firearm going off. He struggled to keep his consciousness.

Breathing deeply, Marcellus tried to steady himself. He placed his hand, absentmindedly, onto a nearby shelf. As his mind began to recover, perhaps through some primitive motivation to survive, he looked up and saw what it was he was now braced against. It was one of the strange, oddly slick daises that held the hideous instruments of the Voul. And there, close enough to touch, in the odd yellow light, was the thing that had once been several human beings, the hideous amalgam that now throbbed and pulsed out the mountain song. He was revolted but couldn't turn away somehow, his mind eroding with each passing moment. Was that an eye? As if in response, it snapped open, revealing an eye he had known in life, his great-grandmother's. In a terrible way, the abomination seemed to call out to react to Marcellus's presence. It was, somehow, still alive.

Marcellus's mind ceased to function and he screamed wildly. On instinct alone, he raced back out the way he had come, his deep-seated need to survive overriding all other impulses. He glanced toward where Hank had headed before he ducked back out the doorway. More Voul now rushed toward the clamorous, violent altercation.

As he ran with all the speed he could muster through the hallway leading out of the lair of the Voul, Marcellus began to notice that the walls and floor seemed to be more flesh than stone and that they were actively moving, contracting back toward the source. He clawed with everything he could in a mad dash to escape and only narrowly made it through the entrance as it closed around him. Marcellus rushed to his feet and made his way into the room connecting to the junction.

Entirely in the grip of madness, he ran. Up the tunnel, through the darkness, the pain in his legs and chest unnoticed by his conscious mind, he ran. Time meant nothing to him, and eventually he could see the faint light of day coming from a distance ahead of him. Could that much time really have passed?

Into the early dawn, he continued out through the forest, not relenting in his pace. Marcellus quickly made his way back to the edge of Hank's yard, but he did not for even a moment, stop. Instead, he made with all the speed he could muster toward his car, still parked in Hank's driveway. Inside the safety of his car, he simply drove off. Never looking back and never hesitating, Marcellus fled as fast and as far as he could. His mind was blank, save for the pressing, primitive need to run.

It was days before his conscious mind again rose to the front of his ravaged psyche. By then, he was deep into the American Midwest, safe amidst the flat plains that harbored no mountains. This was nothing of what he had ever wanted, but now, strange currents drove his decision-making, not the least of which were unnameable fears of things hidden deep below the surface of the world.

Into anonymity Marcellus dove, changing his name and trying his best to forget all he had been before. It was an easy enough fix and would save Marcellus's life, at least physically. He would never again paint and went to great lengths to avoid traveling through mountainous areas, but he would otherwise lay claim to an ordinary life in time. For all intents and purposes, Marcellus Emil Ott never made it out from beneath that dreaded mountain. What remained now was a shell of what he had been before, and he faded into the background of the world around him, happy enough that he had at least managed to survive.

At night, when the sky was immense, he could still faintly hear the mountain song droning out from the depths of the earth. When he closed his eyes, he could still see the deformed body of Granny being bitten in half by a Voul. A part of him worried that he would never be able to stop running.

Epilogue

Plumes of black smoke rose into the sky above Cobbled Hills. All about the town, sleek black sedans sat parked as the buildings burned. Men and women, dressed professionally in dark colors (agents of The Primal Bureaucracy), were piling bodies near the center of town, out in front of the cathedral. About half of the remains were of Voul. All were being burned in front of the only building that remained defiant against the razing. Silent and imposingly cold against the apocalyptic backdrop, the great black cathedral only reflected the light of the inferno.

Outside of the Black Pines Inn, several important-looking men stood watching the blaze as it engulfed the second floor of the inn with a vigorous swell of bright orange flame. Others were routinely coming up to them to deliver reports and snippets of information.

"So, do you think it's over?" The taller of the pair asked as he took a long drag from a cigarette.

"There isn't enough smoke in the air for you?" The stockier one replied as he made a show of adjusting his glasses and glaring at his companion.

"Obviously not, at least not of the right variety." The taller agent gave a wide, toothy grin. "Besides, my vices aren't the topic du jour. I want to know what you think. Do you think this is over?"

"It depends on what you mean by *over*, I suppose. Will you and I ever have to clean up another Voul infestation? Probably. Will we definitively eradicate The One Below The Stone, here and now? Probably not. Does this set things back for them several hundred years? Likely. I don't know what you expect me to say. This is the ending Command wanted. That's good enough for me." The smaller agent shuffled several detailed reports into a briefcase.

From behind a nearby sedan, Leann emerged. She was dressed much as the other agents were and made her way over to the two in charge directly.

"Arturo here says you did a good job, Agent Jefferies. Things have all gone according to plan." The taller agent spoke directly to Leann.

"It's Agent In Command Nunez to the both of you, Agent Creel." The stocky agent interrupted, adding the last part with specific emphasis.

"Fine, fine, be a hard ass. Everybody loves that about you." Agent Creel chuckled, continuing to occupy himself with his cigarette.

"Thank you, sirs. I just did what I was instructed." Leann looked uncomfortable and kept glancing at the pile of corpses being amassed in the town center. "Have there been any reports from below the mountain?"

"It is a bit above your clearance level." Arturo Nunez looked up from his paperwork for the first time, making direct eye contact with Leann for a moment. "But I can understand you're invested. What is it, twenty-six months now?" He produced a further report from his briefcase. "As you can see, extermination teams are hard at work removing the self-proclaimed 'deity' below the mountain. The process should be complete within the day. The local Voul are ninety-eight percent neutralized."

Leann read over the report as quickly as she could. "There isn't anything in here on what we've recovered from inside the thing. Did they find Hank?" The question seemed to hang in the air.

"It is unhealthy to get attached to targets, Angela." Agent Creel spun around in an instant and was standing, towering, over Leann.

The use of her real first name seemed to strike a nerve. "Of course it is, Agent Creel. Do you think I'm some wet-behind-the-ears rookie?! After everything I've done for this case!" She was furious.

"Calm down, Agent Jeffries." AIC Nunez was calm and direct. "Don't let our friend Creel here get under your skin. It has been a while since you've been undercover. Some level of concern on our part should have been expected."

"There is nothing to be concerned about, sir. My question was academic, so to speak. I was looking to see if they had recovered the amulet, which I assume was on the person of Henry 'Hank' Worthy. I understand your concern—and Command's—but I assure you, there is no personal connection between myself and the target." Angela let out an audible sigh. It would take some time to get used to being herself again.

"He wasn't the target. The painter was." Creel glared at Angela.

"Excuse me, sir. Did Marcellus survive?" The part of Leann that was still near the surface of Angela smiled despite herself.

"Yes, of course, he survived. He's wearing the amulet you seem so keenly interested in. It's probably more accurate to say the Stone of Hy'anakc is wearing him now. Isn't that right, Agent Jefferies? The thing is essentially alive if I understand the reports correctly." Creel smiled his characteristic and unnerving smile, a cloud of smoke seeping out through his teeth. "And that's just how Command wanted it. Or did you not get told that part when you came calling for someone to save you."

"That's enough, Creel. Agent Jefferies has performed her duties admirably. She isn't under any suspicion of wrongdoing. Besides, you're just bored and looking for something to do. There are other things we can arrange to occupy you." AIC Nunez might not have looked the part, but he was entirely in command of the proceedings regardless.

"As you wish, AIC Nunez," Creel said as he headed off toward the bonfire in the middle of what remained of Cobbled Hills. He never took his eyes off of Angela Jefferies, and she did not shrink from his gaze.

"Pay him no mind," Nunez said after Creel had gotten out of earshot. He moved closer to Angela and spoke in barely a whisper. "There was one other thing, Agent Jefferies. They found a coat inside of the creature during the initial assault. Large pocket, denim with patches. It matches the description of Hank that we have from your reports. I wouldn't hold out any hope." Nunez nodded sagely to Angela.

"Thank you for letting me know, sir." Angela managed to squeak out while still maintaining her composure. So it was really over then. Hank was gone. And Marcellus was now the hollow vessel of an ancient artifact—his life over as surely as Hank's.

There would be other cases; other work to get her mind off of this terrible end, but it was going to take time. At least they had managed to wipe that place, Cobbled Hills, off the map. If nothing else, she could sleep well tonight, knowing that.

Ancient Memory

I.

In order to understand everything else, I have to tell you something I'd rather not. It has already taken me too long to get to this, but you must understand it is hard to reckon with your own demise. I suppose there is at least some solace in being able to make this record, and what must be done must begin somewhere.

As a child, I ran with a pack. We were human, just like you, with dark tan skin and predominately black hair. I say that we were a pack, but perhaps the term tribe is more appropriate. There were some two dozen of us, comprised of members of five families. There were ten similar tribes that we knew of in the region we collectively referred to as The Wildlands.

Each year, we would follow the migrations of abundant grazing animals amidst the wooded plains and temperate forests of The Wildlands. Though we were never without competition from the predatory large cats and canines that also made their homes in the area, there was bounty enough for all. We did always take care to stay away from the rarer prides of large cats, as they seemed particularly intelligent and were known to hunt for purposes beyond simple sustenance. There were even rumors that an encounter with such a pride of cats had caused the disappearance of the twelfth tribe—those who had vanished five summers past, but such a tale was nothing more than common gossip. Or so we thought back then.

Every year, in early autumn, the tribes gathered at the great mountain that marked the southern border of the Wildlands. Here, we celebrated and shared stories and supplies so that all would survive the brief but typically brutal winters that were common in our time.

At the great gathering that occurred in my fifteenth year, everything changed—the months leading up to that particular great gathering had been difficult for my family. In the spring, my only living sister had been taken by restless sleep and a glut of prophetic dreaming. Though our people commonly took little stock of such things, unlike our kin from the deserts south of the mountain, my sister's change was hard to ignore. Gaunt and wild-eyed, she would toss absurd accusations at others in the tribe. The final push came from her glee at being right after foretelling the death of one of our hunters in the early summer. By the time of the gathering, my parents were clearly concerned both for their daughter's well-being, as well as for our continued prospects of living with the tribe. There were rumblings that perhaps everyone would be better off if my sister were simply no more.

Then the unbelievable happened. The missing tribe, the Akkamu, re-turned to us—beaten, but not lost. Though they had been gone for five years, they provided little explanation outside of the repeated refrain of having followed prey deep into the northern forests and becoming hope-lessly lost. They had suffered significant losses, having only three mostly intact families among their number. All of the others were lost to a nebu-lous "predator from the north," that was only ever glimpsed but deeply feared by the survivors. And though no one openly doubted the trauma of those survivors, a strange air hung about the Akkamu. Only my sis-ter seemed unaffected by their presence, confiding in me that she had dreamed of their return some nights prior but had kept quiet due to the scorn we were being treated with. Whether I believed her or not at the time, I cannot say, but it was clear that something momentous was upon us.

As the great gathering began to draw to a close, our family's fate was decided. It was not uncommon among the tribes for individual families to move from one group to another. Often, if a tribe suffered significant losses, through illness or accident perhaps, other tribes would contribute a family from among their number to the less fortunate tribe. This was done primarily to maintain sufficient numbers of hunters so that all of our nomadic groups could survive.

It was no shock when it was announced that our family would be going to join the Akkamu. Strangely, no other families from other tribes were likewise offered, as would have been expected. Our new Akkamu neighbors were nothing if not observant and attributed the lack of aid as a testament to the strange attitude the others had taken toward them since their return. The Akkamu understood that my sister did not share that revulsion and welcomed us with open arms despite full knowledge of her peculiarities.

Leaving the gathering, we headed east, something our old tribe had never done, to a winter camp in the low hills. That winter was particularly cold and, tragically, claimed both of my parents through disease. By then, however, I had grown to become a much-needed hunter to help the beleaguered hunting troop of the Akkamu, and every member of the tribe was there to support us.

As spring came on, we made further east and began to encounter a strange new species of deer. Thinner and smaller than the elk and caribou we typically sought, they were also slower and exceedingly easier to hunt, being remarkably timid and docile. I had never seen these strange deer before, but they were known to my fellow hunters, and, in fact, they had been searching for them for many seasons.

After pressing the issue later, on the evening of my first kill of the strange deer the Akkamu called Iliti, our tribe elder admitted that it was indeed the hunting and tracking of the Iliti that had first led the Akkamu into the deep forests of the north. I was initially incensed that we had been kept in the dark about the Iliti. Still, my sister calmed me; she had become my most beloved companion and the only other human being I truly trusted.

Though I had reservations, the bounty of the Iliti was hard to deny. Simple to track and nearly effortless to kill, a single Iliti held enough meat to feed the tribe for several days. Further, though I remember thinking it strange, none of the other predators hunted or followed them. Even the dreaded big cats, who were never known to pass up an easy meal, stayed far away from the grazing packs of Iliti. These factors made the decision to hunt the Iliti exclusively a simple one, especially with the limited numbers of the Akkamu.

For three years, we roamed the eastern hills and hunted the Iliti. My sister and I became fully Akkamu, though I had declined a wife in deference to her care. Now the eccentric, mildly crazy soothsayer of the Akkamu, my sister was treated with almost spiritual deference by our new tribe. Still, for a good bit of time, everything was happy and peaceful.

Then, in the spring of my eighteenth year, the Iliti began to move farther east than ever before. After a month, it was clear we would have to make a decision regarding whether or not to continue hunting our strange quarry. On their current course, the Iliti would soon take us too far away to reasonably be able to return to the southern mountain and the great gathering of our people. The far eastern lands, past the swamps that rose up on the borders of the Wildlands, were virtually unknown, and terrible rumors and legends crept from their shores.

In the end, a vote was held, and it was decided that we would pursue the Iliti but that any families that did not want to go east would be outfitted as such that they could return alone to the great gathering and seek lodging with the other tribes. I expected to leave for the gathering, but my sister insisted we stay with the Akkamu. She had seen a great future for us with the Akkamu in the east, or so I was told.

If I am being honest, I must admit that I considered abandoning my sister to the Akkamu then, so great was my fear of the lands beyond the swamps. To this very day, I sometimes wish I would have listened to the sinking feeling of dread that was beginning to permeate my being. I stayed because she begged me to, because she would have died without me, but most of all, because she was all that I had.

II.

The trip eastward was quicker than expected. The Iliti knew paths and trails through the swamps that made travel much easier. They seemed almost as though they were being driven, and the Iliti began to move with a speed we had never before seen.

In two months, we reached the far eastern edge of the swamps, a distance that we had estimated would take us twice as long. As we reached the grasslands sprawling out from the swamp's edge, we saw what drove the Iliti. They were going home.

It is hard to express its majesty; great green fields stretching to every inch of a horizon that had never seemed so immense. And Iliti, countless packs of them, were spread out as far as the eye could see. It was as though we had stumbled through some dream and found ourselves now in a strange alien land. We were collectively struck half dumb by the sheer bounty of it all. In short order, we set up a temporary camp a few miles east of the swamps.

On the second night at our temporary camp in the grasslands, there was a sense of peace among the Akkamu they had never before displayed. It was decided that some final secrets needed to be revealed to my sister and me. I will never forget the look on the elder's face when my sister abruptly interrupted the proceedings with, "Don't you see yet, Brother! They have been looking for this place all along!" I was shocked, but the elder confirmed as much, telling me that while the Akkamu were deep in the Seven-Sided Forest of the north, they encountered a large stone carving that clearly depicted a colossal congregation of Iliti in some distant land. There were several among the tribe that even believed the Iliti themselves had led the Akkamu to the stone carving. Ever since finding the carving, and at a terrible cost, the Akkamu had searched for the resting place of the Iliti. When they were finally found three years later, it was decided they would simply wait and see if the Iliti would perhaps lead them again where they sought to go. Now it had born fruit, and the legendary land had finally been found. By the end of the night, we had decided on our next course of action: we would scout for a location for a permanent camp.

The following day, Triton, Bora (two of our other hunters and my close friends), and I volunteered to scout the surrounding area. In particular, we would look to the east, where the congregation of Iliti seemed the greatest. We were to head out for one month's time, as best we could manage, while the remaining tribe stayed at the temporary camp.

For the first week, our scouting trip was remarkably uneventful. For days on end, we marched across low rolling hills and grasslands, constantly accompanied by the grazing packs of Iliti. It was always the same, and at times, we had trouble maintaining our proper bearing. Then, on the advent of our second week away from the temporary camp, we came to a tremendous imposing river.

The river was wide and moved steadily up from the south, though it did not seem terribly deep or fast. About a half mile north of where we initially came upon the river, we found a suitable spot to cross, not only for us but also, hopefully, for the entire tribe if and when the time came. The water was cold and we greedily drank of it. Clean water had been the hardest thing to locate since we moved east of the swamps.

On the far shore of the river, we decided to follow a minor tributary stream that branched off and came up from the southeast. For days, we followed the small creek, marveling as it cut and darted about the landscape. Eventually, after heading steadily downhill for more than a day, we came to a great basin next to a stark white cliffside. It looked as though the ground had simply erupted at one point, creating a sheltered basin in its shadow. What was most telling about it was its strange color. The oddly colored stone that comprised its bulk was white, almost as if it was snow, and its surface was porous. It was not terribly strong stone and crumbled with little effort into a sort of white sand. Indeed, the sand was all about the basin, making small islands amidst the spider web of the fracturing creek and forming a great beach where the creek brushed up to the white cliff before turning sharply south and continuing away.

More interesting to Bora and me, however, were the strange qualities the sand seemed to possess after coming in contact with the water. In places where the stream-wet, sandy mud had managed to dry (primarily the tiny islands), it had become hard and firm. Enough so that it was not possible to break or alter its surface, even with sticks or tools. Triton, elder to both Bora and myself, reasoned that the mountain must also be hardened underneath, hence its ability to stand and not crumble under its own weight. With some simple experimentation, we were able to recreate the hardening effect on the sand. We all agreed that it would be possible to construct homes from this hardened sand that would suit our people well.

We then moved our exploration onto the nearby cliffside. Steep and gashed with large cracks, there were a myriad of small caves at its base and various places along its face. The south-facing side was far less steep, more of a large hill than the cliffside of its opposite. Near the top of the cliff, we found a relatively narrow path that led to a small but secure and unoccupied cave where we made camp.

Over the remaining course of the week, we used the cliffside cave as a staging point to scout the surrounding area. From the start, we were all strongly inclined to recommend this area as a future site for our people's village. The week's worth of local exploring exposed nothing that drew our concern. At the week's end, we convened in our cave headquarters to decide our course. We all agreed on the suitability of the location as a future site for our village, and in the morning, we set back out toward our temporary camp and the waiting tribe.

Our return trip was slowed, in part because we took the time to mark trails and ensure we would be able to find our way back, and also because Bora sprained an ankle crossing the creek and needed to nurse his injured foot on the trip home. Still, we made the journey more or less without incident and were glad to be back among our tribe almost exactly one month after we had initially left.

The tribe was delighted to hear that we had found a suitable location, and we all quickly set about gathering up our supplies and tearing down the temporary camp. My sister remarked in private that she was excited to see if the great white cliff would be as striking in person as it had been in her dreams. For my part, I, too, was excited as to our future prospects, though at the time, I had no way of knowing how momentous a thought that truly was.

III.

Once our entire tribe arrived in the basin, the little doubts there were as to our path were laid to rest. We were now several miles east of the large river, and, as we had hoped, the crossing was a trivial matter. Here in the basin beneath the cliff, the tributary creek carved the land up into a series of small islands, each separated from the others by small freshwater creeks rimmed with the white sand of the area. The cliff, which stood to the southeast of what would become our village, was starkly white and seemed almost to shine in the light of day. Several of the deep caves that seemed to dive below the base of the cliff elicited shock and fear from the older members of the tribe. We made a note to ensure again that these were not the dens of any particularly nasty local wildlife. The eldest of the tribe seemed especially worried about the potential of some unseen force allayed against us.

I remember thinking often of the trauma the Akkamu must have endured during their time in the north. They weren't dishonest but regularly neglected to inform us of little details from the past that always seemed to play on the minds of those in the present, for one, and not the least among them, that a calm place to settle among the Iliti was not novel to them. That it had ended in disaster was always known, but there was also always the sense of something unspoken among those who had survived the ordeal in the north.

I pressed on, and in short order, we converted each of the basin's islands into suitable habitats for our families. The abundant white sand formed surprisingly strong walls when mixed with some of the local soil and water and allowed to dry. This hardened sand mixture was strong enough that several huts with two floors had been constructed.

Our explorations of the caves at the base of the cliff had found no evidence of any residents, living or otherwise. Deep and surprisingly cold compared to the surrounding temperatures, the caves seemed to be nothing more than cracks leading deep into the earth below us.

With our homes built and our safety intact, we settled into a happy new life. The Iliti were everywhere, and we did not want for sustenance. Indeed, the woods to the west, between us and the river, had provided several sources of nuts, berries, and other wild plants, as well as a much-needed source of wood for construction and heat, though the latter was becoming less and less of a concern with each passing day.

By autumn, we had filled our storerooms with more than enough to survive the winter, and little mention was made of the great gathering, now far to the west. Again, it was my sister whose voice lamented that this would have been her last chance to attend. I thought it strange only that we gave no thought to enlighten our brothers and sisters among the other tribes as to the boundless bounty we had found. By then, I had become accustomed to the doom my sister always foretold. That one last time, I wish I had listened to her.

When winter came, so too came another surprise. Simply put, the winter never came. Even in the night, temperatures never became so cold that we needed a fire. It seemed that winter stopped at the river, though nothing of the sort had ever been seen or heard of. The woods between us and the river were indeed colder, and snow could be glimpsed along the river's far bank. But in the village, it remained warm, seemingly still in summer. One of the elders remarked that it almost seemed as though the cliff was drinking up the cold. Regardless of the cause, it was the mildest and warmest winter that any of us had ever known.

The following spring brought several new construction projects. As the herds of Iliti migrated about the grasslands, our village fell in the path of a stampede. We were never able to determine what had spooked the Iliti, and no one was injured, but significant damage was done to several huts. As a result, it was decided that a wall would be built around the village, made of the same white sand concrete we used in our homes. Additionally, in part at the urging of my sister, a watchtower was to be built on the central island, tall enough to view any approaching trouble from outside the wall.

The Iliti were so abundant and easily trapped that it was possible to feed the entire village with the work of a single hunter. So it was that we freed up a newfound workforce to get to our village's improvement. By the end of summer that season, the wall was completed, and two stories of the tower had been erected.

Though we all claimed ignorance, a strange new quality had begun to occur in relation to the Iliti. Namely, a single hunter could not manage to hunt them exclusively for overly long. Extended contact with the Iliti had been observed to cause derangement and madness to varying degrees, though those affected always recovered with some time spent away from the strange deer. Still, most of us were hunters, at least to some extent, and it was easy enough to justify the rotating hunting schedule as everyone doing their part for the tribe. No one wished to talk about what happened to a person's mind after repeatedly encountering the Iliti in the wild.

The facade held, though, and by the fall of that year, our watchtower was complete. At four stories, it provided a beacon, both to see out and to be seen from great distances. It would come to be more in time, but at its onset, it was a symbol of everything we had accomplished.

As another mild winter began to roll in, potential disaster struck. The tributaries and creeks that fed into our village practically dried up. While it was shallow and narrow, the tributary was particularly long, stretching some one hundred miles southwesterly to where it originally branched from the main river. It was believed that something must have plugged the creek, either along its path or at its other terminal end, one hundred miles away. Bora, Triton, and I were chosen to travel along the tributary to locate and potentially dislodge whatever had blocked the water supply.

I was eager for the chance, having just finished my most recent stint as the active Iliti hunter, but the others were less optimistic. Fear had crept into their perceptions, and it was clear that there was a sense of the Akkamu having been here before. However, such an idea was nonsense. As we made preparations to leave, my sister was sullen. She would say nothing more than "Beware the stars with eyes," over and over as if it was the refrain of some twisted nursery rhyme.

We left the following morning, heading along the course of the tributary creek. We had planned to move slowly along the creek and hopefully reach the river in seven or eight days. On the evening of the first night, we made camp roughly fifteen miles from the village on a slight rise we had once used as a staging area for a hunt. That was during the early days in the basin when we still took preparations as though hunting traditional game. The location provided an ample view of the basin and our village, which was far in the distance. We were all taken aback by the sight of all that had been accomplished in so short a time.

It was three days later, moving at a similar pace, when we ran out of our standard provisions. We had intentionally packed lighter food so that we could bring along tools, two large spades, and two picks. The general abundance of the Iliti had made us complacent, and we had assumed hunting additional game would be a simple matter. We spent the fifth day hunting a small area around our camp to no avail; there simply weren't any Iliti anywhere to be found. Bora managed to find a suitable cache of berries that sustained us for the night.

A strange thing happened on that fifth night. As we discussed our shared difficulties hunting during the day, we happened upon something we all agreed should have been noticed before. There were no other living things, birds, other game animals, predators, or insects anywhere around us. Further, this was not an isolated incident, as none of us could recall seeing any of those beasts since we entered the grasslands over a year past. How such a revelation could have slipped our collective notice as a whole group seemed to me particularly fraught with nefarious implications.

I decided then and there that I needed to finally press the issue of what was being silently kept from my sister and me. I trusted Bora and Triton more than any of the other Akkamu, and here, away from the village, I expected answers. In light of everything that had transpired that day, Triton and Bora agreed.

What they told me I mostly already knew, save for two particularly salient points.

The first was that there was far more information about the Iliti among the carvings depicting the huge pack we had discovered on the grasslands. Much of the information had been kept from both Bora and Triton, as they had been young when the carvings were found. What was known was that the Iliti were not of our world, though how they came here was not clear, even to the elders who had spent the most time pouring over the carvings. Additionally, it was believed that only by following a pack of Iliti could one enter or leave the place where the giant packs roamed.

While this information was shocking to me, it was the second tale that chilled my soul to its core. The Akkamu had encountered an entire civilization in the now dreaded Seven-Sided Forest of the north. These people, whom the Akkamu simply called the Tree-folk, had lived in the forest since time immemorial. They knew of the Iliti and had witnessed their coming to our world in a time almost lost to memory. However, the Tree-folk cautioned the Akkamu against pursuing the Iliti. Ancient Tree-folk legends told of a terrible predator that haunted the shadow of the Iliti. It was believed that this predator alone kept life from the path of the Iliti to ensure the safety of its favored prey.

The elders of the Akkamu had ignored the warning of the Tree-folk, and when the pack of Iliti that had led the Akkamu north had been finally found, the elders ordered them slaughtered. At the time, they believed this would keep any nebulous predator off their path and suitably intimidated. It accomplished neither.

After the hunt, the Akkamu returned to the home of the Tree-folk, hoping to share their bounty and dispel the myths around the Iliti. When they arrived at the main Tree-folk encampment, they found that the Tree-folk were no more. They had not left but had been culled to a man. Many of the discovered remains looked to have been bitten in half, while others were flayed apart with horrible deep cuts. The sight nearly caused a panic among the Akkamu, and they retreated, putting the scene behind them as fast as possible.

Then, the killings began. The mystery predator that the Tree-folk had called Laathix eliminated the Akkamu, one every day, whose body would be found displayed for the others. For the following two weeks, the Laathix hunted them, then abruptly stopped. Both Bora and Triton were confident that this sudden change in behavior was all that had kept the survivors alive. Lost and severely beaten, the survivors worked their way south and left the forest, eventually making their way back to the great gathering.

Hearing the tale almost broke me. I was incensed at the idea that such a viable threat to our people was simply being ignored. More so, I feared for the others back in the village, now sitting in what no longer looked to be a safe haven.

Too many questions now crowded my mind. How could we protect the village from the Laathix? Was it already a threat? Was it hunting our scouting party? And on and on, my mind reeled. By then, it was incredibly late, and we decided to bed down. However, for the first time, we agreed to sleep in shifts, leaving someone always on watch. It would not be the final time.

To my surprise, we all managed a decent night's sleep. I had taken the last shift of lookout and watched the dawn break on the eastern horizon from a nearby tree. Try as I might, I could not reconcile everything I had learned the night before. Still, our immediate concerns were more pressing. We would need food, and the creek was required to keep the village running. Either of which would undoubtedly be more deadly than some mystery predator. The dread of my companions had been palpable the night before, recounting their shared horrors. I could not doubt they believed every bit of what was said.

Once we had all risen, our new plan took root. Two of us, Triton and I, would hunt a west-by-southwest arc, leaving and then returning to the tributary creek a half-day walk upstream. Bora would continue upstream, albeit at a reduced pace, to maintain our original mission. We parted ways shortly thereafter in hopes of managing our immediate problems by nightfall.

The woods of the westerly arc we moved along were denser than any we had encountered before. The eerily silent underbrush accentuated the unnatural state we found ourselves in. Then, as if in response to our ever-growing unease, an Iliti appeared some fifty yards away with its back turned from our approach.

Turned as though it was grazing on the forest floor; something about the Iliti's movements seemed strange. We moved in for the kill, Triton around to the Iliti's flank with pick raised, I with one of the large spades from behind.

The Iliti reared its head up to my compatriot, who screamed in shock. The beast's skull was opened up like a flower, with several bright orange tendrils stretching out from the wound. And were those eyes? Instinct took over, and I swung the spade true to the base of the Iliti's neck, nearly severing it. A terrible gout of black blood erupted from the wound, its smell instantaneously overwhelming, foul, and repellent. I gagged and staggered to the side while the body of the Iliti thrashed away. I could hear Triton coming up behind my position. I tried to gain my composure, but the world swooned around me, and I staggered forward and vomited.

The odor of the blood seemed to have less effect on my companion, who was upon me a moment later. Triton pulled me away from the foulness of the dying Iliti.

Clear air brought me back to reality. Though we spoke little and were both still in shock, Triton and I agreed we needed to be sure the Iliti was, in fact, dead.

The Iliti had fallen about twenty yards from us and seemed dead and motionless. As we came ever closer, a sound could be heard—a terrible squelching, cracking sound.

As we reached the body, I had to struggle to keep from vomiting again. Out of the wound in the Iliti's neck, a sizeable starfish-like thing was attempting to extricate itself from the corpse. One of its arms, the one most out of the neck, was terribly wounded.

Here, Triton saved us both. While I stood dumbfounded, struggling to breathe, Triton drove his pick into the starfish-thing again and again. No gouts of foul blood erupted, but it seemed in a terrible way rather to scream, perhaps even to beg for its life. Regardless, my companion reduced the thing to a pulp in short order and turned quickly to me.

He told me that we would need to gather wood to burn the thing he now referred to as "the abomination." And he would hear nothing in contest to it. I complied, still half in a daze, and in a short time, we had raised a sufficient blaze.

I remember watching the predominantly black smoke rise from the fire after we had thrown the starfish abomination in. I remember saying something foolish in my daze and pining about what that thing was. I had not expected an answer.

I was only casually aware that I had even said anything out loud, but an answer I had received. They had encountered things like the starfish abominations in the north. Giant sea creatures that also lived on land and were known to lay eggs deep inside other living things. He spat then and called the thing a parasite with as much venom as I had ever heard from him.

We waited for the starfish abomination to burn away, but we did not wait long. Something in its foul blood accelerated the flames, and there was little more than ash left in under an hour.

After a brief reprieve, we made our way back east to meet Bora at the creek. Surprisingly, given everything we had endured, we were on time, but we were returning empty-handed.

Once we had made it back to the creek, Bora's camp was easy enough to find. To our great relief, Bora was safe and had even been fortunate enough to find some fruit along his path, so we were not wholly without food.

As we ate, Triton wasted no time in telling Bora all that had transpired. Triton then referred to an immense sea to the north when describing the starfish abomination to Bora. I thought it almost comical that there was still more unspoken about those dark days.

With the starfish abomination dead, we decided it would be safe to continue, though we unanimously agreed to continue a lookout at night. At this point, we believed ourselves likely near the main river. Having our mission to focus on kept more than a little of the darkness at bay.

All of us were up with the dawn, and we quickly finished off what food remained and went back to our task. A new haste quickened our steps and we made along much quicker than before. By midday, the sound of the main river could be heard in the distance.

It was late afternoon when we finally reached the bank of the main river. There, we found what we had sought, but the sight was almost too much for me to bear. An immense fish, far bigger than anything I had ever imagined, clogged the mouth of the creek. It was clearly dead, missing what looked to be a significant portion of its front half. Strangely, there was no smell of death or rot in the air.

More concerning to me, however, were the five starfish abominations that were attached to the gigantic corpse. My companions seemed almost grimly to have expected something like this and were calmly observing the beasts when I asked what we would do. They knew of a way to fight the things, namely with fire. We would make torches, though we needed to work quickly. The poison cloud the starfish abominations possessed was just as explosive as their blood, or so I was told, and it was widely accepted that the things would not emit that defensive measure in the face of mutual annihilation. Then, it would be a simple matter of pulverizing the abominations and burning the remains.

Here, Triton stopped us and instructed us further that he knew of a means of preventing the starfish abominations and other creatures like them from detecting us. The means, however, was fairly grim and required harvesting an organ from the starfish that was located at the base of one of the arms. While I was aghast at the prospect of needing to dissect one of the things, Bora and Triton both agreed it would be for the best, and so it was planned that the last living starfish abomination would be killed carefully so as to prevent overly damaging it.

We were fortunate that the area of the creek near the main river was moderately wooded, and fuel for our fire was abundant. I struggled momentarily with the flint as our commotion began to arouse suspicion among the abominations, but managed to collect myself enough to spark the flame. We bound sticks with strips of leather culled from two of our packs and, in a remarkably short time, had fashioned three large torches, though they would not burn for long.

I could barely form rational thought as we stepped from the overgrown hedgerow, torches in hand. To my shock and horror, the starfish abominations, whose central body parts indeed gave rise to two long orange eyestalks, clearly recognized the threat we posed. Ever more revulsion grabbed me as they made to flee from our advance.

Clearly terrified by the fire, the creatures were as slow and physically inept on land as Triton had promised. As we fell upon them, I remember wondering why I was even participating in this mindless slaughter. The things ran and knew horror; they screamed in their own terrible way, and indeed, the last one momentarily begged for its life before being gutted by the knife our eldest companion Triton always carried on his person.

Using the torches, we burned the starfish abominations where they fell, save for the last. That one Triton carved up, extricating several black orbs from the sickly-looking body section. Then that one, too, was tossed onto one of the blazes already burning.

As we moved back to the cover of the woods nearby, we watched as a towering pillar of smoke rose from the carcasses. For three hours, we waited as the fire roared, eventually consuming all of the remains. Two of the starfish had fallen while still on the corpse of the enormous fish and the resulting blaze had burned away a decent portion of its remaining mass. We were then able to shove a portion of the tail of the beast back into the main flow of the river proper. This was enough to pull the corpse into the greater flow of the river and free the water flow to the creek.

While we were indeed happy to have completed our task, I was deeply affected by the battle, such as it was. Triton and Bora both did their best to put me at ease, claiming what we did was little more than pest control. The things I witnessed were attributed to the strange effect the smell of the creatures has on living things unaccustomed to their presence. I was about to ask how they had gained such customization when our conversation was abruptly interrupted.

The sky to the north was split open as a massive purple comet streaked toward the ground. Moments later, a tremendous crash was both heard and felt where we stood, transfixed in the purple-pink afterglow.

IV.

We all had the same thoughts about the safety of the village and our families. Quickly, we set off back along the creek toward the village, though it was already quite late in the day. We stopped for camp when it became too dark to travel. All our talk then was of concern for those at the village. None of us would get much rest that evening.

For the next three days, we traveled in near silence. We were still without much food but gathered enough as we went to keep from starving. A greater force than our stomachs moved our feet then, as an eerie purple glow persisted in the north and began to color the world around us.

On the morning of the fourth day, we reached the staging camp we had used on our first night out from the village. Our great central watchtower could still be seen, though the purple glow was now perilously close as well.

On the last hillock overlooking the village, still several hundred yards from the outer wall, we stopped to survey our approach. The village seemed strangely empty, and we wondered if perhaps our people had sought shelter in the caves at the base of the cliff. Bora was sent to investigate the caves while we kept our vigil—on high alert in the strange purple light.

Bora left us then and traveled back along the hill toward the creek and the southern side of the village. We watched in silence as he forded the creek. There, at the southern edge of the village, we noticed something we had not seen before. Our remaining building supplies, as well as what looked to be the ruins of one of the huts, were crudely damming up the creek. Though mostly ineffective since the return of the waters, it nonetheless caused a significant build-up of water along the southern wall.

Bora signaled us then, alerting us to the makeshift dam, and continued across the creek. Shortly, he was on the beach and then off into the caves at the base of the cliff.

It seemed then that time passed excruciatingly slowly as we waited for a sign of Bora emerging from the caves. The village remained silent and empty, but there was something else. It did not look abandoned in spite of the notable lack of living occupants. The Iliti were gone here, as they had been while we ventured to fix the creek. Even at a great distance, from an elevated perch, there was no sign of the Iliti anywhere in the basin. This was remarkable and unique in our time there, and it carried with it a sinister dread that seemed to seep down from the clouds.

I was about to say something about my rising dread when Triton spotted Bora emerging from the caves. He moved with no added haste or urgency, and we both remarked that there must not have been anything in the caves.

As Bora reached the creek again and began to cross, we noticed the movement. We had missed the emergence of five of our tribesmen from the central watchtower. They all moved strangely, as if having forgotten how to use their legs properly, and their eyes showed a bright purple glow, not unlike that which was in the sky. Triton signaled to Bora, but he was distracted by the added difficulty of crossing the overflowing creek and was not looking to our perch on the hill.

It was clear that the tribesmen moved toward Bora. Again, we tried to raise the alarm. Even shouting seemed not to attract Bora's attention, and though they moved wrongly, the tribesmen were horrifyingly fast. In another moment, they were at, and then over, the makeshift dam.

Bora saw them then, knee-deep in mud and grime from the creek. At first, it seemed he did not understand the danger he was in. It occurred to me then that it was perhaps strange that I was so sure he was in danger. Our fears were momentarily waylaid when the first of the affected tribesmen to reach Bora was met with his fists. The tribesman wailed and fell back strangely as Bora rushed past him toward the bank of the creek.

Bora gained the bank but was not able to make it far before the tribesmen fell upon him again. By now, Triton and I were in full sprint, heading to Bora's aid.

Mobbed by the tribesmen, Bora let out a mournful scream as a bright flash of light overwhelmed us all. We froze and dropped to the ground upon the edge of the hill, overlooking an altercation that was no more. Bora stood up then, calm and among the other tribesmen, seemingly unhurt, his eyes glowing with bright purple light.

I almost lost my sanity then, faced with this new horror and the apparent loss of Bora, but Triton was calm. He decided we would split up and make for our old camp far up the cliffside. I was nearly lost to the horror then but managed to protest regardless. Triton, to his credit, could see I was in no shape to travel and amended his plan. Fortunately, at least for the moment, it seemed that the tribesmen were unaware of our presence. They returned to the watchtower with haste just moments after having seemingly turned Bora into whatever they now were.

It seemed ages passed as we hid on the hillside, silent and unmoving. Eventually, my stupor passed, and Triton again decided that we would head for our old hidden camp on the cliff. We used it actively when initially scouting the basin and kept a store of weapons and supplies there for emergency purposes.

As the afternoon began to draw on, we headed back along our path and then a ways south along the creek before we crossed. Though we had only seen others of the tribe once Bora came close to the village's border, we wished to ensure that no lookout could discern our presence. We intended to approach the cliff from the southern face, obscured from the view of the village.

As we forded the creek, I remarked how much deeper and quicker it had become since our business at the river. Upon reaching the far bank, I noticed two of the vile starfish abominations crawling along the shore. Mindlessly, I readied my spade and prepared to attack when Triton stopped me. He produced two of the creature's glands that we had harvested after the altercation at the river. I placed one of the oily, foul-smelling things in my pouch, as Triton instructed, and, true to the tales; it seemed the starfish simply ignored us and continued downstream. Though I was repulsed at passing so close to the things, this was still better than fighting them.

As we headed up the far side of the cliff, I was struck by our fortune. Though we were still wet from the creek, we were warm and dry as though it were a summer's day. Even in the mild winter of the basin, this was exceptional. I couldn't help but feel some other forces at work on our cursed journey.

It was early evening when we reached the top of the cliff. From there, it was simply a matter of finding our trail marker and the narrow downward path that led to the cave. Once inside, we availed ourselves of some of the dried meat we had stored there. Something in the character of the Iliti meat had changed; we were both repelled at eating any more of it. Still, the other stored goods provided an ample feast for us, and we both ate substantially.

We had no need for a fire, so mild were the temperatures. The purple glow we had followed since witnessing the comet several nights before provided a strange sort of light. It was clear now from our vantage point above the village that the glow was actually coming from the village itself. Primarily centered around the watchtower, though also running throughout the streams within the walls, everything seemed alight with the oddly deep, bright purple glow. The same light that had been shown from the eyes of the tribesmen and poor Bora.

As we watched the village, still empty and silent save for the glow, neither of us knew precisely what to make of our situation. While we were relatively safe and hidden from the village on the cliff, our supplies would last no more than a few days. And there was, of course, the matter of our friends and family, who seemed unharmed so far as we could tell, save for the strange movements and glowing eyes. Neither of us had any interest in leaving Bora and the others to that fate if they could be saved. I thought of the awful wailing scream Bora had let out when he fell and knew that I could never live with myself having damned someone else to that terrible unknown end.

Far below us, at the base of the cliff, something stirred, and we both froze. A cold anticipation gripped our souls. As I watched the beast move, it seemed at first to be one of the large cats I had known in my childhood, but larger. No, it was longer, not larger. Longer and with an extra set of legs and an oversized, snake-shaped head. I looked then to Triton and nearly fell from the cliff edge. I had never before seen such fear on another face. I knew then that this thing far below us must indeed be the dreaded Laathix.

Worse still, from where it had come, the Laathix could have come from nowhere else but within the caves at the base of the cliff. My mind raced at the implications. Could the thing have been there all along? How could we have missed it? Triton, nearly mad with fear, managed to speak, saying that the hunters had believed the Laathix possessed an unmatched ability to camouflage itself. So much so that it was essentially invisible when not moving.

We watched in muted horror as the Laathix stalked out along the beach and headed towards the village. Inside the village walls, the other members of the tribe had begun to move out from the watchtower. They spread out at even intervals throughout the village, and we were able to account for every tribe member, Bora included, and save for my sister among their number. It seemed then that they all began speaking, though we were too far away to make out any of what was being said.

In an instant, light erupted from the watchtower and each of the tribesmen around town. The new light thrummed with power and formed a strange geometric shape that encompassed the village.

At the sight of the light, the Laathix jumped back and let out a fierce howl. It was clearly not used to being so suddenly gotten upon and charged back toward the nearest wall of the village. As the great and terrible Laathix leaped through the newly erected barrier, it howled again. Writhing in agony, the Laathix dissolved into a sickening array of light and was cast out into the night sky.

At our cave lookout, Triton and I both struggled to comprehend what we were seeing. He, at least, was mildly relieved at the sight of the Laathix's demise and suggested we gather weapons from the cave. It seemed whatever we were now a part of was rapidly racing toward its completion. Our plan was to gather gear and head down to the village, which was still encompassed by the strange geometric shape.

The cave was relatively shallow and well-lit from the continued purple glow, though the prevalence of the color had become unsettling. It was this purple glow that gave us our first taste of genuine terror as a shadow passed across the cave entrance.

A large, clearly snake-like head came into the opening, followed by the complete form of a second Laathix. Triton stifled a scream, and we both froze. The Laathix, now entirely in the cave with us, reared up its forequarter and opened its huge mouth. As it did, its jaw separated at the center and opened along its upper torso to just above its middle shoulder, revealing row after row of hideous curved teeth. The nightmare before us let out a low growl, and my blood froze.

The sight was too much for Triton, and he screamed openly now. Primal instinct took over as the Laathix charged. I thrust forward with a spear I had just unearthed from our stores. Finding purchase in the beast's central shoulder, the spear drove in deep. Seeing me must have jarred something loose for Triton, and a moment later, he, too, had charged and driven home one of our newly found spears. The Laathix thrashed and I was thrown clear to the entrance of the cave. I witnessed in horror as the Laathix's immense three-sided mouth bit Triton cleanly in half. I screamed then as my survival instinct carried me down the path along the cliff at top speed.

After a few steps down the path, the ground shook, and I lost my footing. Turning as I attempted to recover, I fully expected to see the Laathix in hot pursuit. Instead, I saw the cause of the tremors that had sent me to the ground. For a moment, I envied Triton that he missed such horror.

Coming down from the sky were fantastic beasts. They were impossibly large with huge stumps of legs and long distorted necks. Vile, smooth heads sat atop fish-like mouths that stretched and yawed in a blatant mockery of true life. They crashed through the sky, barreling down on the village and the cliff in between. I ran, though I had no hope of escape.

As they reached the cliff, the very ground splintered as though it were old dry wood. I ran for some time, impossibly leaping amongst the raining motes of land, until a medium-sized rock took me off my feet and sent me flying through the air.

I landed in a tree back between the cliff and the creek, somehow still alive. Still, the terrible sky demons bore down on our small village. There was a sound that came when the demons reached the barrier of light that surrounded the village. No term can express that withering sound, and never since have I heard anything similar.

The light intensified and the demons began to dissolve and be tossed back to the stars. Soon, it was too bright to see anything, and the horrible din worked to entirely destroy my conscious mind. In blackness, I tumbled, oblivious to anything else around me.

When I came to, I was still in the tree. Though my body was beaten and bruised, I seemed almost miraculously unhurt. The tree I had landed in was entirely five hundred yards from the cliff face and an easy three hundred feet lower in elevation. Of the cliffside, there was no more, just copious amounts of rubble scattered as far as the eye could see. As I gently climbed down from the tree, the pain inside my body became greater, and I began to suspect that I was not as unhurt as I had believed.

As I moved slowly through the destruction, I tried to take stock of everything that had happened. For one, if I had survived, then perhaps so too had the Laathix or others of its kind still in the area.

Deciding that I had little chance against any predator, let alone that walking nightmare we had encountered the night past, I resolved to make for the village as we had originally intended. The pain in my insides intensified with each passing minute, and I wondered if I would even make the journey home.

I surveyed the area as I went, and it seemed a swath of destruction and rubble stretched back to the east, as far as the horizon. Thankfully, there seemed to be no evidence of the destruction in the sky I had witnessed the night before. I wondered if I had ever seen such a sight, given this new evidence before my eyes. It was then that I realized the color. The ever-present purple glow was no more, and authentic color had returned to the world around me.

Eventually, I reached the village. I emerged from the thickest and most extensive parts of the rubble to the east of the village, having traveled roughly north from where I awoke. To my amazement, the village seemed unharmed. Instead, it looked as though the village had been the epicenter of a great blast that ravaged the surrounding area. It was, however, eerily silent, and I feared the worst for my tribe.

As I entered through the east gate, my fears were realized. My fellow tribesmen, arrayed roughly where they had stood before the great geometric shape had engulfed them, were all dead. Their bodies shriveled almost beyond recognition.

I was overcome then by the sorrow and horror of it all and fell to my knees weeping. I do not know for how long.

Once I had recovered, I resolved to collect the bodies and bury them. I knew I could not leave them in this ignoble state, and strangely, my pains and injuries seemed to have faded shortly after entering the village. Even the worrisome pain deep within my body had become but a whisper.

It was also clear to me, though I could not say why, that there were no threats near me. The village was safe in a primal manner that I cannot adequately express. With my newfound safety in mind and my recovered injuries in my body, I set about my work.

In spite of the awfulness, I seemed to manage the task efficiently and quickly. I had found an undamaged spade and made short work digging a large grave. While going through the village, I noticed that the huts now seemed weakened. It was as though they had been made of sand, whereas before, the dried white sand and water mixture was as hard as a stone. Several even crumbled at my touch, as though they had never held any strength at all.

As I proceeded with my task, I became aware of two significant issues. My sister's body was not among any of the remains I had collected. I accounted for everyone, even poor Bora, but my sister was nowhere to be found.

Along with this, I became aware that I was actively avoiding the watchtower. It was subconscious at first, but eventually, I became aware of it, and a new sensation tore through my body. The sensation brought clarity and the spell on my mind was broken. I could see the tower now clearly, its top glowing unmistakably in that strange purple light and surrounded, almost imperceptibly, by a peculiar geometric shape.

I abandoned my task and headed straight for the watchtower. If nothing else, the collective traumas of the past week of my life seemed then to have bled me of all remaining fear. I entered and quickly made up the ladders leading to the top.

I suppose I should have at least paused at the hardly-there barrier formed by the shape. Instead, I barreled through, stopping only once I had come into the room at the very top of the tower.

In the very center of the lookout sat my sister, though she was now impossibly old. In her arms, she cradled something about the size of a small animal. As I approached, she looked up at me and smiled, her eyes free of any purple glow.

Closer now, I could see that what she cradled was actually a shape made of deep purple light; the shape was reminiscent of the barrier shapes but constantly shifted and changed as it rested in my sister's now-ancient hands.

I moved to speak, but she stopped me and motioned that I reach out and touch the shape. I hesitated in spite of everything, or perhaps because of everything, but I needed answers, and so I relented. I reached out and touched the shape and could feel it talking inside my mind.

Its name was Kamu, and it was ancient beyond comprehension. It had come back through time and space to this moment, or rather the night before, to stop the Yaub, the great sky demons whose footfalls toppled mountains. At the end of time, the Yaub are too numerous, consuming all that is and ever could be. They could be stopped, though, at one point in the ancient past. For Kamu, time was a position, a location, and not a flow to which it was bound, and so it had embarked for the good of all things.

The Iliti had been the key, serving as a sort of homing beacon for the Yaub throughout reality. Attracting them again and again to suitable feeding grounds. When danger threatened the Iliti, the Yaub's greatest agent, the dreaded Laathix, was summoned to protect them. A duty it accomplished by slaughtering all life near the prized Iliti.

Kamu had needed help, however, in order to accomplish its goal. It required a speaker to ensure its will was completed and vessels to channel its great and terrible power through. This was my sister. Kamu had brought her visions and had found a kindred spirit in her strange heart. Together, they had worked to move our tribe along the path of the Iliti and to build on the site of the final battle.

I was shaken hearing the cold disconnection Kamu had in using human lives as so much fodder. And that my sister had capitulated with the thing. She had been the one to send me away at the end, to spare me being used in such a way, but it was through no benevolence or love. Now Kamu needed one last thing.

The final attack had drained much of Kamu's life force, as well as that of my sister. It needed another willing vessel so that it could be remade within our reality. There was an amorphous fear lingering of some potential danger caused by its actions against the Yaub that Kamu worried would need addressing. My sister and Kamu were both dying, as was I, it revealed, though I had already guessed as much. I was kept upright now by Kamu's remaining power.

I could barely think as I drew back my hand. I was so angry that all of this had been orchestrated from the beginning, yet still, I had no urge for the release of oblivion. And so I agreed. Kamu needed a willing vessel, and in the end, I was more afraid of what the end would mean than I was about this strange new dawn offered by the thing in my sister's lap. I opened my mind to Kamu, and for a time, all I recall is color and shape with no reason or meaning.

When the world reformed around me, I was changed into what I am now. I am powerful beyond reckoning but lost and disoriented in time. I do not believe the merger worked as Kamu had intended. Perhaps that was my sister's doing. My poor sister must have expired sometime while I swooned amidst the formless colors and shapes, for she was dead when I awoke. I felt barely anything, but still, I decided to see to her burial. There was something cathartic about putting to rest all that remained of the life I had known.

All that remained of my village was rubble and sand. I did not know my purpose then, and still now, I only guess at the causes of the nebulous fear that dogs my mind. But I persist, all the same, recording all that I see and encounter in the hopes of someday seeing a pattern or a solution to my plight. Of my purpose, I would learn in time.

I left the basin and then headed back to the west. Something in me wished to see the lands of my birth again—to walk the fields my feet had known in childhood. I sought to gain some comfort in the knowledge that my people persisted, even though my tribe had been wiped out. What I found was worse than the threat of extinction, but that is a different tale for another time.

I can recall walking toward the setting sun on the third day after the altercation with the Yaub. Those were as if they were my first steps, my first real memories in this body that are my own. What I had been before lay buried, along with my sister and our tribe, under the stark white sands and rubble of the once beautiful basin we called home.

Conclusion: Rook's Story, Part 3

The dark blue sedan was off the side of The Nightroad, partially lodged into a bush but stopped at least. Its headlights cast strange shadows through the leaves of the bush. For a moment, everything threatened to come crashing down on Rook.

It had been chiefly luck. As he passed out, Critter's leg had pressed forward onto the gas, and the car had taken off wildly. Rook had grabbed the wheel, but it took him several moments to forcibly remove Critter from the gas and regain any semblance of control. By then, they were off the actual pavement and into the bushes and shrubs that dotted the shoulder. It was another 200 yards before Rook had managed to get one of his legs over and onto the brakes, bringing them to a grinding halt. He reached over and put the car into park.

Critter was only barely conscious, moaning and delirious, crammed into the driver's side door. Rook hopped off his perch on the console and proceeded out the passenger's side. He paused and scanned the surrounding area. There was never any telling what might be lying in wait if you stopped along The Nightroad, and Rook had already had a long enough night.

Seeing no immediate threats, he proceeded around to the driver's side door to attend to Critter. The battered Critter practically fell out of the seat as Rook opened the door. He was bleeding from the mouth and didn't look to have long for the world.

"Aw no, fuck, fuck. Don't fucking die, you hillbilly maniac! You can't just kick it and leave me out here!" Rook shouted as he held Critter in his arms. Apart from the bruises on his face, there was no apparent cause for his sudden turn for the worse.

Critter coughed and managed a half smile. "Don't even think about it ... ya pansy ..." He coughed again, this time spitting blood into the dust. He pulled himself up with Rook's help, and the two managed to move him to a leaning position against the back of the car. Critter was battered but seemed to be rousing from his earlier stupor. "Fuck me, this is bad." He said as he pulled his right arm out of the sleeve of his flannel shirt. The bandage he had applied was wet with blood. "You're gonna have to help me with this."

"Shit! When did that happen?" Rook had never been good with blood.

"Fighting that thing, I figure. I thought I could hold it off, but I'm gonna need something from the trunk." He stepped away from the car and leaned against Rook. "Open it up and get the first aid kit."

Rook complied and found the kit easy enough. Opening it, he saw three large syringes, each filled to varying degrees with brightly colored liquids that seemed to glow faintly. "What the hell is all this?" He asked.

"More emergency plans." Critter groaned. "Just grab the reddish one, quick." He seemed to be in a great deal of pain.

Rook picked up the syringe with the faint reddish-pink glow and held it up for confirmation.

"Yeah, that's it. Give it here." Critter said.

Rook handed the syringe to Critter. After a deep breath to steady himself, Critter jabbed the needle into his neck and pressed down on the plunger. He groaned loudly and strained momentarily against some unseen force.

Rook busied himself at the first aid kit, gathering more gauze and bandages for Critter's arm. After Critter settled for a moment, Rook removed the blood-soaked bandage. As it revealed the wound, he stopped with a gasp.

What had initially been a deep puncture wound just below the triceps seemed now to have rotted away the surrounding tissue. A purplish-black coloration spread out from the rotten hole in Critter's arm, engulfing his shoulder and reaching down near his elbow. Rook struggled to maintain his composure. "What the hell are we supposed to do about that?" He said plainly as he applied a fresh layer of gauze to the wound.

"Yeah, tell me about it," Critter said. "Look, that shit I just took should give us a little time. At least enough to figure something out, ya know. Fire up the Beacon. Let's see how far out we are."

The Beacon. The thought hadn't even occurred to Rook. It was their fail-safe, an unerring compass that always pointed towards home. Just turn it on and drive back to safety if anything goes wrong on a mission. And this was about as wrong as it got. Rook reached into the center console from the driver's side. A large dial that looked like a silver ball embedded into the console was Rook's target, and he spun the dial until a glowing blue/green light appeared on its surface. He aligned the light with the appropriate markings along the outside of the dial and waited. Moments later, the digital display on the console blinked on. The readout was clear: 3 hours and 48 minutes to the Eagle Creek exit and home.

"Just under four hours." He called back to Critter.

"Well, shit," Critter exclaimed. "That's a bit longer than I imagine I've got. Those meds will help keep it at bay, but I can still feel it. Like a nail along the inside of my skull." He grimaced in pain. "Time for plan B."

"You can't be serious." Rook was exasperated. How would he ever manage to find Critter help out here? Where else could they turn but to the safety and support of the others among Exodos Omnis?

"As cancer," Critter smirked. "Hear me out. Best case, I've got an hour, maybe a little more. Then I'm gonna be another one of those fang-mouthed freaks we burned to the ground back off the exit. Not enough time to get us home, but it's enough to get us back to where that Roadog chewed up our original target. With any luck, they've got some antidote or magic hoodoo that can set this straight. 'Cause, other than that, I might actually be out of ideas." Critter coughed, a haggard look crossing his face.

"As far as your ideas go, this one's pretty lousy," Rook said. His mind raced to come up with alternatives to Critter's plan, but events of the evening had had an effect on Rook's thoughts, and he had trouble focusing on anything in particular. "What if we just cut it off?" He said. It was all he could come up with in the end.

Critter instinctively drew his arm back. "Yeah, it's not on the top of my list. Plus, I don't think it'll matter. I can feel it inside me; it's too late for that." Critter put his arm back into the flannel shirt and buttoned it up. "C'mon, my plan's all we got. You're gonna have to drive." Slowly, he walked to the passenger side of the sedan and got in.

Rook stood for a moment outside of the car. So that was just it, then? What would happen if he just turned toward Eagle Creek and made a run for it? Maybe they could make it. And maybe Critter would turn into some hideous monstrosity en route and try to chew his face off. No, Critter was right. His plan was all they had to go on. Reluctantly, Rook climbed into the driver's seat and started the engine. "Alright, let's see what we can find at the cultist's car. Hang on, man." He said, and they were off.

Given how far away it had been from them earlier, the drive should have taken about fifteen minutes. Rook pushed the sedan as fast as he dared, racing through the strange perpetual twilight of The Nightroad. He could hear Critter's breathing from across the car, each successive breath more ragged than the last.

It was only five minutes until they spied the cultist's car, its headlights now gone out but still primarily intact along the side of The Nightroad. Rook drove near the vehicle and parked. "Okay, so what am I looking for?" He asked. It was easiest if he kept his mind focused on the task at hand.

"Slow down a sec. We gotta make sure it's clear. I don't see anything, but that doesn't always mean much." Critter scanned the area from within the car. "First off, the trunk, grab a headlamp and the Icer. It's the medium-sized shotgun-looking one with the can of blue goop attached like a clip. You can't miss it. Just aim and shoot if anything's out there; it has about as much recoil as a garden hose. Search their car, any scrap of funky writing, or vial of who-knows-what. That is what we're looking for. At this point I'll try most anything." Critter coughed again. "And be quick about it, yeah?" He added.

"Alright. Screw it, let's go." Rook hopped out of the car. This part was almost like being back on the court if he didn't think too hard about it. Just run the play and everything will work out. Two seconds later, he was at the trunk; another five, and he was inside with the gun case open. The Icer was indeed impossible to miss, a single-barreled shotgun with a metal stock, the strange can of "blue goop" attached just in front of the trigger. Rook grabbed the gun, almost forgetting to secure a headlamp.

It had been twenty seconds, and he was headed toward the cultist's car. It was hard to ignore the human remains scattered about, though most had been cleaned up by the beast from earlier. Dark blood stains colored the ground in all directions. "Stay focused!" He thought to himself.

He reached the car and peered in through the torn-off driver's side door. There were remains in the back, the lower half of a cultist that hadn't managed to make their escape from the back seat, and the smell was nauseating. Still, there didn't seem to be much else inside the car; there were a couple of bottles of water and refuse scattered about the car floor, but nothing else. Rook opened the glove box, but that, too, was a dead end. Then he tried the console and found that it was locked tight. There was a tiny keypad attached to the top of the console. "Shit," Rook said out loud.

Rook searched desperately for a solution. Prying the console open didn't seem to work, and no one was alive to get the code from. Then he thought about the Icer and an idea formed. The Icer was like a backward flamethrower, casting out a cloud of super-cooled chemicals that caused molecular disintegration rather than physical combustion. Perhaps it would be enough to dissolve the console and get Rook inside.

As he stepped out of the car to implement his plan, he was startled by the sudden cacophony of noise that erupted from behind him. Critter was lying on the horn and gesturing wildly toward the darkness beyond where Rook was standing.

Rook turned, and the light from his headlamp fell upon the sight both of them had been dreading in the back of their minds. The Road-og. It was almost on top of Rook. The great beast let out a fearsome roar as it charged. Rook turned the Icer on it and fired, but the recoil, combined with the shock of the event, proved too much for Rook to handle, and the cloud of chemicals emitted by the Icer missed high and to the right of the Roadog.

The beast swung a huge black-furred paw at Rook and sent him flying into the hood of the sedan. The impact partly caved in the hood and left Rook stunned and helpless. Dazed, he tried to fight back, but all he could clearly tell was that the Roadog was stalking ever closer to him. He could smell it's breath. Then he felt a sharp pain as the thing bit down on his leg. A harsh yank sent him again flying through the air, this time colliding with the ground with a painful thud.

This was it then, he thought. Eaten by some horrible monster in the inexplicable darkness surrounding reality. Not exactly the way he had pictured going out. But then again, nothing in his life had gone according to plan after that fateful day two months ago when he lost his fiancée and started rolling with Exodos Omnis. He probably should have expected this.

The blast from the Icer made a sickening crack as it impacted the Roadog's front quarter. Then, another crack as the beast turned on its attacker. Critter was barely standing, braced against the passenger door, the Icer firmly in his hands. The third shot caught the Roadog in its massive lupine skull and it let out an anguished howl.

That had been enough for the horrid thing, and it fled, still smoking, into the darkness. Rook was still mainly in a daze, the pain in his leg threatening to wash away his consciousness with each successive throb. Critter ambled toward where Rook had landed.

"You all right?" Critter said.

"Leg's hurt pretty bad and burns like hell." Rook forced himself up into a sitting position. "You think that thing's really gone?"

"I don't wanna find out. Can you walk?"

"I can try." Rook stood, putting most of his weight onto his uninjured right leg.

Critter came over to help support him. "So, no luck at the car then?" He said.

"Not sure," Rook struggled to walk, the pain in his leg white-hot with each step. "There's a lock on the console. I was going to turn the Icer on it before we got interrupted."

The pair made it again to the back of the car. Critter helped Rook settle into a sitting position behind the bumper, then immediately went for the first aid kit. After just a moment, he returned with the greenish-colored syringe in his hand.

"The fuck is that?" Rook felt things spiraling out of control.

"Calm down, it's just a clotting agent. Keep ya from bleedin' out till we get back home." Critter injected the mysterious substance into Rook's leg. Almost immediately, the bleeding stopped, though it did nothing for the pain. Critter bandaged the wound as well as he could, but it seemed that the longer time passed, the more his maladies affected his abilities. They weren't out of the woods just yet.

Rook tried to steady his thoughts. His right leg was still fine; he could drive well enough. It was high time they fled for the safety of home. But what would they do about Critter?

"Yeah, I only have one idea left," Critter said. Whether Rook had been thinking aloud or just wore his thoughts on his sleeve, he was unprepared for Critter's response.

"Syringe three, the white one." Critter passed the first aid kit to Rook. "It ... should ... put me into a coma that resembles being dead. The problem is that half the time, it just kills ya. It's kind of a last-ditch, ya know. Gimme the shot, throw me in the back seat, and drive our asses home. They can wake me up there and hopefully figure something out for the rest of it."

"And how do we know it's gonna stop you from turning into a monster?" Rook was beginning to hate Critter's plans.

"Hell, we don't. Just figure if I change, I'll still be a monster in a coma, right, at least for a bit. It should give you a chance." Critter had settled onto the ground next to Rook and looked knackered.

"Okay, fine. But why do I have to give you the shot? You didn't seem to have an issue with this earlier." Rook was doing his best to process everything.

"You really gonna make me say it? I'm fuckin dying here. I just can't be the one who does it alright." Rook had never seen that look on Critter's face before.

"Yeah. Alright. Help me get up; let's get you into the back first." Ever onward, Rook thought.

They got to their feet and made their way to the back seat. Rook removed the spent mine and tossed it into the trunk. Then, with Critter seated in the middle, he injected the thick-looking white substance into Critter's good arm. "Good luck." He said.

"Yeah, thanks. You know, you turned out alright, Rook. I had my doubts at the beginning, but I'm glad I was wrong about you." Critter replied.

After about ten seconds, Critter was unconscious. Rook adjusted him into a lying position along the back seat. It was impossible to tell if he still lived. Then Rook secured both Critter's hands and feet with zip ties. No sense in taking any chances.

As he limped back into the driver's seat, Rook began to let himself hope that this last effort would see them safely home—less than four hours. Just follow the Beacon home.

Rook started the dark blue sedan and prepared to turn back onto The Nightroad. He fired up the Beacon and waited. Minutes passed, but nothing happened. He had surmised what had happened by the time he looked up. The hood, where he had damaged it from his earlier impact, was right next to the all-important antenna for the Beacon. The antenna now hung over the side of the car, barely still attached to the vehicle.

Rook was no good with repairs, but he had an idea of the direction he needed to head from the earlier activation of the Beacon. And a rough idea of how long it should take. He started the timer on his phone. Critter was counting on him; Rook was his only chance, if he still had one at all.

Rook rolled down the window to his side and looked out. Above him, a boundless starlit cosmos laid bare. Below him, as always, spread the road. Under such alien stars, Rook decided there was no other choice but to drive on.

Acknowledgments

I hope you've enjoyed this first trip down The Nightroad. It has been many years in the making, and as such, there are a number of people that I'd like to thank. Without any of these people, the book that you've just finished would be markedly different.

First and foremost, thank you to my incredible wife, Megan, and my wonderful children, Jackson, Elwood, and Mylo. It is their support that gives me the strength and courage to walk the path of becoming a fiction author. They, along with my extended family, have read more early drafts and rough copies than anyone should have.

To my friends Matthew and Mason, thank you for always being available to discuss story ideas and help me learn the craft of writing. I know I can always count on you two for honest feedback.

To Mary Jo and Jodi at Batavia GOArt!, you made the process of acquiring funding through the local grants way easier than it initially sounded. In the end, this made all the difference in the world and directly led to this book getting into publication this year.

To Bill at Media Hatchery, your edits and timely contributions have greatly helped to polish the book. Thanks to your efforts, the book is now in a state that I am truly proud to offer to people around the world.

I believe it's a book that was worth your time and I hope you feel the same.

Lastly, but certainly not least, thank you to everyone who read the book. Your support and feedback will be instrumental in shaping the books to come. You took a chance on a first-time author and I humbly thank you for the opportunity to show you a piece of my fictional world. I hope you enjoyed your stay. I look forward to showing you what we have in store for Anthology Two.